Human Scale

a novel

Kitty Beer

Plain View Press
P. O. 42255
Austin, TX 78704

plainviewpress.net
sb@plainviewpress.net
512-441-2452

ISBN: 978-1-935514-42-8
Library of Congress Number: 2010923424

Cover art: Photograph by J. Regan Hutson
          Painted rendition by Barry Shuchter
          Cover design by Susan Bright

The last of June burns to the third degree,
Sun swelling like a blister on the sky.

Elton Glaser
in *Ozone Alert*

For Zachary, who will be fifty-six
when this story takes place

Part I

1

Down the hill where it is said a sports field used to be, the soy crops look healthy in the jellied sunlight. Purple and white flowers bright and static in glare so strong it congeals the air. Along the rows ragged figures toil, bending, watering, crouching, pulling. Beyond, the sheen of the lung-shaped pond glitters green.

"We could go up to New Hampshire, to those settlements…" starts Vita.

She's standing by the window after breakfast. Drake is behind her, still at the table. She anticipates his outburst before it comes.

"That's enough," he growls. "I won't have my wife sounding like some subversive. Don't let anybody hear you talking like that. You'll get us all in trouble."

She does not turn to look at him.

"We'll just say we're going for a visit," she replies mildly. She's used to his anger. It's one of the few emotions he allows himself to show. "She's still only thirteen. They won't suspect us of leaving. Why would they, you're an important man."

"You bet I am. And you know why. I'm a loyal Zorian, and so are you. So keep your mouth shut. Subject closed. Do you want to jeopardize everything we've got?"

Vita weighs another reasonable response, but instead finds herself blurting, "Sure I'm a good Zorian, but I'm loyal to Lorna first of all, and you should be too! She's just a child."

"Nonsense. Don't be melodramatic. All the girls have to do it, if they want to be accepted." His tone reverts to sadly patient. "Look, Vita. We've been through all this before. Be sensible. We want her to keep the position we've worked so hard for—I know you want her to have that security. I know you want the best for her, you're just wrong. All heated up about nothing. Relax. It will be good for her."

"Good for you, you mean."

But she has gone too far. Drake comes to stand close behind her. "Watch it." His hands are on her arms turning her to face him. His grip is tight enough for discomfort. "Forget it, I said. And I don't want the girl getting any of your treasonous notions in her head. Don't you dare try to put her off. She has a bright future in this enclave and I won't let you rob her of it with your silliness." His tone mellows. "I won't let you endanger yourself, either."

He relaxes his hold; his body warmth softens her.

"Drake dear. I'm sorry. I didn't mean to upset you."

"It's the best thing for her," he urges quietly. "Nowadays there's just no choice. Use your head."

He smells of soap and chicory coffee. Impulsively she kisses his cheek. He laughs shortly, hugs her, dismisses her.

"Let's clean up the dishes or we'll be late," he says, in a tone both light and firm.

She watches him gather their plates and cups. He's stocky and broad. At nearly fifty he's more handsome than ever, no gray yet in his black hair, heavy shouldered, hard-jawed, an imposing rock of a man. But as soon as he's out of sight, she turns again to the window, no less concentrated on her idea.

Even with Drake's credentials, they know they're lucky to have been admitted to the upper levels of the Boston enclave. They moved here in 2053 when Lorna was four, and were granted this apartment not long after, in a house they share with five other families. It's one of several on the hill that form an imposing line of renovated triple deckers reminiscent of better times, slanted roofs crowned with solar panels, in what used to be the town of Arlington. The original city of Boston has been under water for twenty years

10

now, though the tops of the tallest buildings still rise out of the waves. From the temple steps on clear days, you can see the insurance building with some of its intact glass glinting like a mermaid's castle in the sun.

So Vita would really have no quarrel with their situation if it weren't for the recent amendment to the Zorian virgin decree, announced just this spring. Now every upper class girl turning fifteen is required to be delivered to the temple for Affirmation, no exceptions. It's one more sign that the priests are consolidating their power. But people feel too vulnerable to resist, memories of chaos are still too raw. Nothing is predictable, terrible things keep happening; even the children know survival is a question. Of course it's comforting to look to, cling to, authority.

Vita feels guilty about her rebellious thoughts. Maybe Drake is right that she's being disloyal, ungrateful, even reckless. She knows he could be right about Lorna's future. If they defy the law, they'll lose privileges and worse, whereas Lorna's Affirmation will benefit their whole family, with added status and luxuries. But Vita in her soul recoils at the price.

She hurriedly dresses for work. Sensible knee-length dress, but light and sleeveless for the heat, flat sandals that show off her painted toenails. It's a challenge to look both virtuous and feminine—the proper appearance for women is the subject of more and more commentary by the authorities. She vigorously brushes her pale hair that frizzes in this humidity, pulls it back with a small blue ribbon, sky blue that matches her eyes. Drake has already left and she longs to linger, to fuss and putter, stroll through their spacious three rooms, strategize about Lorna some more. But the office is waiting; she must immerse herself in processing work, helping to evaluate the overwhelming demands at Services for healthcare and emergency food supplies.

Boston's territory now encompasses parts of northern Rhode Island and southern New Hampshire, under the enlightened and popular leadership of Chief Barry, though he is advised by the usual clutch of priests. People even come here from elsewhere, seeking its relatively benign protection. The Hartford enclave just to the south, for example, is ruled by a priest inclined to cruel and arbitrary punishments.

Vita checks the weather flag by the pond. It's still orange, as it has been most of May this year, so she packs her oxygen mask just in case. Among Drake's privileges are bus passes for his family, allowing Vita to ride to work in a small creaking van smelling of its fuel, stale cooking oil. The road to the center of town runs along a ridge that long ago was a train track, and then for a while a bicycle path in the days when bikes were playthings. Now cycles of all shapes and sizes are precious transportation that greatly outnumber fueled vehicles. Weaving in and out, some are so crammed with goods or possessions that the rider is invisible. Some of the pedicabs carry whole families.

On the left side of the road fruit trees anchor the slope; along the other side march lines of wind turbines, and below them jumble the ramshackle homes of the poor, or the Nons as they are often called. Disintegrating apartment buildings, lopsided shacks, ragged tents as far as the eye can see. Rivers of barefoot people carrying bundles on their heads. Vita turns her face away and does not allow thoughts of them. Instead, she ponders sounding out Lorna on the subject of leaving Boston, risking Drake's serious rage. She imagines the conversation. "Lorna, baby, do you know what happens in Affirmation when you turn fifteen?" How can she pierce Lorna's innocence and trust like that? It would be brutal.

Then the jagged idea that maybe Lorna already knows all about it. Vita struggles to grasp this and can't. Her memory of herself at that age conjures up only an image of embarrassed awkwardness, a dreamy unrequited crush on an older boy, the desperation of trying to belong to a group, any group. Her real pleasures were giggling with her sister and running along the lakeshore with her dog.

At lunchtime Vita sits with co-workers around a table in a back room. There are no windows and the attempt to cheer it up with posters has not worked. As usual they talk about the heat and the latest storm damage. Someone boldly wonders if this new priest influencing Chief Barry is going to mean tighter controls. Vita suddenly wants to sound out their opinion about running away with Lorna. The thought of doing this scares her so much she starts to sweat, she's swept with all the symptoms of nausea. Of course, she wouldn't dare say anything like that in a public place. But the idea has her by the throat.

Finally she says, very timidly, "I wonder if it's possible to ask for a dispensation for the virgin decree?"

"Why would you want to do that?" queries one woman who has two grown daughters. "If my kids were young enough, we'd jump at the chance. Maybe we could even get some airconditioning out of it."

"Yeah," chimes in a young man, studying Vita suspiciously, "what's the problem?"

"I don't want..." She starts passionately, but bites off her words in alarm. "I mean. I don't know. Just wondering."

They all shrug, all except for Diamond. She turns her gaze full on Vita and comments, "What an interesting idea. A dispensation. Sounds almost medieval."

Diamond is a recent employee in the visuals department, assigned to the video team. She's about fifty, short and compact, with dark curls lighted by graying wisps at her temples that make her high forehead seem even higher. Slashing black brows add to the drama of her exotic face, shades of harems or gypsies, sultry, opaque. Vita is taken aback by the directness of her stare and the slight sarcasm of her remark; she sinks back into herself, thinking grimly that she has opened an unfortunate door.

Sure enough, Diamond crosses her path as she leaves the office that evening.

"Heading for the bus?" asks Diamond casually, in her pebbly low voice. She falls into step beside Vita. "Heat always seems better this time of day, doesn't it?"

Diamond's words are bland, but her tone seems suggestive. Of what? Does she think she can trap Vita into revealing something worth reporting? Father Rose has recently persuaded Chief Barry to expand the powers of the Citizen Watch, ostensibly to spot spies. But the new CW has already summoned some average folks to quiz them about trivial things.

"Oh for sure," she responds. "It does start to cool down around now."

"How far do you have to go?"

"We live over on the hill. How about you?"

"Right up there."

Diamond points to the third floor of a square brick building they're approaching, above a store selling bottled water. In the display window a cardboard polar bear is lifting to its lips a scintillating blue cup. A prettily painted sign proclaims, "Crystal Clear. Buy Your Water Here."

"The polar bear lives on," sings Diamond with a smirk.

Vita knows this is a reference to the bear's extinction, and also knows it's not quite politically correct to refer to it. The woman could be trying to trap her, but then again, maybe she's being courageously honest. Vita is drawn to the mystery.

"See the geraniums?" Diamond says. "That's my place. But I have to go to the market first."

"So do I," Vita confesses.

Glancing sidelong at Diamond's neatly clad form, she decides that since the woman lives in an acceptable place and has a market pass, besides working for Services, Drake could not object to her, at least not as casual companion.

They turn down a narrow street and present their passes at a barbed-wire fence. Here the roofed market begins, its stalls crammed with everything from toothbrushes and diapers to potatoes and dried eels. Nons are not allowed in; they have very little valid money so would of course try to steal.

"You have a daughter?" asks Diamond as they stroll past the stalls, comparing prices.

Of course. Her indiscretion did find a ready ear. How can she play it down? "Yes, Lorna. She's thirteen. A handful. Do you have kids?"

"A son."

That's it? Diamond is not exactly forthcoming. But just then Vita spots the pigeons she's looking for and buys three for dinner, though they are small and scrawny. Their heads are still on, their little red eyes staring up, their claws piously curled together. Both women then decide on hothouse oranges for a treat.

"Do you live alone?" asks Vita quickly thereafter, keeping Diamond safely on the subject of her untidy former roommate until they separate.

2

Without having consciously decided to, that evening Vita says to Lorna, "Hey, come sit with me for a minute. I want to ask you something."

Drake has gone out to a meeting after dinner. Lorna has cleared the table and spread her textbook out on it, flipping through the pages. She looks up at her mother with a frown.

"Now you don't want me to study?"

"It'll just take a minute." Vita pats the seat beside her on the couch.

But Lorna goes to flop down in a chair opposite her. "What is it? I've got tons of homework."

Vita ignores her attitude. "Listen."

As she realizes what she's going to do, Vita's hands start to tremble. She presses them together. Lorna's eyes widen with alarm.

"Okay," says Vita, mostly to herself.

"Mom?"

"Okay. You remember Affirmation, what the priests require? When girls turn fifteen? How much do you know about it?"

"I know we have to go to the temple and stay there for a while. I heard we have to drink wine. Yuck."

"What else?"

Lorna pulls her feet up under her, looks down, twists her lips, wiggles uncomfortably. She has beautiful abundant honey blond hair of which she is proud, but she's still lanky and spindly, walks shoulder-hunched and hipless like a boy, her half-formed breasts ignored by the boxy shirts she usually wears. She's very pretty already though, with more delicate features than Vita's. Instead of her mother's round face and almost sullen mouth, Lorna's are sharper and sweetly refined. And she inherited her father's eyes, velvet brown depths deepened by long lashes. Vita's heart winces at this loveliness in bud, this impending beauty sounding alarm.

Vita chooses the cowardly route. "You know, there's a serious problem with fertility these days. Many men and women can't have children, it's a chemical in the environment." She stops. This is pointless. It's no news to Lorna, who is looking hard at her hands waiting for her mother to get to the point. "Parenthood is highly regarded..." Nope, going nowhere.

In the nervous silence Lorna rolls her eyes at the ceiling with such arch impatience that Vita blurts, "Affirmation means they require the girls...the daughters of people in our class, important people...they require them to have sex with priests." She is stunned by her own crude bluntness, but she goes on, in a rush. "I don't want you to have to do this, darling. I can fix it so you don't. Just tell me what you think. Your father doesn't agree with me. He says..."

"I know all about it." Lorna still isn't looking at her mother.

"Oh."

"We get to be like queens. We can have anything we want. We wear beautiful white dresses. It's not so bad, sometimes you get a nice priest, and handsome. It's sort of romantic."

"Lorna, baby, is that what you think? I don't believe it."

Her daughter raises her eyes and they are clear and cold. "I don't care one way or the other."

"I don't believe that either."

But Vita is stunned by Lorna's raw indifference. Her little golden girl, her cuddly baby child, comes across in this moment like a cynical siren.

"I signed up for early preparation classes," Lorna tosses at her defiantly. "We start in the fall. Lots of the girls choose it. We learn the proper rituals, how Zoria's gospel blesses us, how we're special, the priests' mission, the history, things like that. Might as well get a head start on how to do it graciously."

"That's what they tell you? Just what does head start mean? Graciously! What in God's name are you talking about?" Vita babbles in horror.

"Relax, mom," Lorna replies with a mixture of tenderness and scorn. "What's the big deal?"

"Remember your friend Marta's older sister who graduated two years ago? She has a baby now."

"She doesn't get to keep it. They'll take it away. Anyhow, hardly anybody gets pregnant, mom, come on. And then when you don't, you have to go into the military anyway. So why not put that off for a while? My friends say it'll be sort of fun."

"What about love?" Vita realizes how pointless that sounds, and adds, "I mean, I want your first time to be...I don't want that to be your first sexual experience. It's not right. I won't let you do it!"

"What you want! That's all you're interested in. How about what other people want?"

Vita tries to breathe evenly, looks around the cozy living room, at the bookshelves, the cleverly concealed kitchen corner, the rugs and curtains, the vase of daisies—the rich white petals with gold centers that she had just today purchased with such pleasure. Her world that finally had come together in recent years now fragmenting, breaking up into flying pieces.

When Drake comes home, Vita is lying in bed starkly awake and rigid. He climbs in beside her carefully but she says, "I'm not asleep."

"Good," he murmurs, and begins his hand on her thigh.

She doesn't move in response, but her mind willingly goes to follow his caress, and she realizes before she lets everything go that this is what she needs right now, his heat and passion, her heat and passion. Their coupling without words. There's nowhere else to go that is not fraught with fear and pain.

∂∞∂

With June, the heat becomes almost unbearable. All athletic events are suspended until fall, water is rationed again, Lorna starts summer camp. Drake and Vita set up their rusty old airconditioner in the front room, in spite of the serious dent it makes in their budget to use precious fuel. All three of them sleep in that room, leaving as early and coming back as late as they can. Reports of heat stroke deaths seep into the news, though they are played down as usual.

After work one day, Vita and Diamond are sitting over coffee in the television arcade by the market watching the news, when suddenly Drake's face flashes on the screen. He has been chosen as part of a delegation to the October summit. The four chiefs of the northeastern region—Albany, Burlington, Boston, Hartford—have decided to come together to solve major problems, especially the disputes over water.

"A historic moment as the 21st century moves into its later, and we trust happier, phase," someone proclaims, while Drake and his fellow delegates stand together looking suitably important and stalwart. "Cooperation will be the watchword to see us forward."

"So that's your husband," Diamond says.

Vita is excited and proud. She knows that Drake coveted this appointment and she rejoices for him. Sharing his dreams about it has meant their closest moments lately. Just last night holding her he confided his prayers. Smoothing his hair back from his forehead, seeing his dark eyes alight, she thought here is my real Drake, the way he used to be. Maybe this political honor will mitigate the religious obsession that's been consuming him more and more. She has a surge of hope for the future if the worth of such fine men is recognized. And Lorna will benefit, she's sure to be petted by her teachers and classmates today. Vita tries not to look too smug smiling back at Diamond.

"A good-looking man," Diamond adds.

Vita shrugs. Was that necessary? Diamond is always puzzling her with remarks in such an offhand tone they sound snide. Vita no longer fears that she's an informer out to report heretical tendencies, but is still uneasy over some obscurity there, a curtain that fuzzes her outlines.

"I adore him," she counters, very smugly.

Diamond sips coffee and says, "Look, there's a shot of that weird frost in April. Remember that?"

"Right. They never explained it. Barely any frost all winter, and then bang. Hey, there's that spy they just arrested. Looks kind of sinister, doesn't he?"

"Who says he's a spy?"

Vita turns to stare at her friend, looks quickly around to see if anyone else heard. What a curious question. The authorities say so, and besides who cares? "Well, he's done something," she replies.

"I think," says Diamond slowly, "he simply disagrees with the government line."

Well, there goes my good mood, frets Vita. She has to admit it's probably true. She doesn't like being reminded that she herself has to watch her tongue. Her moment of pride and glory is shrouded over by her awareness, piqued and growing since her subversive thoughts over Lorna, that the happy face put on by official Boston is far from the truth. She suddenly and reluctantly feels a huge gap between herself and self-righteous Drake, and a pull to Diamond's brave skepticism.

"Hey," she grins. "We're too old to be rebels."

"You're ten years younger than me," Diamond points out. Her long, almost Asian eyes under the dramatic brows are dead serious and penetrating. "And you are a rebel at heart."

"No I'm not," breathes Vita in a panic. "For God's sake, keep quiet."

Then Diamond lets out a sudden sharp laugh. "Just kidding."

"Who knew," says Vita, but she does know. Diamond is a risk.

3

A few days later Vita and Drake are at a reception honoring the summit delegates. It's an elaborate affair, held in the climate-controlled greenhouse adjacent to the Chief's headquarters. Vita is wearing her new silky pale blue dress with frills at the V and hem. She has only been here once before; this is truly where the elite congregate and she feels timid and important. She stands cool under overhanging palm trees where multicolored parrots chat and float, looking through heavy glass down the hill at her own neighborhood where people are staggering in the heat. Months of drought have yellowed everything that's supposed to be green; the air itself is yellow. She sips fizzy grape wine from a champagne glass and nibbles little pastry rolls. Chief Barry and his favorite priest, Father Rose, are sitting at the other end of the hall. Vita would like to get closer and she looks around for a suitable path through the crowd.

"I think I'm going to faint, " says a hysterical voice beside her. "I'm just that nervous. I'm not at all well, this is too much for me, I'm just going to faint."

Vita turns to see a frail trembling woman with thin grim lips. She starts to reply but the woman continues, not looking at her but staring around as if at specters."I hate crowds, you know, they do frighten me so. Oh, where is my husband, why did he leave me here all alone? I'm not at all well. He does know that. I only like to have a few friends about, people I know. This just won't do. Why did I come? It's so hard for me, he does know that."

Vita has taken a few breaths getting ready to answer, but now she realizes that no reply is expected. She goes on half listening while scanning the room for Drake or someone else she can escape to. She has spotted a couple she met a few months ago at some function and is getting ready to excuse herself from the breathless monologue, when she sees a striking man making his way towards them. He is tall, square-shouldered but lithe, with a full mouth in a broad brown beard. His solicitous smile broadens when he sees Vita. He beams down at her with a gratitude clearly mingled with admiration.

"Thank you for entertaining my wife," he says. "Gloria has trouble with strangers. I'm Alex Cohen."

"Vita Gordon."

"Alex, you know I'm not at all well," whimpers Gloria. "Why did you leave me alone? Can't we go home now? You know I hate crowds. You know that."

"Ah," says Alex to Vita, "you must be Drake's wife. I've just been congratulating him."

"It's quite exciting," Vita concedes, locked into his probing green eyes. When he moves closer she doesn't step back. "Our whole family is very pleased and proud."

"Of course. He's just the right man for the job."

While she's enjoying the mutual warmth behind their conventional words, she watches his eyes turn from fiery to guilty, Gloria plucking his sleeve.

He pats his wife's shoulder and pleads, "Whatever you want, Gloria dearest, don't get upset."

Vita is intrigued by this couple who seem so ill-suited. The sensual sensitive man, the harsh neurotic woman. As she comments somewhat automatically on hopes for the summit, she starts to ease away, making her eyes roam the room. Alex tells her he's on the staff of the ambassador to the Albany region, and they'll be returning to the embassy there soon. But he's expecting to attend the summit, yes it will be a momentous occasion. During most of the conversation Gloria keeps up a strangulated twitter. Soon Vita rather abruptly excuses herself and takes off. She's viscerally aware that behind her Alex's eyes are following.

She meets good-looking men all the time, of course, and is well acquainted with suggestive glances, but she can't remember when she's been so stirred.

She finds Drake holding forth to a small group, and he acknowledges her with pompous pride.

"Most of you know my wife, my lovely Vita. Does a bang-up job at Services, making some hard decisions, doing her bit. Right, darling? Folks, there's got to be a better way. These Nons are draining the economy, they are sick all the time and don't pull their weight for all the resources it costs us just to keep them alive."

The others nod sagely.

Someone says, "And when they die, we have to bury them, that's a burden we could do without. After the last flood you remember there were so many, we had to do another mass grave."

Another adds, "Some of them make passable soldiers, and we do need them in the fields and factories, but they're always fainting and dropping like flies so what good is it?"

"Zoria says we're all her children," states Drake authoritatively, "but now she's decreed that Nons are different, they aren't as blessed. The proof is in how destitute they are. God is punishing their sins."

"Poor things. I feel sorry for them," pipes up one woman. "We send over our stale bread when we can."

Vita looks out over the complacent faces to the sky beyond, which as she watches turns from the smiling pink of sunset to a strange purple color. At the same time, shapes of trees through the thick glass begin a crazy dance cut by a swath of lightning. Vita has a moment of eerie unreality as the palm trees around her stand in complete stillness above the heads of the murmuring genteel crowd. She even takes a sip from her glass and smiles vaguely at some clever remark.

But her mind has already gone out there into the vicious storm, and in another moment a clap of thunder like a bomb shakes the building. The flow of polite conversation ceases for a split second of dead silence, and then bursts into a barrage of rising consternation.

Chief Barry jumps up and urges calm. But everyone is either pressing their faces against the glass to see what's happening or hurrying for the exits.

Vita cries, "We've got to get home. Lorna!"

"She'll have the sense to go to the cellar, don't worry," says Drake. But he grabs her and they join the crush at the door.

Outside water is pouring from the sky, blown sideways by ferocious wind. Debris flies though the air. The vans are all full and are taking off, so they have to settle for a wagon pulled by a horse that rears every time thunder claps. Vita catches a glimpse of Alex carrying Gloria like a child, the two of them soaked to the skin, his mouth shouting soundless words into the gale.

Overnight the storm only worsens. Everyone in their house cowers in the cellar. The must and cider smells of stored potatoes and apples soon mingle with that of nervously sweating bodies. Wrapped in an emergency blanket, Vita anxiously listens for the crack and crush that would mean the house is hit, cradling a trembling Lorna. The cynic and the siren are gone, the condescending adolescent has vanished like a veneer. It's her tearful little girl that Vita holds and croons over. Vita's own fear is absorbed into the welcome well of Lorna's need.

Drake and a couple of others make periodic forays to check the weather. But when morning comes, their report is disturbing. Hail the size of apples, and snow covering the ground.

26

Nobody knows what to make of this. June is always so brutally and unrelentingly hot, and during the past few winters there has not been one flake of snow. Some people start laughing at the absurdity. Some wonder if this doesn't mean maybe the Earth is regaining some equilibrium. Vita is one of those shaken with dread.

"These extremes," she says quietly, "are getting worse and worse. What about the crops? What about the food supply?"

Drake says, "It's God's will."

Lorna says, "I remember snow. It's cold! Can I go upstairs and see it, please?"

For a couple of days after the freak snowstorm, people are staring at and picking through rubble, apathetic and numb. The damage was severe, mostly to buildings hit by falling trees or hailstones, or dislodged by melting mudslides. Even Chief Barry's magnificent greenhouse hall cracked in one place, causing more anxiety than anything, because it had been such a symbol of invulnerability. The realization that it could be damaged drops it achingly into the mortal realm. Is nothing safe?

Before television reception is restored, Father Rose makes resonating speeches from the portico of the temple, backdropped by a still angry dark sky.

"Sinners all! Haven't you listened to Zoria? God has had to remind you again. Just look what he's had to do! Just look around at the horrible punishment he has had to mete out. Heed his warnings or he will punish you again. Zoria cannot bring Jesus back to you until you are clean, until you give yourselves to her Word. She has been pregnant with Jesus for so many years! She longs to bring him forth to you for the Second Resurrection, oh glorious day! But how can he come among us when his flock is so corrupt, so full of devil's work? Fall on your knees and beg God to restore the Earth's health. Promise him virtue and obedience in all things. If you don't, it will only get worse. Weep, sinners, pray for forgiveness!"

With everything closed, people flock to the temple and the chapels, Drake among them. Vita has never seen him so pale and moved. He really believes Father Rose. Vita, guiltily, does not. To her worried astonishment, neither does Lorna.

"I don't want to go to church," she tells her father. "I don't see the point. I already know exactly what they're going to say."

"What!" Drake barks. "I don't believe my ears. Can a child of mine be spouting these heresies? Get down on your knees and beg God's mercy!"

But Lorna stands defiant, hands on hips, until he pushes down on her shoulders and then kneels beside her, urgently invoking forgiveness. The girl's voice joins his in a sullen monotone.

On the third day the sun returns full blast, and Chief Barry calls for action. First of all, the dead Nons must be buried. Dozens were crushed or drowned in the storm. Most Nons don't have cellars, and the old subway tunnel they used to flee to has been flooded so many times it's now only a dank dripping cave. After that, the rebuilding must begin. Teams are assigned, and a date for reopening offices and shops is set. Suddenly there's activity everywhere, sounds of hammering, shouts of instructions, even laughter again.

4

Lorna continues to amaze her mother. Late one evening the three of them are sitting in their beds in the front room reading, with the creaky air conditioner going full blast. Outside the dark window a hazy half moon presides over still excruciating heat. Curled up on pillows with her teddy bear, Lorna suddenly drops her book to her lap.

"Did you know," she announces, "that global warming is causing this deranged climate?"

Drake slowly puts down his notebook and begins an apoplectic glare.

Vita intervenes diplomatically, "That's one opinion I've heard. What about it?"

"Well," Lorna explains, "global warming was caused by burning fossil fuels in the last century. God didn't have anything to do with it."

In the tense silence the air conditioner wails plaintively.

Drake gets up and strides across to stand over his daughter.

"I don't ever," he seethes, "want to hear you speak like that in my house. I don't ever want to hear such filth in your mouth again. That's not in the book you're reading."

"No, daddy, this is the one you gave me about dedicated teens," Lorna replies, beginning to cower.

"Where did you hear such abomination?" His hands are balled red fists.

"Summer camp," she whispers.

"Vita!" he shouts. "I told you that place was anathema. Get her out of there at once! I'm going to report that camp to the authorities." He turns and grabs his daughter by the arm. "Who's been telling you these lies?"

"I don't remember."

"You'll remember, you'll remember." Drake shakes her. "Beg our merciful God for forgiveness. Beg. Let me hear it."

Lorna starts to cry and babbles, "I'm sorry God, I'm sorry daddy."

Now Vita jumps up, pulls at Drake, cries, "Leave her alone. What are you doing?"

Drake pushes her roughly aside, bellows, "I want you both in heaven with me. I won't stand for this devil's work. I don't want to hear it, you understand?"

Wife and daughter succumb to habit and bow their heads.

After Vita comforts Lorna, holding her and drying her tears, she turns out the lamp and lies down under the sheet beside Drake. She can sense that his fury is spent, and knows that he now longs for her touch. The room is sultry and pitch dark except for a crooked thread of moonlight. For a while she stays well away, doesn't move.

Vita and Drake met when she was barely twenty-one. She was still mourning her mother's prolonged death from cancer. Cancer was everywhere, surging to epidemic proportions already by then, but her feisty, hard-nosed mom was not supposed to be defeated by it. Two years earlier her father had been killed "in action" somewhere out west, though they had never been able to unearth what kind of action or any details at all. Orphans now, she and her sister were living on the second floor of the family house on Cayuga Lake; the first floor had been flooded so many times it was a soggy moldy mess. Vita had a job of sorts in town, helping restore damaged library books. Drake was part of a team setting up a refugee camp in the area, for the hordes of people heading north. Back then there was still hope that if you could just get to northern Canada, you'd find normal weather again.

After meeting Vita, Drake took a great fancy to the library, and soon they were spending most evenings together. He would come for dinner, always bringing a treat they could not afford, and then sit with her in the dark on her porch overlooking the lake, soothing her with his talk. Way before she fell in love with him, Vita was mesmerized by his certainties, his core of strength, his shining view of the return of Jesus, waiting for rebirth in the womb of the great Zoria. She found it easy and so comforting to embrace his burning faith. That he was nine years older reinforced her awe and acquiescence. With converts throughout the South, the Zorians were at that time beginning to make headway in the rest of the country, though still regarded by many as an obscure cult. Drake was among their most fervent believers. Vita recalls vividly the calm solid resonance of his voice, the restfulness of his steady embrace.

"My family in Tennessee lost everything in the floods," he recounted. "The streets of our town were raging rivers. I saw my father drown. Yes I saw him drown. I was only twelve years old. I can still see his horrible eyes, like empty glass. But you know, Vita, all this suffering, Jesus feels it in his every fiber. He knows what suffering is. When he returns he'll bring joy and peace. That's the promise of Zoria."

"But what happened to the world?" she insisted once. "To me, it seemed that suddenly everything went wrong at the same time."

"It wasn't sudden," he assured her. "It just went from bad to worse. God was really getting fed up. Some people say the balance tipped in '42, 'the 29th Day,' they called it. But God gave us plenty of warning, years of warning."

"That's right, I heard about the 29th Day, the tidal waves over Boston and New York. The government had to leave Washington. My parents said burning fossil fuels was screwing up the weather and oceans. And chemicals poisoning all the water. But, Drake, after that they stopped using coal and oil, didn't they, and banned the chemicals?"

"Vita," he replied with gentle force, the muscles in his arm around her tightening, "fuels and chemicals are the toys of man. When the natural way of things is destroyed like this, you may be sure it is the will of God. Don't despoil your precious little mind with such thoughts again. God condemns and punishes and saves us as only he sees fit. It's not for us to ask questions."

After that she never interrupted, nor asked for more explanations. She accepted that Zoria had been pregnant with Jesus for many years, and that the world must be punished before it could be blessed. Drake's faith was a cloak that salved her own raw grief over her parents, and merged in some vague but delicious way with the burn of his sexuality.

Even after he had to leave for duties farther east, the eviews they exchanged through the library computer kept her close and dependent on him. She often wonders what her fate would have been if Drake had not rescued her at that frightening and vulnerable time.

Now in the heavy darkness he inches closer, and when she remains still his hand creeps to cover her breast. This gesture of peace and affection turns her slightly towards him, and he lets out a great sigh. They sleep.

જ્જ

"But I want to stay in summer camp, mom. Can't you persuade him?"

"He's too upset, I couldn't. And besides, you're going to have to tell him who gave you those ideas."

"Never."

"Histrionics won't work either. Was it a teacher?"

They are cutting up vegetables for dinner at the counter by the cooker. The airconditioned front room is closed off and this room is steaming hot. Lorna stabs a carrot. "No."

"Who then?"

"If I tell you, will you promise he won't get into trouble?"

A boy, then. Vita smiles to herself. It's probably Garth, the kid from Williamstown. Gawky, with snapping black eyes and butterscotch-brown skin, soccer player. Lorna's crush on him has been apparent to her mother for some time. But she keeps her face severe.

"I can't promise anything. Your father will have to know, and what he does about it is up to him."

Vita turns to flip the soy cakes simmering with onions. To save fuel they're making enough for tomorrow as well. Their stored solar supply is running low, though probably Drake's new appointment will mean a larger amount issued to them. For dessert they'll have mulberry tarts from the bakery. Lorna, her hair bundled up from her neck in a twist, her lanky arms bare, continues concentrating fiercely on the carrots.

Abruptly she says, "Do you think we could live on a farm?"

The question is so irrelevant and unexpected that Vita's mind stops while she watches herself go on mincing basil leaves. Dimly, deciding on the diplomacy of registering her surprise, she's aware of the minty aroma of the spice layering into the smell of toasted onion.

"I don't know," she replies neutrally.

What kind of answer is that? She must get at the source of the child's wild question—she's convinced it's not whimsical.

So she tries, "I used to live in the woods you know, by a lake. We grew pumpkins and tomatoes. Sort of like a farm."

"I think this farm," Lorna tosses off casually, as if it's purely interesting speculation, "would have goats." She sweeps the vegetables into a pile, brushes her hands together, wipes her sweaty forehead with her wrist. "I think it would have chickens, and a cornfield."

Vita puts down the knife carefully. She has the sense that Lorna is reaching out to her, as clearly as if she has in her hands something precious and is proffering it, and that what Vita says next will result in receiving the gift or in seeing it disintegrate. She wants to encircle Lorna, capture her eyes, but she does neither. She slides the soy cakes to a plate, stirs the vegetables into the onion sauce.

"I think," she says, matching Lorna's tone, "that we might be able to manage that. It sounds like a good kind of farm. Where do you think it might be located?"

"Oh, I don't know. It could be west. It could be near Williamstown."

Now Vita does turn to look fully at her daughter. Lorna has taken off her apron and is twisting it in her hands. Strands of her hair have escaped their confinement and curl darkly wet on her neck. She's scanning her mother's face while trying to maintain a display of candid innocence that doesn't work. Under other circumstances Vita would laugh at her lame ruse, but she answers with dead seriousness.

"Lorna, doesn't your friend Garth come from Williamstown?"

"So?"

"He knows about this farm?"

"I guess."

Hanging there on the verge of complicit communication, they don't hear the sounds of Drake's arrival until he calls, "Where are my girls?"

In guilty unison, they busy themselves so that when he comes in, Lorna's getting out knives and forks to set the table, and Vita is blowing on a spoonful of sauce before tasting it. She receives her husband's kiss on her cheek with a merry chuckle and the kind of half playful deference she knows he likes.

5

Diamond jerks from a doze, pulls away from her lover.

"Hadn't we better get moving? It's late."

He mumbles, squeezes her thigh, "Sleepy."

"You've already had a good snore. Okay look, you can rest some more if you want, I'll make coffee. But I don't want to be late back to work at a job I just started. I have to be a model employee, remember? And you haven't got much time yourself."

She resolutely removes his hand, goes to wash at the sink. He watches her, looking good in the shaded light, generous breasts, nice thighs and buttocks. Of course her years show in the thickened waist and shoulders, but she still holds a young grace. She fixes her face, combs her hair, dresses again in the neat cream-colored outfit. Frankly enjoys his watching. Comes to gaze down at him affectionately.

"It was good, Alex," she smiles.

"Terrific." He rolls up. "Shit, look at the time."

"I told you."

While she cleans up the remnants of their lunch and starts the coffee, he washes, pulls on his underwear. Comes to sit casually at her little round table, ankles of his long legs crossed. He feels very good.

This fling with Diamond is a wonderful extra. In fact, the Credos suggested to them when they were assigned to team up that they could use the pretense of an affair to cover their meetings. Diamond is no threat to his marriage. Just because Gloria hasn't wanted to have sex for years doesn't mean he's in danger of falling in love with anyone else. He's sure that Gloria, deep in his soul, enfolds his whole capacity for love. And Diamond's as wise as she is practical. She's made it clear the casual convenience is mutual. She makes love with calculated ferocity, wasting no time on abandon.

She says, "Perk up there, Alex my man, we have decisions to make."

She hands him the coffee, sits down opposite him, responds to his grin with, "I know it's hard to be revolutionaries when we're so relaxed. But let's try. Now listen. I have a chance to shoot Chief Barry's private quarters, the crack in the roof they need to repair. They only asked for a photo, but I'm planning to film it as well, in an excess of zeal you might say, to get the whole layout. What I need is a way to zap it to your contact right away. I don't want to hold on to it."

Alex sits up straight. "That's risky."

"Your computer reception in Albany is safe, isn't it?"

"I meant, risky for you."

"No, not really. At least I don't think so. The cover message will rant about the urgency to fix the Chief's damage. As long as they don't get excited when they see the video camera, it will be routine. Once I get back to the office, I'm home free."

"Delete it right away."

"Of course."

He gives her the site address and to help memorize it she takes a few turns around the room, repeating it out loud. Alex drums his fingers nervously.

"That footage will be dynamite," he concedes, "especially if you can get the location of the generator. But someone will be watching you every minute."

"Don't worry. By the way, I'm cultivating Drake Gordon's wife at the moment. He's one of Father Rose's golden boys, so there's potential for getting inside info. At any rate being seen with her is a good maneuver."

"Yes I know Drake. Good work. You have a talent for subversion, my pet."

"And who knows, she could be a possible recruit."

"Be careful with that. Recruiting among the powers that be isn't something I recommend."

"But what a coup it would be to get Mrs. Gordon on our side! She's a bit of a wimp, but I think she's starting to wake up. Anyway, look who's talking. You're part of the elite yourself."

"No, I wasn't when I was brought in. I was just sitting on the deck of my boat seething at the world. The first Credo I ever knowingly met was a fisherman. He'd been hauling up fish with tumors all over them. He got me thinking."

"You make the most adorable spy," croons Diamond, coming to flick her tongue over his lips briefly. "Gotta go. Listen, don't forget to lock up. I'll see you Monday, same time, okay? Good luck."

"I need to brief you before I go back to Albany. Update you on what I learn this afternoon. We need to figure out how everything fits together."

"We will. We'll spend the whole time on it. No hanky panky."

He laughs, but by the time she has hurried out he is all business. From under the bed he pulls out a laundry bag and from within it everything he needs. He reddens and blackens his face—red for sunburn, black to look like he hasn't washed for weeks. Draws on a frayed ragged shirt and trousers missing knees, shoes missing toes. Pulls down the handle of the door in the ceiling, tosses a rope to a hook, and clambers up into the crawl space. Worms his way to the round rear window. Peers out at the back of the market place, where Nons and their children are pawing through discarded rotting food. Takes a breath, readying himself to change worlds. It happens every time. It's as if he takes off his head and screws on another one. He's already half-starving, craven, desperate, beyond anger.

As soon as Alex has dropped to the ground, he pulls the rope after him, circles it around his shoulder like a workman's, and steps into the open. The Nons don't give him a second glance. He takes off down the steep path. He has about an hour. If anyone is watching the front of the house, he can be expected to nap in his mistress's bed not much longer than that. Of course it's unlikely there's any official doubt about him, but busybodies are everywhere, willing to whisper to the authorities in exchange for favors. As the priests gain steadily in power, sedition is going mainstream. It used to be that if enough nosy neighbors ratted on you, you might lose a few privileges. But lately intimidation is taking a more serious turn, especially with the ramped up Citizen's Watch. There have been instances of public condemnation from the pulpit, jail terms on trumped up charges. Of course sexual flings are fine—what gets targeted is any kind of anti-government activity.

Alex makes his way through narrow dusty streets, elbowed and jostled by barefoot crowds. From various directions come the wails of children. The smells turn his stomach until he gets used to them. He stops at a squat shack, pushes open the lopsided door. Inside, two women look up from their sewing. He makes the Credo sign—arms crossed over his chest—but there's no need.

"Alex! Welcome!" The older woman gestures him in, her leathery face beaming. "How's everything with you? They're all here."

"I'm fine, Lema, thanks," he answers, amazed again at the civilities preserved in such squalor.

In the back room, four men and a young woman are sitting on the floor in a circle on straw mats. They make room for him.

"Good," says Alex. "Let's get started."

6

That afternoon Vita seeks out Diamond in her cubicle.
It's Friday and it's been a hectic week for Services, with several crises at once. Father Rose persuaded Chief Barry to stop wasting precious fuel purifying the Nons' water supply. So dysentery has struck them again, with their children particularly hard hit, dehydrated and dying. Then a skirmish with the Hartford enclave to the south has brought in ten wounded. And just when medical care is most in demand, a girl at the temple is having a precarious pregnancy, so the best doctors are tied up continuously hovering over her. Vita has been processing and coordinating priorities and schedules hour after hour until she has a headache.

She flops into a chair beside the desk while Diamond hastily closes out a program and turns to her.

"What's up?"

Diamond puts the question with characteristic snap, but Vita senses a defensiveness she can't pinpoint.

"We missed you at lunch," she hazards.

"Had some errands."

"Our department's in a frenzy, how about yours?"

"For sure." Diamond twists a wry smile. "And on top of that I had to drop everything and go shoot the Chief's roof."

"I hope it's not too bad."

"The damage? Not in the general scheme of things."

"No," Vita agrees sadly. "Some of the soldiers' wounds are really awful. I hope it doesn't screw up the summit to have this violence cropping up again." Then she decides to risk it. "Listen, let's go to your place after work, skip the news. It's much more relaxing there, I really had fun last time." When Diamond hesitates, Vita at once regrets her boldness. "Well," she stammers, "maybe not today…"

But then Diamond responds with a reassuringly snide remark. "And miss the big story on whether the temple primadonna du jour is 'experiencing discomfort' again?"

"That's right."

"It must be my hard cider."

Vita laughs. "Might be."

In what seems a short amount of time, Vita has come to relax with Diamond, drop her guard. She admires Diamond's sharp edge, her common sense approach, her brisk confidence, her wise irony, her worldly malaise. Vita wishes she could be more like that, instead of always worrying and fretting, often losing track of who she is, what she is, outside of Drake's sphere.

So shortly after five they're turning into Diamond's door. The two flights of stairs are narrow, but her room is spacious and attractive. Vita is astounded to see that the airconditioner has been left on, meaning that Diamond must have the wherewithal to keep it running all day. On top of the fact that the machine is newer than hers. They stretch out their arms standing in front of it, with little exclamations of relief.

"What bliss to come home to a cool place," Vita sighs.

"I forgot to turn it off," Diamond explains crisply. Then she adds, "You know, it's a gift from my son."

Diamond's son is a sergeant in Zoria's Guardian Angels. Vita decides he probably arranges for its fuel too.

"How is he?" she asks politely, when she really wants to get on with the main purpose of her visit.

"Still touring out west with Zoria. They're getting a very good response. It's the wildfires out there. Going on and on—as soon as one slows down another one starts up. Ten million acres and counting. People are scared to death. They need the promise of Jesus."

Diamond pours out cider, hands her a cup. Vita has heard the slight irony in her comment. She knows that protecting Zoria was not the career choice she wanted for her son. But Vita has come to find such hints of heresy more refreshing than frightening. In these final weeks of June since she began plotting Lorna's escape in earnest, she's started trusting and confiding in Diamond more than she feels is wise. It's just that she needs a confidante so badly, and all her other women friends seem bland and timid in comparison. She envies and aspires to Diamond's cool, courageous detachment. She looks around the pleasant room and tries to think of a word to describe it. Elegant, organized, sumptuous, practical, whimsical, down to earth. It's such an odd mixture, from the alphabetized spices and stacked file boxes to the spacious rumpled bed and big stuffed unicorn with a gold ribbon around its horn. What's strongest is the feel of the space, curled and rounded, as if the four walls are irrelevant to its shape. The room is visceral, intense, and sure of itself, just like Diamond.

"You know," Vita plunges in, "Lorna has a crush on this boy Garth? She met him in summer school."

Diamond nods. They take their cider over to sit on the couch together.

"Okay, well, I think he might be the hook I need to get her out of the virgin decree."

"Sounds promising."

Vita is tired, and lulled by the cool air and heady drink. Here at this moment everything seems easier. She relaxes, leans back against soft fabric, turns her face fully to her friend's.

"You see, Diamond, I think I'm going to have to leave Drake, at least for a while."

Diamond's reaction is amazement. "What? But you have a pretty good marriage I thought...don't you?"

"We do. At least, well, in its way. But he'll never consider refusing to offer his daughter to the priests, he's so holy and devout. He doesn't even think it would be bad for her! So I have two choices. I wait two more years—really only one and a half now until she turns fifteen—and make myself accept it and even prepare and encourage her as I'm supposed to do…or I get her out of here."

She stops, takes a gulp from her cup. Her foolhardy words hang in the air. Diamond's look is calm intensity, unreadable. What is she thinking? Is she shocked and horrified, worried, or is she dawning admiration?

Diamond waits a while for more, then comments calmly, "So Lorna's feelings for this boy are making her think twice."

Vita sits silent for a moment studying Diamond, taking in her neat composed form, small square hands, arms flecked with dark down, her startling eyebrows, thin arched nose, long flexible mouth, face from another sphere where self-confident people know what they're doing and what they're up against.

"That's it," Vita decides to continue. "I'm convinced that her attraction to a real boy is making her aware of what sex could mean. It's only been a fairy princess idea up til now."

"If the girls are lucky enough to get pregnant," Diamond smirks, "all sorts of wonderful things happen. The kids fathered by priests get adopted by elite couples, and they've proved fertility so they get to marry the best men. The whole deal only takes a year or so out of their lives."

"Diamond, spare me your irony. Don't tease me on this subject, please."

Diamond gives her sympathetic lopsided smile. "Sorry. It just gets to me, the way they make it sound like it's for the good of the human race. They're using the drop in fertility as an excuse to molest young girls, that's all it is. Just part of their power grab."

Vita takes a deep breath. The anxiety she expects to feel listening to such heresy doesn't materialize, instead she feels energized. Unexpectedly a picture of her sister emerges, hands on hips, challenging her. She feels sure Ellie, always unafraid to speak her mind, would have admired Diamond too. Why shouldn't she tell Diamond about her? Even as she hesitates, Vita knows she will. Her need to share is heightened by the self-confidence she feels surfacing.

"You see," Vita confides, "I have a sister, Ellie. She disappeared when she was seventeen. We were still living at the lake. Drake had just left and I was feeling so terrific about him, but missing him too. One day I came home from work and Ellie was just gone."

Diamond widens her eyes, but doesn't question the abrupt change of subject.

"The military?"

"That's what everyone thought at first. The scouts were all over, grabbing young people and forcing them into uniform. But when I didn't hear from her at all, I realized it wasn't that. I was going crazy, but the police decided she'd run off, they had other things to worry about and they got tired of me harassing them. Nothing was missing, all her clothes and things were in place, and of course she never would have left me without even a note, that's ridiculous."

"Kidnapped."

"Yes. But who? I've decided it must have been the slave trade, what else could it be?"

"Twenty years ago, yeah, there was a lot of that, with all the chaos. Now not so much, it's more institutionalized. The Zorians have got it legalized. They have their young girls and the Nons do the work."

"She'd picked blueberries for dinner. She'd fixed our broken fan, she got some milk from our neighbor's cow... she knew I loved milk with blueberries...and then, I figure she went for a walk, or maybe she was just working in the garden..." Vita gazes away and feels tears smarting. "I think she's dead."

Diamond pats her hand and gets up to refill their cups. "You were close?"

"She was my little sister, I took care of her."

"And now you're afraid you'll lose your own little girl."

The remark hurts so much that at first Vita feels Diamond has attacked her on purpose. But then she realizes it's the truth of it that stabs. She sobs into her hands.

Diamond gives her a handkerchief and waits. After a while, she says, "You've got a problem. Your husband will never let either of you go."

7

Alex stares out at the yellow fields. He's on the first leg of his trip home to Albany, riding in a rickety bus that makes a god-awful noise. Sounds like a wounded seagull. He's been away for almost two months and he's worried about his wife. After the big June storm she'd insisted on being taken home right away, wouldn't stay in Boston another minute. She says she's fine, she looks okay in the eviews, but you never know with Gloria. Something could have happened, some new physical affliction, or maybe another flashback. Those are the worst, those flashbacks, when the whole nightmare happens to her all over again.

In the seat across the aisle from him there's a gorgeous young woman who has eyed him more than once. He admires her legs and the curve of her breast, and forces a stony response. He won't get mixed up with her, he's not even tempted. Partly because he's sated with Diamond, but mostly because he never would risk a liaison where the woman expects any emotional commitment. This lovely thing would want to marry him, or at the very least insist on assertions of love.

When Alex met Gloria twelve years ago, he was living on an old fishing boat in Gloucester Harbor. Times were harsh, there wasn't a lot to eat, drinking water was scarce and selling at sky high prices. Bandits ruled. By the late 2040s the tide had turned from confusion to panic and chaos, with the federal and state governments in total disarray. The only police force to be found anywhere had to be privately hired, at exorbitant rates. The rich who could afford protection became richer because of it. Schools were closed, hospitals had no equipment, and everybody was trying to buy a gun. Communities were broken and scattered, with hordes heading north to escape the stupefying heat. Makeshift

47

funerals were happening everywhere, on street corners, by the seashore, at abandoned malls.

The boat was called, according to its hull, the "Julie Anne." It was tied to the chimney of a house now underwater. He could stare across the harbor at Gloucester's hills, where buildings were still standing but no people moving. The tall white church with its brilliant blue roof looked grotesquely serene. All life was on the water, families crammed into boats of every size and kind, even the old gas powered yachts, now sporting makeshift sails. Alex sat on the deck late into the night coming to terms with the loss of his mother. She had died of pneumonia in a hospital that ran out of oxygen. After he'd wept his insides out, sleeping on her grave three nights in a row, he listlessly took to the road, not caring where he was going. He was sure he would never recover.

One day Gloria came floating towards him clinging to a board. She was naked and her eyes were insane. She didn't speak a word for weeks. She only ate because he fed her. She was like a baby bird he'd rescued as a boy—a creature that did not register him, that only automatically went through the motions of being alive. When had he started loving her? In those first moments of her desperate need, or later when she smiled at him, kissed his hands calling him her savior? Whenever it was, her spirit had since then occupied his soul entirely.

Eventually, she told him what had happened. At first he gathered only that she'd been raped. Gradually it came out there had been six men, who kept her tied up at their camp for a long time—months? Then they threw her in the water to drown.

When at last Alex ventured to touch her in a sexual way, she screamed and wailed for hours. Finally, when she did let him make love to her, ever so slowly and gently, it was only out of devotion to him. She hated every minute of it. He ended up feeling like a rapist himself, ashamed of his manhood and its persistent urge to invade. When he made it clear he was going to try very hard not to do it any more, she wept with gratitude. She likes to be cuddled and rocked, like a child, so that's what he does. He'll do anything to make Gloria happy. She has rich mahogany colored hair exactly like his mother's, and the same piercingly touching way of holding his hands in tenderness and supplication.

Outside Northampton they switch to a wagon pulled by two horses. There's a canopy over the top, but the sides are open to the rows of benches. The gorgeous young thing takes a different route. Alex fully enjoys watching her very nice hips as she walks away. His remaining fellow passengers are nowhere near as interesting: an elderly woman with two young children, a man in overalls, a couple of minor diplomats like himself. Their vehicle merges with those heading north, and traffic is slowed by the glut of haphazardly concocted conveyances, from cooking oil campers and horses pulling trucks, to a man shouldering a rope attached to a wagon piled with belongings on which perches a solemn little boy. The freakish snowstorm has been followed by more months of drought just when harvests should be ripening, driving many to leave their homes for the chimera of food and better weather elsewhere. Along the side of the road cluster groups of haggard people resting; some look as if they may never get up again. Some hold out empty cans to the passersby, begging for the water no one can afford to part with.

Going over a hill they pass a mile of slanted solar panes, and ranged along the hills beyond, a forest of wind turbines. Alex knows well that the precious fuel they generate never reaches those who need it most, but is carried directly to the elite in the Albany enclave for their homes and offices. Including his own quite luxurious flat of two large rooms, where Gloria no doubt awaits him now. He wishes she would seek out other people, get interested in more things. But her main focus is her myriad phantom physical ailments, her favorite companions the health aides she frequents.

He dwells on a memory from years past, when Gloria was living on the Julie Anne with him. One day when he returned to the boat she was radiantly waiting, wearing a white dress that she had sewn herself from some old shirts. Her sweet haunted face full of love, holding out her hands to him. Her breasts lifting the soft drape of the fabric. She had let him kiss her deeply, he could have sworn that she responded, her body pressing close. This treasured moment is his mantra, his hope that one day she may yet heal enough to truly give herself. When he pleasures himself, he imagines her pulling him in, opening her beloved body willingly.

The memory brings him in spite of himself to his last encounter with Diamond, when she mounted him with such fury. She had been laughing, and her laughs became howls of pleasure and conquest, black curls flying, breasts thudding wildly. His hands on her bucking hips slippery with their sweat. Ah, he could get used to Diamond! Too bad he's not going back to Boston for at least a month.

And there is much to do before then. "Disable, Depose, Distribute," the Credo slogan, pulses continuously in the back of his mind. Disable the polluting plants and machines, depose the priests from their autocratic rule, distribute life essentials fairly to all. In the past, this has been done piecemeal, without much success. Many Credos have been jailed or executed. The plan now is for a widespread coup, with everything meticulously in place so that the transfer of power occurs everywhere suddenly and thoroughly, with as little damage as possible.

When he'd told the Nons about Diamond's video of the greenhouse, several voices called for immediate action.

"We have the info, let's strike now," cried a restless young man. "Just think, no more greenhouse palace pigging out on energy. What a win!"

"Relax," Lema had countered. "Sure, it will be great for a little while. Put a scare into them and leave us some power for our own projects, God knows we need it. But look, we've tried that before and you know it's just a matter of time. They'll fix it, and then where will we be?"

"Right," Alex pursued, "and they'll use the sabotage as an excuse for a crackdown, as usual. That's why the jails are full of Credos."

"So what, we've got nothing to lose," snorted the young man.

"Yes we have something to lose," Lema insisted. Her puckered old face was glowing with urgency. "Our children, our gardens, our homes such as they are. No, listen. This time we're going to wait. Get everything in place at the same time as the other three enclaves. That way, we'll be like mosquitoes, all over. The priests and Security Forces won't know where to turn to fight back."

"Of course we'll use the video," Alex assured them, "study it, integrate it into the whole plan. When we shut down that greenhouse, the lights will be going out in every damned infernal palace from Burlington to Albany to Hartford."

He and the young man had both jumped to their feet. At this point he put his arm around the youth's shoulder, face close, eye to eye. "I want this as much as you do. More. This tyranny and injustice make me furious, this continuing raping the planet makes me furious. Believe me, I wouldn't ask for patience if it wasn't the best way to win."

"When we rev up that greenhouse again," crows Lema, "we'll be using it to grow food for our kids."

In the end, cooler heads prevailed, ferocity coaxed into strategy.

Besides plotting with the Credos in Albany, Alex will be working hard to make sure the October summit goes smoothly. With Ambassador Ladd still in Boston, he's responsible for meeting with the Albany authorities in a careful mix of diplomacy and firmness. He's got to soften them up for the demands that Rose and Barry insist on, in spite of his own disapproval. The irony is not lost upon him: he's using all his smarts to shore up the northeastern alliance at the same time he's aiming to undermine their regimes. Both his jobs take restraint, diplomacy, courage, focus, all things he prides himself on possessing. Before he can think about it, he reaches out his canteen, still half full of water, to the grasp of a woman on the roadside holding a wailing baby.

8

Vita and Diamond are watching the news after work on August 28, when a full-screen image of Father Rose appears. This is not rare, except that the timing is odd. He usually gives a benediction and blessing just before six, toward the end of the broadcast. Now it's right after the newscaster, a toothy woman with masses of hair, has launched the usual preliminaries: "All there is to know in Boston." Uplifting theme music, a shot of Zoria brandishing her signature inverted cross, Chief Barry delivering his friendly half salute, half wave, and a distant view of the pond area in pink dawn. But today this is followed not by updates on skirmishes, crop yields, and temple pregnancies, but by a close-up of Father Rose. His meticulously groomed iron-gray hair caps his senatorial face like a helmet. He is not smiling.

"Citizens of Boston," he intones.

Everyone in the café stops with cups or forks in midair and falls silent.

"Citizens of Boston, God is angry. Not a drop of rain for months. His bounty withering on the vine. Why is that? You know who's to blame, just look at yourselves. Glorious Zoria is still pregnant with Jesus, after all these years. Imagine her sorrow that she cannot yet bring him forth to you. You are not worthy. Will you ever be? In her love for you she has had great hope. She sheds tears for you and constantly prays to God the Father for mercy. Tirelessly she travels far and wide over the land, bringing the sacred Word to all. But there are those who do not, will not see the light. Even the great Zoria's endless patience is running out. God must be obeyed."

Diamond mutters under her breath, "He's taking over, I knew it."

Vita's temples pound with confusion and anxiety. She knows that Drake is watching this announcement with resigned humility. She knows she too is supposed to feel dread of the divine, open her heart to deserved punishment and penitence. She envies Drake his certainties. What has happened to her own comforting confidence in Zoria? Vita is beset with incredulity, she wavers in longing for logic, and she can't stop herself from seeing that this man is only a man. He's no messenger of God. He's greedy, immoral, power hungry, and sinister. For these disturbing heresies she blames Diamond, and she's almost as angry at her as at the priests. What is she going to do with her new insight? It can mean nothing but trouble.

"Shut up," she hisses at Diamond.

But Diamond has never let Vita's qualms bother her. She chuckles maliciously and replies, "You can swallow it if you want. Go ahead, if it makes you feel better."

The ruddy skin of Father Rose has taken on an almost magenta hue as he waxes more ferocious. Vita looks at the faces around her, all upturned pale moons reflecting his glory. If any of them are questioning, they don't show it. He informs them of several new decrees. All citizens must attend religious services every day or be fined and publicly chastised. Nons who are very sick will no longer receive medical care. Children at the age of seven will be taken from their parents for a year of religious training—even the Nons, in a separate cloister of course. The traitors and heretics known as Credos will be actively hunted down. These are the highlights. The priest ends his declamation with the standard blessing, and a wan, limp Chief Barry is briefly featured calling for calm and obedience. Vita once thought the Chief handsome, but now his eyes seem colorless and his reddish hair greasy dull. His broad face has flattened out, lost a dimension. Then the newscaster is back, nodding and protruding her teeth in an eager grimace of admonishment.

Diamond drains her cup. "Let's go to my place."

Vita gets up and follows her without a word. This is subversion already.

When Diamond has turned on her air conditioner and they're doing their little dance of thanksgiving in front of it, Vita realizes how much of a sanctuary this has become. She counts on it to maintain her balance and explore her disturbing new thoughts. But its very comfort makes her uneasy, because her friendship with Diamond is also the impetus for her increasing skepticism. She hears the voices of her various religious counselors, especially those she frequented when she and Drake were first married. In such a situation, they would say, avoid this temptress at all costs, and report your suspicions to the authorities. These voices always used to at least give her pause, but now they echo through fog, like a fiction. Vita feels she's cutting ties that have sustained her for many years; off she floats alone, anchorless.

At one point about a month ago, she'd tried to pull away from Diamond. She found excuses to hurry home or attend some function. Diamond would shrug and turn away. But Vita had the sense even then that she herself was the suppliant.

Then one day as they were leaving the office Diamond said, casually and softly, "I found out some interesting things about that farm near Williamstown."

Vita of course turned to her abruptly, clutched her arm, to shush her and encourage her at once. As they imitated a relaxed stroll, she replied, "Diamond, you haven't told anyone!"

"What do you take me for?" Diamond squeezed her elbow in response. "I'm hurt you'd think so. I only made inquiries."

"What kind of inquiries? Who? How do you know those people?"

"I don't know them."

The scrape of impatience in her voice made Vita apologetic. "Sorry. But I thought only Garth knew about that place."

"Well I don't know what Garth knows. Maybe not much at all. What I can tell you is I've heard they're great folks, and they help people in trouble."

As they hurried up Diamond's stairs, Vita wondered again about Diamond's connections. How would she know about sanctuaries for fugitives? But she couldn't confront her. This friendship was too important to keep shying away from. She vowed to accept Diamond once and for all, stop listening to Drake's voice in her head. Besides, what counted was getting as much information as they could about the farm. Garth's lead only went so far as to recommend it. What did it matter that mystery seemed to cling to Diamond's edges?

In any case, Vita saw she couldn't put her plans for Lorna on hold any longer. The child was tense, fidgety, losing appetite and weight. Vita could not put her off, didn't want to. Their clandestine conversations had reached the point where a time frame was being formed, where talk of what clothes they would need to take had been touched on. In addition, Vita had discovered a blank in her life without the stimulant of meetings with Diamond. It was as if she was shaping her new self around those few hours after work, as if her backbone were located in the round perplexity of Diamond's home.

Now, doing homage to the air conditioner, swaying with her arms raised, Vita laughs out loud, tasting for an instant an almost wild freedom. Diamond does a mock salaam to the machine, chiming in with her throaty chuckle.

"This is what I worship if anything," Diamond crows, "on any hell hot day!"

Then she turns to watch Vita. "Look at you dancing, you're like a goddess, tall and blond and graceful like the wind. Plus, sweet and feminine. I'm jealous…I hate to say it but you're the kind of daughter my mother always wanted."

Vita stands still looking at her friend in bewilderment. "I think you're beautiful, Diamond. In your way, Egyptian, exotic. I could never be like that if I tried."

Diamond's wistful, envious look melts into laughter. "Well don't try! You never could succeed, that's for sure. You're an angel. Everyone likes you, especially men."

Vita takes this more as mockery than flattery. "Now that's not true, come on. First of all, I'm not tall, I'm average, and my face is too plump for a goddess, look at my nose, it's like a knob in profile."

"Oh forget it. Let's have some cider. I want to get a buzz on."

They curl on the couch with their mugs, legs tucked up.

Vita urges, "Now tell me."

"Okay here's my news. It turns out the farm complex includes a bunch of cottages, tiny though, only one room mostly. Apparently they were moved sometime back in the 2030s from an old motel. It's where the folks live for the most part, and there's a good possibility one will be free about the time you're thinking of going."

"October? I can't believe it. What luck." But Vita knows she has gone pale. With a place to live, she'll have no more practical excuses. "What's the catch?"

"There is a catch. You and Lorna would have to commit to taking care of the goats, feeding and milking and all that. It's not easy work. And the owners will need some money upfront."

"Goats. Lorna will be thrilled. She already talks about the goats," Vita says heavily, not trying to hide her ambivalence. "I believe Garth is a fan of the goats. What can I say. I've milked a cow, I suppose a goat's not much different."

"Just feistier," chuckles Diamond. "Hey, think it over. I know this is a bit of a shock. I never thought it would be this easy to find a place."

"Thanks, Diamond."

Thanks for not pushing it, Vita thinks morosely. It's as if now that she has what she thought she desperately wanted, it's like a small death. Goodbye to security, to comfort, to pleasant predictable routines. Goodbye to Drake. Will he repudiate them entirely, or will he come around eventually?

Then a terrible scene erupts in her mind, Drake bellowing and calling for the Security Forces to hunt them down, Drake himself pursuing with murder in his eyes, being thrown in prison or being cast off among the Nons, reviled and alone.

She says almost whispering, "What if he comes after us?"

"He might. You knew that."

"I can't put Lorna at risk."

"They won't hurt Lorna. Only you."

Vita puts her mug down and presses her hands together. "I guess I can handle it. Besides, how will they know where we are? That area south of Williamstown is a no man's land. The Chiefs don't pay any attention to it."

"No, they won't know where you are, that's the beauty of it."

Diamond now is watching her with detached interest. She knows Vita's in the throes of a searing life decision, but she seems to be observing her like a specimen in an experiment: Which way will she go? Will she persevere or break? It's in this moment that Vita stops looking for strength outside herself, and finds it within. Her annoyance with, even suspicion of, Diamond's motives bring brief vertigo, and then she hits smack up against her own backbone.

"I'll do it, " she says, without hesitation, without gratitude, without asking for approval. She says it with fierce and final serenity.

Diamond gets up and paces. "Look, Vita, I know this is an awful decision for you."

"Tell them we'll take it. The cottage, the job, anything. We'll be there around the 20th. The summit starts on the 18th, so Drake is sure to be out of town by then."

She stands up too, stretches. She's elated with fear and resolve.

"I'll tell them, Vita," Diamond sighs, "but oh, I'm going to miss you."

That night Vita begs Drake, "Can't we talk about it just one more time?"

Lorna's asleep in the front room, and they are in the stultifying living room, she in a chair, he standing in front of her. Light from the lamp is dim. Sweat is rolling down his neck, the pulsing angry muscles of his neck.

"Why?"

"Because…" Because I need to, because it's your last chance, because I still love you. "Please, Drake, try to understand how I feel about this."

"I understand that I don't recognize you. I understand that some devil has got into you. I understand that I have to pray to God every day for you so he doesn't strike you dead."

"Drake." She feels a terrible tiredness, realizes she'll have to lie. "I'm sorry I'm such a trouble to you. I swear I'm trying to see your point of view, I'm trying to come to terms with it. Of course, if you really think it's best…"

He moves closer so his legs are touching hers. "Oh, Vita, yes. You will see the light. You will return to the fold."

"Just please, don't condemn me for wanting to keep our daughter from a bad experience. It's only because I love her so much."

"I love her too, I want a good life for her. We must follow Zoria's way."

His beautiful dark eyes that have so often heated her, his hands that have taken her to ecstasy, this man who stands before her, her husband. She hopes her face does not reveal the chasm of distance she feels, the longing loss.

9

September brings precious rain, providing a few days of relief and celebration. The water tanks fill again, the surviving crops spring jaunty from the brink of drooping death, children leap around opening mouths to the sky, people strut the streets without umbrellas reveling in getting soaked. A collective drunkenness, the repressions of decorum barely clung to. Like everyone else, the Gordons brush aside their troubles. While the heat's at bay, they all come home earlier, Lorna after spontaneous rain dances with her friends, laughing gloating at her sopping clothes. Even the newscasters, even the priests, are grinning. Drake and Vita tryst in their bedroom while their skin is still damp and cool.

Vita embraces this magical chimera with conscious abandon. While aware that every moment with Drake, from serving him dinner to pulsing against him, is among their last for a long time if not forever, she avoids thought. Her life merges with the precious rain, she moves yielding with it, even the tears behind her kisses come from the wet sky.

But of course, the rain doesn't stop when they've had enough. It doesn't stop for weeks. Drought has weakened the trees and other vegetation, so they uproot easily in the torrents of water. Mudslides topple the Nons' hillside shacks, carrying the ruins along at whitewater pace to smash on those below. The Gordons and their housemates circle their building with sandbags, working with Security Forces to keep them in place around the clock.

At one point, when the dam of sandbags threatens to break through, everyone heaves their bodies against it, holding it in place through the night out of sheer will. Finally towards dawn, Vita insists on pulling Lorna away, both of them shivering and spent. Inside, they strip, wrap themselves in towels and blankets. Lorna collapses on her bed, Vita huddles in a chair beside her. In the wavering ashen sunrise, Lorna's face looks as drawn and pale as sickness. But she offers clearly with a small smile, "I'm sure goats can swim." Then she falls asleep before her eyes close.

Vita goes to the window. She can make out Drake below, one shoulder braced against sandbags, the other arm gesturing, and farther down, her neighbors reinforcing their own dams. There's no wind, just steady rain, a curtain of certainty as if there never was anything else. The pond has risen to pour through the fields, but Vita knows soy is hardy and withstands both drought and flood. As long as the plants aren't submerged, there's hope.

Vita trundles blanketed out of the front room, closes the door, and sits in darkness listening to distant shouts garbled by the merciless metallic pour of water. She should make up her mind and either get dressed again and join the others, or go to bed and rest. But she doesn't move, as if not deciding, simply sitting here instead, rescues her.

As solace, she tries to remember what it sounds like without rain's relentless wash and beat, its crescendo of opposing sounds—pummeling, bruising, disintegrating, spitting on leaves, thudding on roofs, pounding its own wet self in puddles, galloping on mud, gushing in streams. Behind that malevolent roar are billions of tiny drops no bigger than a tear.

The last year that Vita and her family were living contentedly together in their shambling old house on Cayuga Lake, she was sixteen. The weather had been getting weirder ever since she could remember, but the first time she truly felt alarm was that spring, when the lilacs bloomed in February and were killed by frost, and the dogwoods didn't bloom at all. Then there was a rain like this one, endless.

"Not to worry," her father had said. "Mother Nature knows her stuff."

But she was old enough to tell when he was protecting her from what he knew. She had never seen the sky rage in this way. She began to put the pieces together, forming a dread. She remembered her third grade teacher talking about the planet's fragile balance; that was the last time environmental studies were taught. Vita concluded that Earth was ill, and not getting better.

That same spring, her father was reactivated to military service. They said they needed his engineering expertise to help restore storm damage to bridges and highways. He was whisked off to Louisiana. She missed him terribly, but she was sure he'd be back soon. She was wrong about that.

Vita is warm now, and knows she's drowsing off. But before she lets in oblivion, she grasps at an image of her father's loving face. It has blurred a bit over the years, but it's as bitterly beautiful as ever.

10

Alex's return to Boston has been delayed by the floods. As it is, the horses are often up to their shanks in mud, and going is slow. Braced against wet wind whipping through the wagon, he huddles in rain gear trying to keep his mind on business. He needs to plan carefully on two fronts: his role in the upcoming summit, and his role in preparing the Credos' coup. He's gratified to be helping formulate peaceful agreements among the enclaves, and by the growing reliance on him of his boss, Ambassador Ladd. Alex has a dream that when the Credos take over, they'll maintain the saner aspects of the enclave system, stability and order, simply adding equality and safety for all. But he knows, better than he often admits, that there are factions among the Credos who have destruction foremost in their minds.

Take Vinsky, for instance. Alex has only met him once, but he's a character both shadowy and charismatic who bears watching. His message is so simple it can be hypnotic: tear everything apart. He has a strong if very small clutch of supporters in the Akron territory, west of Albany. But the majority of Credos, especially those Alex reports to in Vermont, are compassionate, sensible people, although perfectly capable of eliminating a true enemy when necessary. When he meets with the Albany Credos, he'll be helping them chart area communications, including filling them in on Diamond's video methods. Operation Onion, crafted to peel away power layer by layer, will go quickly and smoothly. If only they don't act too hastily, if only Vinsky doesn't get his violent way.

When making the switch from wagon to bus at Northampton, Alex is able to buy a bowl of hot soup. The sensation in his hands cupping the warm ceramic bring him a heady memory of Diamond, who will soon be in his arms, by tomorrow if all goes well. Now that their next encounter looms, his body is rousing, though he hasn't thought much about her while he's been at home. Gloria was alternately adoring and sharp, keeping him on his toes, and on his tiptoes. He usually manages to gauge her mood in time to respond accordingly, but once in a while, just often enough, she surprises him.

Take yesterday. They were having lunch in a restaurant with a friend of hers, a sly, placid old lady who loves to dwell on doom and gloom, interweaving tales of horrendous events with her own multiple maladies. She and Gloria were deep into a discussion of headaches when Alex excused himself to visit the bathroom. Gloria went white and grasped his arm.

"Alex, no, don't go," she gasped. "We women just can't manage alone here, there are men all around." She didn't wait for his reply, but pulled him back into his seat, and into her arms, keening, "If you leave me now, I won't be able to take it. I'm warning you, I won't be able to take it." Her friend started soothing noises, but Gloria continued at a high pitch, "Oh please, my darling dear, don't desert me now, there are men all around," repeating it all over again. It was getting embarrassing as well as alarming.

"Dearest, keep your voice down," he tried, holding and patting her.

The waiter hurried over and all faces in the room mooned towards them. Gloria looked as if she were in the throes of serious illness. Alex was hunched over her now, keeping her from falling off the chair. Her friend was trying to get her to drink some water. Then suddenly it was over, even more quickly than it began.

Alex explained lamely to nobody, "Just swallowed the wrong way I guess."

The color was back in Gloria's cheeks and she calmly took a bite of dessert. The waiter backed away in relief and the spotlight faded from their table.

She said, "I just don't want to lose you." But it was more by way of summary than apology.

Alex felt annoyed, and then guilty because he felt annoyed. The episode had been some version of her dreaded flashbacks, clearly horrible for her—how could he be so callous? Her delicate nerves had already been frayed by the prolonged drought and flooding. Should he postpone his trip? But she has to accept my going at some point, he reasoned, struggling with himself. He can't bear it when she accuses him of abandoning her. He knows he never could, why can't she believe it?

When they got home, he said, "What happened?"

"What do you mean?"

She stood in the hallway looking at herself in the mirror.

He said with an edge, "You know what I mean."

She turned her face to him slowly, with an expression he couldn't fathom. Fear, accusation, satisfaction, pleading—yet darker. Grim. Fierce. Resentful. As if she hated her need for him. He took a step towards her. His soul hurt.

She said, "Leave me, then. Leave me alone." And she turned back to the mirror, folding her hair behind her ears, leaning close into her own image.

He stood there astounded to realize that he had no desire to reassure her, no desire to even touch her. No desire of any kind. If she took her clothes off there and then it would not have moved him. So, she finally had killed his physical yearning. It was a huge relief, after all these years, to not want her. But it was like a death, too. To have his body drop out of the situation was as if a support had collapsed from a bridge. He tried to rekindle, took his eyes over her shape, her glorious hair and beloved profile, her hands, legs. Nothing. He felt absurd in his sense of loss. Hadn't he strived for this, tried so hard to train his groin into stasis, drilled himself in paternal platonic responses, manufactured sexless dedication? His heart cried out, brought tears to his eyes. It was almost as if now that he really did feel only spiritual attachment, he loved her all the more.

He walked past her into the livingroom and collapsed into a chair.

"I'm exhausted," he muttered. "Let's just forget it."

"I'm not going to forget it," she answered, standing in the doorway.

And she didn't. She brought up his abandonment continuously while he prepared to leave. Her litany riddled him with guilt. "You don't have to go away, you do know that. You can get a job here. Of course you can. You want to leave me, you want to make me suffer. You don't even try to imagine what it's like to be betrayed like this. You don't love me, no you never did." One moment she was covering his hands with kisses and tears, the next moment screaming and keening, one moment kneeling to him, the next pointing an accusing finger, arm extended like an avenging angel.

He begged her to forgive him. He knelt too, he held her and crooned, he scolded, he wept, he explained over and over. At last, this morning when she was still lying in her bed with dawn anointing her sleep-softened face, Alex fully dressed with travel bag in hand leaning down to kiss her forehead, she said, "I do love you." His spirit soared.

Everything will be all right, he consoles himself as the van jolts and squeaks beneath him. Yes, he does take the best care of her—his pride in that struggles back. She does know deeply how he treasures her. From his briefcase he pulls out the papers he needs to know backwards and forwards for his briefing with Ladd this evening, but they lie limp in his hands while he recalls Gloria's face last week when he gave her the pretty little set of painted boxes to keep her medical powders in. She looked like a little girl, flushed in her thrill.

"Now I'll be sure which is which, now I can keep track. I need to know exactly what and when, you do know that. I'll be so proud of them, I'll never get my meds mixed up now. Oh, my favorite colors, oh Alex!"

She gave him a hug of happiness and he tasted joy. It was a beautiful moment, and she looked beautiful, eyes luminous with devotion. This is the image he forcefully decides he will nurture all the time he's away. He won't remember her face haggard, her voice harsh, nor his alarmed loss of desire, but only this image, his princess.

Some miles later the van chokes and stalls. Alex looks out to see water half way up the tires, and ahead a lake where the road should be. The driver stands up and says, "We're sending for a boat. Should be here in half an hour. Thanks for your patience."

Alex tunes out the voices of consternation around him as out of fogged memory beams a boat ride he took with his mother when he was nine. It was her birthday. His father had gone off to work that day without mentioning it, surprising nobody, but she had been cast down nevertheless. Mrs. Cohen was a tall woman, taller than her husband, almost as tall as her son would become. But she did not stand tall. Rather, she rounded her shoulders in apology and hung her head, glancing at people tentatively from beneath her brows. There she sits opposite him as he rows, her always untidy but luxurious caramel colored hair cascading down from under a floppy straw hat. She's smiling at him proudly.

"Muscles, young man, look at those muscles won't you."

Had he smiled too, had he shrugged, had he replied? That doesn't conjure up. What does, what flames, is his anger at his father and his sense of power in righting the wrong. He was man enough for his mother. He was giving her what she wanted. All that summer afternoon, to the music of birdsong and water ripple and her peaceful voice, floating in the shade along the riverbank, arms aching, he was brilliantly happy. But in the evening his father gave his wife a new ironing board as a present, and they went out to the movies. Mrs. Cohen glowed then as thoroughly as she had in the rowboat. Alex was deflated and confused. He was tempted to tell his father about their afternoon, but he knew that would only spell trouble. At the very least, a shouting spree on the part of his father, probably some smacks across his son's head, perhaps even some uppercuts to his wife's jaw. Nobody knew just what Mr. Cohen would do when crossed, so they kept many secrets from him. Calm was preserved if they could just stay under his radar.

Alex goes slowly over the memory again, his mother's shining face, his childish pride, the sweet summer air—he'd forgotten how sweet the summer air sometimes used to be. His arms ache again with the vividness. He finds himself smiling.

11

So Cohen, what've you got?"

Ladd is giving him the go-ahead, and Alex eagerly leans forward. He and Ladd had conferred at length the evening before, after his arrival in Boston, and he feels well prepared. Around the oval table in the conference room sit the ambassadors to Burlington and Hartford and their assistants, as well as Chief Barry and Father Rose. Alex morosely notes that Rose has now claimed the head of the table, with Barry seated at his right, instead of the other way around.

"Albany has agreed to holding the summit in Kingston," Alex reports. "Of course they wanted it on their own turf like the rest of us, but they're satisfied with the consensus. Yes, Kingston is a no-man's land, but that's just why it appeals—it belongs to nobody. They've also agreed to contribute funds for cleaning up the old hotel there that we talked about, to house all the reps and provide some tech for the discussions."

"How much money?" interrupts Father Rose. "Fair share?"

"Right," Alex responds respectfully, annoyed. "Yes, the exact amount we suggested. Now, on top of that, Albany would like to contribute wine for the dinners, from their northern vineyards. Quite generous, I think. And further…"

"Generous," snorts Rose, "when we're providing the meat for the opening banquet! You're getting soft, Cohen."

The bastard, thinks Alex. He knows I hate him. He's so smart he might even discern that I plan to throw him and all the other power-mad priests out on their ears. He dips his head apologetically and says, "Just diplomatic, I hope, Father. I assure you, I was adamant about the agenda.

Albany dropped their opposition to putting the water issue first. They're damn protective of their lakes."

"Look," growls Rose turning to Ladd, "your man Cohen is great at delicacy. But we need some strong-arm tactics here. We need water. What do we have to do to get it?"

Ladd is taken aback. At his best he has an air of quiet nobility, but now he suddenly looks very frail, his aquiline nose nearly trembles. "Negotiate," he replies lamely.

Rose turns to Chief Barry. "Chief, don't these people know what's at stake?"

Barry looks around the table. "These are good folks, Father," he says mildly. "Loyal and intelligent. I rely on them."

"That's not what I'm talking about!" Rose raises his voice, lending it a sonorous accusatory tone. It's the voice they all know from dramatic religious proclamations and ceremonies. It has a stunning effect.

Barry hastens to add, "Of course you're right."

Beads of sweat have sprung to Barry's pale forehead. He's been gaining weight lately, his benevolent solidity seems to be melting into fat just like his willpower. He's no match for the priests' relentless push to power, thinks Alex with a mix of sorrow and anger. But then, what can he do as Chief? People aren't paying attention, or rather they are melting, too. It's so much easier to blame all your troubles and terrors on sin. Especially when the consequences of not doing so are getting bolder and harsher.

Rose stands up. "Albany has a string of lakes," he proclaims, "the Finger Lakes, cleaner than anything we have. We have the fuel to transport a regular supply from there. We want that water."

Alex takes out his handkerchief, burying his furious expression in a simulated sneeze. He's beside himself. This guy has got to be stopped. He's going to ruin everything. He doesn't know the meaning of the word diplomacy. Of all the points Alex was able to gain in Albany, negotiating the water question was among the best. Ladd had been warm in his congratulations on just that issue. What the hell is Rose after? Does he really think he can strong arm the Finger Lakes folks, or is he just out to drive Alex nuts?

Ladd says tentatively, "That's why we've got it first on the agenda. That way, everyone knows water is a priority."

The ambassador to Hartford agrees. "Follow the water. You'll see my report focusing on Hartford's request to share our desalination plant, if we can get it up and running again."

"I think you'll find…" Ladd starts to conclude.

"Citizens of Boston," Rose intones, "Your duty is to your own territory first and foremost. Compromise must be the last resort." He continues for ten minutes, mixing Jesus and God in freely with his political machinations until nobody is sure what manner of address they are experiencing. The only thing that's clear is that Father Rose is boss, and that Alex has lost his chance to shine that day.

Later that afternoon, Alex bounds up Diamond's narrow stairs and grabs her in a hug, sighing, "You feel so good."

She returns his kiss, but then pulls away.

"Later," she laughs. "We've got to work first. Wow are you ready!"

He chuckles in embarrassment. "Too many weeks without, I guess." He hastens to add, "Besides, you look great."

And she does. She's wearing a dark blouse of some kind of silky fabric dipping low in front, with short sleeves that show off her lovely little arms, wide red belt, earrings with purple lights in them, eyes bright with affection and promise. They sit at her table over mugs of coffee while he tells her about Rose's steamrolling. She joins him in his bitter anger.

"He'll be out of a job when we're through with him," she says, to Alex's great gratification, even though they both know the man's a deeply serious menace they may not be able to stop.

"We could rebuild and run the old desalination plant for not that much more fuel than it would take to transport Albany's water," he points out. "Unless they cart it here by horse and wagon, which would take weeks. Besides, Albany would fight. Rose can't be serious."

"I don't think he is. The Zorians have a big agenda, and at the top is proving they run everything. And you know what that means. And worse. My friend Vita Gordon has a daughter up for their charming new virgin decree. I think I told you about Vita. She's a bit of a wimp, but she's turning heretic fast. You'll see, these decrees and dictates will be the priests' downfall eventually."

"You're an adorable optimist. No, my pet, instead the jails and graves will be full of folks who refuse to invoke Zoria and flagellate themselves every minute. There'll be constant war. You know Rose is making noises about running the whole northeast, crowning himself some kind of pope or imam. What infuriates me is that finally, with the enclaves starting to recognize common goals, we had a fighting chance at some kind of future."

"Well, you're an idealist, my dear," she counters, getting up to pour him more coffee. She briefly strokes his cheek with the back of her hand before sitting down again. "So now, update me. Have Marcel and Miro decided to move sooner?"

"No. I've got a meeting down the hill in two days, I'll get a first hand report then. But I gather they're very worried about a possible leak in the Hartford ring. One of ours who's managed to become a priest is seriously jeopardizing everything by resisting orders. We've got to shut him up or get him out of there. So our leaders have got their hands full concentrating on that."

"How are they going to do either? If our priest disappears it will look suspicious."

"Don't know. Hopefully he can hold out and keep quiet. He's in such a good position for us, would be a pity to lose that. But even worse if he's discovered. He could spill the beans."

"On us?" Diamond shudders.

"I doubt he knows about you and me. But he could ruin the Hartford effort and set us back a year."

Alex wonders if he should tell Diamond about Ladd's revelation at their briefing last night. He knows he should not spare her; Diamond is tough and she's his partner. But he fondly observes her expectant warm face and doesn't want to cloud it. Afterwards, yes, afterwards he'll break it to her: some Nons who have worked with Alex in the past are being interrogated. Suspicions are very vague, so all may be fine. But Nons who are interrogated don't fare well, and they could break.

Through Diamond's geranium-shaded window the afternoon sun cuts one last bright slant before dimming. She looks luminous and delicious recounting details of her video plans and recruitment efforts. When she finishes, and with a small triumphant smile waits for his approval, he drains his cup and goes to take her in his arms. Down he goes, falling away from everything, into grateful whirling unconsciousness. For all its brevity, this respite, this driving mindless need, this soft heated safety, gifts a fleeting peace.

12

Vita says, "Lorna, she'll be here soon. Isn't the tea ready?"

"What, are you nervous? You said she's a good friend. She's not going to mind a little hustling in the kitchen."

Lorna takes her time gathering her books from the dining room table and resetting it with mugs and spoons, a pot of honey. As the weeks before their flight dwindle, she's become more laconic, while Vita is getting tenser by the day.

Drake is hanging around on purpose to see what this Diamond person is like. He's supposed to have left half an hour ago. Vita chose Saturday afternoon because he has a doctrine briefing every week at this time at the temple, and wouldn't dream of missing it. She should have known. Though he has made his usual official inquires about his wife's new friend, he wants to judge for himself. In particular he needs to reassure himself that Diamond won't be any kind of subversive influence on Lorna. He doesn't trust Vita with this, doesn't trust her insight, doesn't trust her even to really care.

She has warned Diamond. "Be careful. If he's there, remember you're visiting just to give Lorna some pointers on digital imaging, to help her out with her communications course. Keep on the subject. Don't act interested in anything else."

"Hey, relax," Diamond smiled. "I'm as pious and patriotic as the next guy. You know me."

No, I don't, Vita felt impelled to reply, but she only quizzically raised an eyebrow and noted, "You can pull it off."

Vita checks herself in the bedroom mirror, combs her hair again. She's wearing a bright blue blouse and a necklace of blue beads, bringing out the sky of her eyes. Behind her she sees Drake looking at her curiously but pretends she doesn't.

He says, "You've known this woman how long?"

Of course he knows the answer, but she tosses off, "Oh, let's see, since April or May I think. Four or five months. I don't know her that well, but I see her at work every day. Did I tell you Lorna and I are making pumpkin pie tonight?"

He smiles thinly and comes to give her waist a casual possessive squeeze. "My girls are good to me."

But he's on edge. He has sensed something amiss for weeks, Vita can feel his wariness. She has gone out of her way to act normal, to be and say all the wifely things, but though he's not a man given to emotional speculation, his wife and daughter are treasure and he is watchful. Look at him now with Lorna. He's standing by the table, dressed up for the priests in his new high necked tunic that all the most dedicated administrators have taken to wearing lately—one more way to identify the true Zorians. His eyes flick over his daughter's movements like radar, as if reading them. Lorna, lazily pouring cooled mint tea into a pitcher and arranging cookies on a plate, hardly would seem engaged in anything significant. Her only admission to the advent of company is a white ribbon around her ponytail. Otherwise, she's wearing baggy Saturday clothes. What is he thinking? What's he looking for?

Diamond is late. Good. He'll have that much less time to study her.

Vita goes into the front room and looks out the window, but her gaze is focused inward. Her mother used to caution her and Ellie about lying. "Lies are like spider webs, you tell one it catches you to death." Her mother's calm severe face in its dark frame of hair; her mother patting the papers always in front of her assuring herself and everyone else that she had better things to do. She was a lawyer, a good one, constantly saving hapless people from the chaos of the courts, and Vita was proud of her. But often as a child she wished her mother was there when she wasn't. Bedtimes, sick times, mean friend times, it was always her father who came through. It was true though—about lying to her mother—who knew every time.

The lie she's living now in deceiving Drake is taking its toll. It's beginning to sicken her, like something foreign stuck in her throat that she can't get her breath around. Her damaged love for her husband claws at the betrayal she's constructing out of love for her child.

Down the hill the hardy trees that withstood the flood are starting autumn yellow, here and there a reddish tone. Around them remnants of others lie where they were flung by mudslides, upended, roots exposed, grotesque tentacles. The weather flag is white, indicating fairly breathable air, but it hangs limp and damp in brooding heat. The pond is a dull pickled green in the clouded light. The lines of busy Nons in the fields look like worms or crabs concentrating on some kind of unfathomable life purpose.

Diamond comes striding into view under a broad sun hat, clad in a rose colored sundress with subdued frills at the neck. Nothing out of place, not a hair, not a hem, not a gesture. As often at first sight of her, Vita feels unnecessarily loose, disorganized, disheveled, unprepared. She automatically pats her hair and skirt, straightens her spine. Here we go. She tries to siphon strength from the compact figure as it hurries out of sight, up the stairs to her front door.

"Mom, she's here," calls Lorna in a moment.

Vita turns slowly, letting Drake get his fill first. She hears him say, "Welcome, pleased to meet you," in a tone meant to be neutral but loaded with innuendo.

Diamond's casual low voice is reassuring; Vita feels its familiar cadence, at once self-confident and confiding, soothing her frayed nerves. She comes into the main room to witness the three of them posing like old buddies already, Lorna shaking Diamond's hand, Drake holding a chair for Diamond, Diamond grinning amicably. Vita almost feels excluded from this sociable trinity.

At last Drake leaves reluctantly, unsmiling. It seems that Diamond has not succeeded in charming him out of his suspicions. In the few minutes of their exchange, his face darkened. He's angry that he fears her and doesn't know why. He's angry that he's puzzled. Drake is rarely confused or uncertain and this woman unnerves him.

"He doesn't like me," comments Diamond brightly.

Vita cautions, "I wouldn't be proud of it."

"Hey, I tried."

Lorna says, "Who wants tea?"

They pull chairs closer to the couch to make a circle and curl up with fragrant mugs, plate of cookies in the middle.

Diamond begins, "So October 20th, okay? That's what I told them."

"Yes. Right, Mom? In two weeks. We're ready."

Vita says, "We'll send our stuff on earlier, so when we get in the van that morning we'll say we're just going out on a day trip, to visit Lorna's former teacher in Sterling. That's the story. From there we'll catch the Northampton bus."

"You'll be met in Northampton," Diamond confirms. "The woman's name is Clove. If she can't come, whoever does will use her name, so there shouldn't be a problem."

"Could you," breathes Lorna, "tell us more about the farm? Our cottage and the goats and the people and stuff? Garth has told me some things."

"I've never been there, but I know all about it," Diamond replies, and starts a rambling but vivid description, mesmerizing Lorna. Vita watches their interaction with nervous concentration. Lorna clearly has no reservations about Diamond, is awed and excited by her. In turn, Diamond openly admires Lorna, treats her like an adult. There's a spark between them unmarred by the reservations Vita still harbors, the complexity of resentment and envy woven through her dependence on Diamond. Along with Vita's relief at rescuing her child, down her spine runs a chill she can't dispel or ignore. This can't be as easy as she has convinced herself. This is a terrible thing they are doing, against all dictates of her society and her hitherto devoutly held beliefs. Not to mention betraying and abandoning Drake.

Vita puts down her mug and rubs a tear of sweat from her forehead. She takes a bite of cookie but has trouble swallowing it. She can't back out now. In fact, she realizes with a stab that if she did, Lorna would leave anyway, without her. For a moment she's awash with loss and fear mangled together, coursing over her being corroding everything.

Lorna peers at her face. "Mom, it's not going to be that hard. We don't have to make the cheese ourselves, do we Diamond?"

"Other people make the cheese, you just collect the milk," Diamond agrees, studying Vita. "Getting cold feet, are we? Don't worry, Vita. Everything will be fine."

Lorna says fervently, "Thank you for helping us, Diamond."

"Why are you helping us, Diamond?" Vita dares to ask.

Instead of protesting friendship or the liberation of women, Diamond smiles with unfathomable eyes and says, "Well, I told you, Vita, you're a rebel at heart. Rebels are good for this world."

Part II

1

March. It's been especially warm and spring planting is under way. Vita sits rocking in the back of the wagon returning from the Williamstown market, embracing a package with a new dress for Lorna. It cost just about what their apple butter brought. Up front Clove and Beasley are chatting, going easy on the horses. The late afternoon is mellow and the view of the farm, as always from this far hill, is idyllic. There's the main barn, nestled amid greening trees, its extensions reposing like relaxed arms; the house and some cottages clustered to the right; and farther off to one side near the orchard Vita's cottage, which is really two stuck together to shelter the goats. All the dwellings are on piles because of the floods, from this distance resembling alert insects. Squinting, she can make out the goats nibbling languidly in their pen by the stream that once was a river, now a silver thread. The fields are fresh bright brown furrows, and in the cornrows green points already appear.

"There's Noam," cries Clove, pointing out her husband behind the horse and plow.

Beasley comments in his usual whine, "I'll bet he hasn't brought in the water for dinner yet."

"Oh come on, Dad, the girls took care of that long ago I'm sure," Clove assures him. "They're very responsible. Chances are dinner's almost ready."

As they begin the descent, the sky opens out before them in a dazzle of rose and blue strands, here and there a high white cloud puff. Vita is so pleased to hear Clove praise her own daughter and Lorna together. In the four months they've been here, Lorna has gone through many moods, from terror and thrill to disillusion and disgust, to acceptance bordering on eagerness. Vita's own mood has not paralleled. Instead, she's maintained a numb skepticism throughout. Life here is what she expected, though not quite as she imagined. Shoveling goat shit had not been on her horizon, but neither had the surprising satisfaction of communal labor. To help cope, she has reached back into girlhood, conjuring up details of weeding vegetables, cleaning fish, picking berries— even though that had been more family fun than a matter of survival. Sometimes when she watches Noam's big red hands at work she sees her father's, sure even in their heaviness, those beloved hands with rough knuckles and golden hair flecks, tucking her in at night.

Lorna's biggest trial, besides the dawn to dusk work expected of her, has been the absence of books and her sophisticated group of friends. In Boston she had not only the intellectual challenge of school, but also pretty clothes and parties, and public events like sports matches and parades. Here, her only steady companion is Clove's twelve-year-old daughter, and everybody wears overalls. Their idea of entertainment is singing around the piano. They don't have any access to television or even a radio most of the time. The machines are there, but not the fuel or the spare parts to run them. Lorna spent the first months, through Christmas into the new year, anxious, exhausted, and bored. Then Garth arrived for a visit on her fourteenth birthday, bringing books and news. Lorna revived and even after he left, she had a new bounce.

Vita is grateful to see Lorna avidly reading again. As soon as they overcame their fear that Drake would arrive in pursuit of them at any moment, Vita began to worry about schooling. She'd been determined to tutor Lorna herself and perhaps even Clove's daughter Sienna, but so far that's been sporadic at best.

Noam waves as they pass. They pull up by the barn and Beasley unhitches the horses, Lorna running from the house in time to help him lead them to their stalls for a rubdown.

Pix the dog, stalwart German Shepherd mix, streaks across the field in welcome. Sienna appears on the porch wearing an apron too big for her boyish form, ringing a large brass dinner bell. She's a broad-faced, wonder-eyed, impish bit of a girl, who seems an ageless eternal child. She has Clove's wavy brown hair and overbite smile, but it's hard to believe she'll ever inherit her mother's jolly girth.

Over dessert, the conversation turns from crops and weather to politics.

"I hear this Father Rose is tightening his grip on poor old Barry," notes Noam, taking a big bite of pie, brushing drips from his chin.

"Sienna," says Clove, "pass the cream around. Yep, we've had another request for sanctuary. Things are getting rough in Boston."

"Can't do it of course, can't take in any more people," says Noam. "We had a good harvest this past fall, but we shouldn't rely on that happening again for a while. And we don't have room anyway."

"Why can't we build another cottage?" Sienna pipes.

Her father stops chewing to regard her pityingly, snorts, "Just where would we get the building materials? And anyway, who have you noticed has nothing to do around here?"

Sienna glances quickly at the two men at the end of the table, lean and gray with tight faces, who have recently arrived and taken over the last living space.

"We could help," one of them offers.

"No, Marcel." Noam says shortly. "While you're here we need you in the fields. Forget it."

"Who is it wants to come?" asks Lorna. "Do we know them?"

Vita splashes cream on her pie and holds her breath. But she doesn't recognize the names. On the Williamstown road today she had seen crowds of refugees, with their belongings heaped in any kind of conveyance they could muster. Heading north, prey to everything from hunger and epidemics to bandits. She'd been careful to keep her dark glasses on and the big hat pulled down, fearful of a chance recognition, but her eyes ached searching hard for familiar faces, praying not to find them, both for their sake and hers.

Clove says, "Ever since the summit was called off, the buzz has been frantic. That summit was Chief Barry's baby I understand. Of course they blamed the breakdown on the other enclaves, but everybody knows this Father Rose was behind it. Now anybody in trouble with the Boston priests wants out of their territory. Better safe than sorry."

"But where are they going to go?" asks Lorna.

It's not a question anyone tries to answer.

Stomping on the porch heralds arrivals from the other cottages, come to join the evening sing. Six-year-old twins with their tousled mother, two anxious-eyed young couples, a white-haired man and his lively nephew. The big old room clamors with life. Clove shares the remains of her pie with the twins and signals Lorna and Sienna to clear the table. Beasley sits down at the piano, flexes his fingers ostentatiously, and begins pounding out "This Land is Your Land," accompanying himself in a trembling baritone. He's going deaf, and his voice roars through the house.

Vita sets up her station at the kitchen sink, rinsing dishes as they arrive and plunging them into hot water. Marcel appears with a full tray, offers a bit sheepishly, "Can I help?"

"No, no," Vita laughs. "Noam says you relax after dinner. They'll be working you hard again come sunup tomorrow, the cabbage and peas are going in."

Bustling through the door, Clove orders, "Out, out! No field workers in the kitchen."

Vita works rapidly, ears tuned to the swelling sounds of singing, the mingled voices of her new world. She's very tired, as always at the end of the day here, nearly gives in to closing her eyes. But the music is beautiful to her. She thinks she can make out Lorna's eager soprano, reaching into air where she's free now, free to grow and become herself. Vita shifts her weary legs, pushes hair out of her eyes with a sodden wet wrist, and finds herself smiling.

Suddenly it stops, the song, the piano, everything. Then after brisk total silence, eerie contrast, a chorus of consternation. Wiping her hands on her apron hurrying into the other room, Vita sees Garth standing by the front door encircled by alarmed faces amid rising cries.

"Quiet! Quiet. Shut up!" Noam is bellowing, no one paying attention to him.

Garth is wild-eyed, catching his breath. Sweat has plastered his black curls across his forehead in twirls like script. He's shouting, "...here in hours...ice...crank up the radio...already started over in the New Hampshire settlements...days of it...danger...bring the animals... food for a week...urgent...now...hours, I said...no I'm not crazy..." Lorna has made her way to within a few feet of him, her face flushed and pale. Garth gestures to her, a hand held out as if asking for help or comfort but also oddly distant: he belongs to the crowd.

It's only a matter of a few more minutes before everyone at River Bend comprehends. By morning they'll be consumed by a powerful blizzard. Noam gets out the radio, hastily winds the crank, and official voices blare warnings. But they all already know what to do.

Beasley helps Vita and Lorna herd the goats from their pen up the ramp into the back room of the cottage. Normally the animals spend the night underneath the building. It hasn't been cold enough to house them inside more than a few weeks in winter. Lorna has to hastily push aside her desk and bookcase, resentfully, hysterically.

The goats are annoyed. They bleat and cough and glare. All six plus the two little ones must now crowd close, and after their feed is brought in, they barely have enough room to lie down. Vita gives them an extra treat of pumpkin seeds, Beasley clucking disapproval. As he leaves, he admonishes them to bring in more firewood.

Vita collapses onto the small sofa in their main room, feet up, head back, a mass of ache.

"I can't move another muscle."

"Garth said days," Lorna wails. "We need supplies for days. We'll be snowed in."

"We've got enough food. Water won't be a problem, with all that snow."

"What food? I don't want to eat that stuff. Pickled peaches? Yuck!"

"You will when you're hungry."

"I'm not staying here."

Vita's not sure she heard correctly. She unshades her eyes to look at Lorna.

"What did you say?"

"I'm not staying here with you."

Lorna is standing by the window with arms crossed. Her hair is escaping from its hasty constraint, spilling over her shoulders and shining in the lamplight. She's still wearing her chocolate colored sweater, the one she's mended herself several times, its color conspiring to deepen the luminous brown of her eyes. Eyes that are now piercing her mother's heart with calculating rebellion.

"Sienna has a cot in her room," Lorna continues. "Clove already said I could."

"I need you here."

"No you don't."

"The goats must…the paraffin for the jam has to be…we were going to make more apple butter…"

"Mom."

Lorna looks away and takes a slow breath to calm herself. In that breath Vita recalls Garth's gesture of supplication, that hand reaching for what it wants, Lorna's loveliness. She sees him put his arms around her. She sees her laughing with Sienna, eagerly bustling along with Clove in household tasks, crafting her own importance. In that long breath of Lorna's, roles are reversed, Vita for an instant the self-centered needy child, her daughter the mature and rational force. Within that breath, Vita gives up. Hurt drowns in understanding. This person no longer belongs to her. She astounds herself by bursting into tears.

"Oh for God's sake! Mom, you can't be crying! It's too ridiculous."

Poor Lorna is torn now, her security of mission shaken. She stomps around, circling closer, wanting to comfort, furious at this turn her stand has taken.

But Vita shakes her head, blowing her nose. "No, sweetie, don't worry. It's fine. I'm not crying about that. I'm just…I can manage."

"Do you want someone else to stay here? I can ask. Shush now."

Vita wants to retch out sobs, but she gulps and swallows them instead. Plenty of time to primal scream when she's all alone. Right now she has to shape up and try to be an adult.

2

Vita wakes slowly, at first believing she's in her bed and it must be morning. The rustle and breathing she hears would be Lorna in the next bed. Eyes still closed, she feels herself in an oddly cramped position, begins to stretch, can't. She tries to snuggle down for more sleep. If only she can get back into that dream, where she was running with her sister Ellie after a deer in the woods, soft cool leaves brushing her arms. Starting up with sudden realization, here she is on the little old sofa, the lamp almost out. All alone. Except for the goats.

A deep and panicked sense of loneliness engulfs her. It's as if her spine and brain have disappeared, leaving her swollen helpless heart to dangle pointlessly. She's breathing too quickly. Vita stumbles to the window, sees only whirling snow, tenses her eyes to make out a light from the main house. And there it is, just barely visible, which means they can see hers too, and there's absurd comfort in that. Now she's aware she's cold. She'd been covered by only a light shawl. She banks up the fire in the stove, rubbing her hands gratefully at the red coals. Goes to look in on the goats. Now that they've gotten used to their crowded quarters, they're contentedly oblivious, curled together in sleepy acceptance. Only Daisy gets up and comes to greet her, with a desultory nuzzle, snuffling, "What's this human fussing about in the middle of the night?" Vita scratches the animal's warm floppy ears, kisses the top of her head.

"Go to sleep, Daisy," she soothes, "Everything's ok."

Who am I fooling, she reflects, gently closing the wooden door again. Just about nothing is ok. She goes to the bedroom to look at the clock, but nobody wound it so it has stopped, at eleven. She sits back down on the couch, pulls the shawl around her. Why would it matter what time it is? She'll know when the sun rises, and that's time enough.

When she was fourteen, her life was so different from Lorna's. Her family was still living happily together in the old house on Cayuga Lake. She and her sister were in school, Vita enthusiastically studying bird behavior and Harry Potter and French history. She did have a friend who was a boy—she liked him because he taught her things about the woods and its ways, for example, how to recognize rabbit prints or a squirrel's nest. But he never did get to kiss her, though he tried. Her sexual feelings were all wrapped up in herself at that point, discovering the pleasure of rubbing her new breasts, and perfecting masturbation. She'd lie on her bed using her hands or sometimes a lipstick for stimulation, though it never occurred to her to actually put anything inside. That only changed two years later with Reno, when she was sixteen.

Reno was a brawny, swaggering youth, a senior and something of a star on the soccer team. Back then in the 30s, it was still acceptable for boys with influential parents to arrange to escape the military draft, so he was headed for one of the few remaining law schools. This impressed Vita's mother deeply, since she herself was a lawyer and her job was the most important thing in her life. Reno was thus so elevated in her opinion that it obviously never occurred to her how dedicated he was to ending her daughter's virginity. Added to her mother's adulation was that of the most popular girls in school: though Reno was not handsome, his credentials and his muscles made him coveted. So, when he had Vita on her back on his bed, she felt silly saying "stop." Which she did, two or three times. But he paid no attention, and it was soon over, in a surging cry from Reno that scared her to death. Vita lay there, somewhat gratified that she'd joined the ranks of the non-virgins, but puzzled as to what the fuss was all about—she'd had no climax and wasn't even out of breath. Still, the event made Reno so tender and grateful, she went about holding hands with him in quite a smug state, swinging her hips to advertise her glory.

Surely Garth would not do that, Lorna's still a child. Surely Lorna has too much sense, knows she's not ready. But Vita knows she's constructing denial. She ends up only hoping they will stick to kissing. And she vows another conversation with her daughter, this time making all the disadvantages blatantly clear. No euphemisms—she'll spell it out crudely.

Vita hugs herself, slowly caressing her arms, thinking of Drake. Right now he's lying in their bed all alone, missing and wanting her. She feels sad for him. Poor Drake, he never did get his moment of summit glory, and then his family abandoned him. Or is he in another bed, with someone else? Is he hating her, vowing revenge? How hard is he trying to find them? Even though she dreads the sight of him, the idea that he'd repudiate her adds to the present press of loneliness and isolation.

She has a sudden thought, goes quickly to see if the new dress is still there. Lorna had unwrapped the package with glee, fluffed out the silky material with tender gloating care. It had been spread out on her bed. It's not there now. So, she took it with her. What an irony. The purchase Vita made to placate her daughter has ended up as part of the spiral taking her away. Oh yes, she will wear it for Garth, with flaunting pleasure.

Vita watches the lamp go out. In the darkness the smell of scorched oil. The light from the stove identifies furniture shapes in pale orange. She undresses, pulling on her heavy long nightgown, and gets into bed, wincing at the icy sheets. The wind accelerates outside, a violent lament. She crunches up shivering and thinks about her father, the best consolation she can retrieve. If only he were here, wouldn't he be able to fix everything, just as he always did? But that's ridiculous, he's been dead for years. When he was recalled to military duty, not long before she succumbed to Reno, her life changed abruptly and completely. That was the last of the happy years. As she learned to do then in her girlish grief, she conjures up his kind face and voice, weaving them into a dream.

When Vita opens her eyes again, to blackness, she's afraid. Not of anything she can identify, just a pit of fear in her chest. Snow is attacking the windowpane with malicious hisses. Creaks and clunks signal fierce wind—just how solid is the cottage, she suddenly worries. She sits up, lights a candle, and peers around the room: the four-tiered dresser Lorna decorated, its round mirror, the small chair with her clothes thrown over it, the shabby floral rug, Lorna's empty bed.

She gets up for no particular reason, with only vague alarm. The room is too empty, the sounds too strange. She would much rather stay warm and asleep, but she doesn't. She carries the candle through the main room, opens the door to check on the goats. Some of them regard her bleary eyed without bothering to raise their heads; the rest don't even wake up. She steps in among them, somehow soothed by the air stuffy with their breath. One more step, and she sees the man.

He's lying face down on hay bales, splayed as if he has fallen. Melted snow drips from his boots, his hat, his heavy coat and mittens. His eyes are closed and his mouth open, he could be asleep or dead.

Next thing she knows, she's back in the other room with the door closed behind her. She has not recognized him, he could be dangerous. Maybe he's been sent by Drake. She doesn't have a weapon of any kind. She could barricade the door, but of course in a few hours she'll have to feed the goats. He's helpless enough now, maybe she can just bash him over the head with a chair. Get a grip, she tells herself. He may be perfectly harmless, probably is. Could be a friend or relative of Clove and Noam's, or just a traveler lost in the storm. She paces, shivering. She should get dressed. She should look strong and aloof.

She's startled out of this self-absorbed tremble by his little moan, not a goat's, a pitiful human sound. He could be ill, he could be dying! With that realization, she hurries back into the room to gaze down on him again, peers closely. He's forty or so, with a brown beard; he's large, tall. His clothes are top-quality, not even mended. There's no blood. But she realizes she may have to touch him.

She tries, "Hello?"

The man stirs and moans again, his lips move, his eyelids flutter. That's it, he's really in trouble and she'll just have to throw caution to the winds. She gently pulls off his hat and mittens, touches his skin. He's ice cold. She goes to get blankets and wine.

While she's working off his coat, his eyes open. His head is on her knees, her nightgown pulled tight over them. Her hair is in her face, she's grimacing with effort.

He says, perfectly clearly, "Mrs. Gordon."

She drops his arm. "Who are you?"

He coughs, croaks, "Cohen," coughs again.

"Never mind, be quiet now. We've got to get you warm."

3

Alex lets her feed him more wine, though he's pretty sure he can hold the cup himself now. She's sitting on the edge of the sofa where he's lying propped up on pillows, wrapped in blankets, beginning to be able to feel his toes again—in fact they ache and burn like hell. She dips the spoon in, brings it to his lips coaxingly as if he's a baby. She's a vision in her pale gown, her white soft neck, her yellow curls springing around her head like Botticelli's Venus rising from the sea. He reflects amused that he had to get lost in a blizzard and nearly die to achieve this heavenly situation.

"Are you hungry?" she asks.

He nods, looking into her eyes, deep blue eyes, large and sultry. Her mouth is generous and malleable, it will laugh and cry easily, he can tell. Now he remembers where he has met her—Chief Barry's party. She had been talking to Gloria and he'd been so grateful. He watches her move about the kitchen area fixing him food. She's lean and lithe, breasts high and full. A beautiful woman.

"Can you eat this?"

She's offering him a spoonful of oatmeal. He smiles and opens his mouth to receive it.

"I can do it myself, I think," he offers.

"But, your poor fingers."

"Oh I can feel them ok now. They're tingling so much they hurt, but they function. Let me try."

She hands him the bowl anxiously; he holds it with his two hands.

"It's warm," he says.

She sits there a bit longer watching him eat. The sensations are delicious. The hot nourishment revitalizing his body, this lovely woman mothering him.

There must be something in his eyes because abruptly she says, "I'll go get dressed now. Be right back," and hurries off to the next room, closing the door.

Alex scrapes the bowl empty, looks around the simple room. He has no idea where he is. Why would Drake Gordon's glamorous wife be living in a place like this?

Then he recalls some gossip he hadn't paid much attention to. The wife ran off with the daughter, nobody knew where to; it was suspected they were trying to escape the virgin decree. Of course, now he remembers what Diamond told him—she helped get them to River Bend. So he has arrived, after all.

His meeting here with Marcel and Miro was hastily arranged. When it turned out they would be on their way from Burlington to Hartford at the same time he was returning to Boston, they suggested it. He jumped at the chance. An adjustment of a few days on his part, and their paths were set to cross at River Bend. He's as anxious as they are to strategize about the Zorians' unexpectedly bold power grab.

When Vita returns, the angel has been replaced by a brisk, skeptical creature in shapeless overalls and clunky boots.

She takes his bowl, comments, "I think you've recovered," and puts away the wine in a cupboard. She looks at his watch lying on the table with a little pile of his other belongings. "It's working. It's five o'clock." She sits down in a chair at a disappointing distance, and looks at him hard. "Are you going to tell?"

Busy recovering from his sensual dreaminess and adjusting instead to projecting gentlemanly gratitude, Alex replies guiltily, "What do you mean?"

"Are you going to rat?"

"Oh. Well why would I?"

100

"You must know we've broken the law. My daughter's fourteen. The authorities are looking for her."

"I heard something about it. Not in the news. They're not screaming scandal or anything because they don't want to look like idiots. But I would bet there's plenty of outrage behind the scenes. They won't want you to get away with it. It won't look good."

She reflects at him. Even in her testy new persona she's beautiful, the candlelight playing on her fair hair and skin. She says grimly, "You're some kind of official. You're one of them."

"Not really," he answers carefully. He would love to tell her the truth so she would trust him, but how can he?

"Meaning?"

"I'm not involved with the priests. I'm Ambassador Ladd's assistant. I'm in Albany half the time. So you see…"

"Everyone in government is involved with the priests now."

He nods reluctantly. "Look, you saved my life. Let's just say I'm returning a favor. I won't say a word."

Still the interrogator, she probes, "What are you doing here?"

"I'm on my way to Boston. We got caught in the storm."

But even as the words are leaving his lips, his mind is racing to the reality that she must have met Marcel and Miro. Will she start drawing dangerous conclusions? He gazes at his clothes drying on the line she has strung between the stovepipe and a nail on the wall. Keeping his expression thoughtful, he tries to decide what to do. Will he have to confess that he came here to the farm on purpose? What kind of story can he concoct without letting her in on the whole situation?

She presses on. "Where are the others?"

"They're probably ok, they stuck to the main road. I took off on foot about three miles from here."

"How do you know where we are? You haven't answered my question, why did you come here?"

"Hey, I swear I've got nothing to do with your problem. I came here to meet some guys about a deal." He yawns widely. "Can we talk about this a little bit later? I'm totally wiped out."

She gives a little smile somewhere between anxiety and compassion, and apologizes, "Sorry, I'm a bit obsessed you understand. Come on, you can have Lorna's bed for now. You need to sleep."

Swaddled in bed, warm and obliterated by exhaustion, Alex falls asleep without being able to conjure up another useful thought.

When he wakes, the room is lighter but the window is covered with snow. The cottage could be buried for all he can tell. He thinks he still hears the sounds of wind and fury, dimmed by the snow's cocoon. But he feels utterly refreshed and it's hard to worry. He lies there luxuriously listening to Vita quietly moving about in the other room. Okay, he'll tell her he has business with Marcel and Miro, which is true. Something slightly shady he'd rather not discuss and would appreciate her not mentioning to anybody, also not a lie. She should be satisfied with that, surely.

Alex calculates that at the latest, he can dig out of here in another twenty-four hours, giving them time for a quick meeting, and still be in Boston by Thursday. Nothing will be happening there anyway, with this weather. He frets about Gloria in Albany, but assures himself that assuming she stayed home, she's safe and cared for, even though no doubt hysterical.

Ambassador Ladd in Boston needs his Albany report. After the summit was cancelled, Rose made some noises about Finger Lakes water that put Albany into a fever of indignation. Alex has been using all his skills to smooth that over. But his first concern in the coming weeks is helping the rebels pinpoint contacts, developing a wider communication network. Credo operations are expanding across the northeast, but not fast enough. There's more risk of exposure, but the stakes are higher too. The time is right. There's even been talk of picking a date, say a year from now, to make the final move. Alex represses his adrenalin surge of elation at the prospect of justice victorious: the prisons emptied, his friends with enough to eat, Earth given a chance to breathe again. He'll need to get to Diamond's first thing, so he can meet with the Nons.

Thinking about Diamond's familiar room, he feels his body stir with anticipation. But to his surprise, his mind conjures up Vita, not Diamond. He puts Vita on that bed naked, ready for him. Now this is absurd, he lectures himself. But he doesn't insist on obedience from his imagination, and continues to dwell on the sensual possibilities it suggests. He particularly enjoys Vita's skin flushing pinkly while she caresses him, and her wonderful pleasure noises. She must be a wildcat when she gets going, he decides.

But before he finds out he's hungry enough to get out of bed, his mind reverts to business, and how he'll handle Rose. Alex's report on his diplomatic efforts will be met with dismissive taunts. He allows himself a cheerful fantasy of choking the vile old fellow to death.

"Guess what time it is?" Vita smiles when he emerges from the bedroom, dressed but in stocking feet. His boots are still drying by the stove. She's crumbling stale bread into a simmering pot on the stovetop. "Two o'clock. You slept for almost eight hours!"

"I feel great. Whatever that is, smells delicious."

He stands a bit awkwardly, ashamed of his sexual thoughts, she looks so maternal and innocent.

"Sit down, you can have some in a few minutes. I'm just thickening it up a bit."

"Let me help."

"Not yet. But I must confess there's a bunch of things you can do later on, if you feel strong enough."

"Sure," he says eagerly, still standing. "Anything. Just say the word. I'm fine, back to normal now."

She sets bowls on the table, spoons, mugs, flowered cloth napkins. The windows are snowed over but the room is bright enough, with an odd grayish luster, to get by with one candle.

"I fed the goats, no problem. But their straw needs cleaning out, it's starting to really stink. I tried opening the door but it's blocked by snow."

"Great, I'll take care of it." He grins readily. A physical task is just what he feels like. He comes to sit down at the table. She brings the steaming pot, smiling down at him indulgently.

"Help yourself." She chuckles. "You must be starving. Your eyes are bulging like a hungry kid."

They laugh together.

"How about you? Join me."

She does, and lets him serve her, ladling the stew into her bowl, the steam curling soft and gently damp around them.

Alex finds himself telling her about his upcoming meeting with Ladd and Rose, the dilemmas he faces.

"Sounds like you have an important role," she comments. "Not easy, with Father Rose so antagonistic."

"He hates me," states Alex with a mix of irritation and satisfaction. "He hates Ladd too, he thinks we're namby-pamby wimps who prefer talking to killing. Which is true."

"But Chief Barry is relying on you to be the voices of reason." Vita sips her spoon thoughtfully. "Drake, my husband, used to be a peaceful man. But he believes the priests are always right, they speak on behalf of God."

"Drake's a dedicated man."

"He really believes that," she repeats, in wonder. She looks at Alex hard. "I don't." It's a challenge.

The perfect opening and he seizes it. "Hey, I'm not Zorian. In fact, I think the bunch of them should be relegated to their temple and stick to spiritual advice. They've got no business meddling in politics."

"I don't really believe Zoria is pregnant. I think she's just fat." Vita bursts out laughing. "I can't believe I just said that. Oh no."

"You sound like a rebel."

"That's what Diamond says. She's the friend who helped us get this place. That sort of remark used to make me angry, scare me. But I think maybe she was right, in a way, that I'm a rebel at heart. After all, look at what I've done. It's downright subversive, you know."

She's not smiling now, and Alex would be more sympathetic but for the reference to Diamond, which brings up his guard. He decides on truth as far as he can go, and says casually, "Yes I know her. A nice lady."

"Nice lady is not quite how I would describe Diamond. But she'd enjoy hearing it. How do you know her?"

"She does video work around our offices occasionally."

"That's right. Dear Diamond, a tough cookie but I miss her. She's so strong, I envy that."

After a careful pause, he says, "You're strong too. Deep down."

"Only where Lorna's concerned. Lorna makes me a lioness, tooth and claw."

4

After an hour of struggle, Alex gets the outside back door open an inch. Then he has to chop away bit by bit at the snow to produce enough of a pathway to discard the soiled straw. He pokes the shovel up as far as he can, making a hole so he can see the sky. It's still snowing, though no longer raging, just a steady beaded curtain of white. They'll be here another night, at least. It's getting dark by the time he finishes, and he distributes clean bedding for the goats while Vita milks them.

"Stand still now, Daisy," she's crooning. "That's a good girl."

He says, "That's right, Daisy. Be a good girl." The goat fixes him with pale green knowing eyes, and her lips curl. "She's loving every minute."

"I know. I used to love nursing Lorna." Then she hastens on, "I mean it's a primitive sensation, I'm sure it's common in all the animal kingdom, otherwise why would mothers bother?"

Alex runs his fingers over the animal's bristly fur, diplomatically comments, "What are we going to do with all this milk?"

"We could make yogurt. I'm not very good at cheese or butter yet. And of course sour cream. We'll have to freeze the rest if we can't get it to the others within another day. But don't you think…" She turns to look up at him from where she's perched on the stool. Milk dapples her hands, a dab of it on her cheek where she's swiped at the hair escaping the kerchief keeping the gold fizz of her curls in place. "Don't you think we'll be able to dig out tomorrow?"

"We can make a start," he agrees. "The storm's mostly over. But just the two of us, it could take days. Let's hope they're working at it from the other end."

"Of course they will be. Oh, I hope they're ok."

"As cozy as we are," he assures her. "Listen, what about milk beer? I can make milk beer."

"I've heard of it, yes. What a great idea. Noam and the guys will really appreciate that."

"You're going to like it too, I promise."

After supper they enthusiastically collect and measure the ingredients. Three quarts milk, 12 teaspoons sugar, 3 teaspoons yeast. Alex pours the mixture back and forth between two pails.

"Now we let it sit over night," he explains. "In a warm place, so over here by the stove. Then tomorrow we toss it back and forth some more until it's foamy and kind of smooth. After that we'll need a container with a tight lid, wait another twenty-four hours. And presto!"

She calculates. "Today's Saturday—so we'll have beer on Monday. Hopefully we'll be sharing it with the others. For now," she grins, "have another glass of wine."

They settle in comradely fashion, she on the sofa against cushions, he ensconced in a stuffed chair that has seen better times but is ample enough for his tall form. She props her feet, clad in knitted slippers, on a small wooden stool. She has changed into soft dark trousers and a lovely pinkish sweater. He thinks, this must be an outfit from Boston, from when she was a society lady. He's touched that she's wearing it for him.

"Do you miss it?" he asks. "All the comforts of home? Wearing pretty sweaters like that?"

"Not a bit." Then she smiles to soften her shortness and adds, "Thanks, about the clothes. I'm grateful for an excuse to wear them. But we're happy, nothing to complain about really. Each season here has its plenty. You're so tired of tomatoes by December you welcome the root vegetables you'll be hating the smell of by March. But the people are wonderful, everybody looks out for everybody else."

The room is very quiet. There's no wind or any kind of sound from outside. If it were not for the animals stirring and snuffling, the occasional pop of the fire, the silence would be total. He wonders if she misses her husband.

"This is a good refuge for you. Was it hard to get away?"

Her beautiful face dims in a grimace. "Terrible. You see, we'd been counting on the summit to give us a few days lead time. So when it was cancelled we had to wait for a day when my husband was going to be out late, and then race to get far enough before he came home. As soon as he walked in the door, he'd know. I kept playing that image over and over. His rage." She presses her temples, shakes her head casting off the spell. "Fortunately, all our connections went smoothly."

"It still haunts you."

"Yes, but I've stopped worrying that he'll show up any minute."

He ventures to chuckle, "Nothing will find us tonight anyway," then hopes she doesn't find that suggestive.

But she gives him one of her dazzling half grateful, half shy smiles, and goes on to chat easily about her past, her parents, her sister who disappeared, then leaving Cayuga Lake and moving to Boston with Drake, her job, her daughter. He enjoys hearing about her life, watching her tell it.

"How about you?" she asks, startling him. "You said you're from the south?"

"Maryland, if you can call that the south." He hesitates. Clearly she now expects confidences from him. "I was an only child." He hopes she'll help him out here. He's not used to discussing his personal life.

"So is Lorna. I think only one child is harder for everyone, but that's the norm these days, if people are lucky enough to have any."

"I took good care of my mother. She was never well, but she got really sick when I was a teenager. My father was very busy, not the caretaker type anyway." He smiles. "I was a model son."

"And now you're a model husband."

She's teasing him a bit and he laughs. "And the perfect guest as well."

"Definitely. So are your parents still alive?"

"I'm not sure about my dad. He went off on some expedition and never came back, just when I was about to leave for college. So I stuck around, went to the college nearby, until it closed down like so many others. Mom died of pneumonia in 2049. Twelve years ago it is now. Doesn't seem that long. May 4th."

"Oh, how awful for you." Vita's eyes are luminous and sad, she leans forward stretching out her hand as if to comfort him.

Alex clears his throat and his mind. This has gone far enough. He pulls his emotions back from the brink, plunges into a more comfortable subject, grabs facts.

"I headed north, along with everybody else. By that time they were trying to escape the epidemics as well as the weather, especially cholera and malaria. And the crops were just sizzling in the fields from the heat and drought. Problem was, you remember, the federal government was out of commission by then. They'd moved from Washington to Chicago because of the tidal waves, but it was only a shadow. No functioning Congress, no centralized effort to organize the streams of refugees. Chaos."

"Yes, I remember. The news from everywhere was confusing, strange, frightening. In Ithaca even in the early

40s we were feeling the effects, everything seemed to be breaking down. The schools had to keep taking days off because there wasn't enough electricity, then they just closed. The library closed. It was hard to get the kinds of food we were used to. Do you think there was a turning point, when nobody hoped or expected any more that things would go back to normal?"

"For us, heading up north, we had this idea we'd find our old lives again somewhere. Maybe you people in Ithaca were more realistic."

"Not for long. Everyone was talking about Canada, how it would be ok once they got there, seasons again and predictable weather. The roads were clogged with people dreaming of Canada."

"All hell broke loose."

They sit in the silence for a while, stunned by the immensity.

Finally Vita says, "Do you think it's going to get worse?"

He looks at her, contemplating lying. He would love to see her face light up. But he replies, "Yes, it will get worse, and worse. Not only the weather. The political straightjacket." He hesitates, takes energy for anger from her sad eyes. "It's evil. Even though most people have stopped using fossils and toxics, these guys in power do whatever they want. They still use gasoline and plastics for the military, can you believe it? The safe fuel we do have, solar and wind and so on, is squandered. Look at that monstrous greenhouse of Chief Barry's..." Alex stops in alarm. He had not meant to show his colors so vulnerably. "I mean..."

But she chimes in eagerly. "That's true! I've often thought about it. Those poor Nons, with nothing, and the priests with every luxury. I'm glad to hear it bothers you too. It's hard to talk about it with most people."

Alex stands up, stretches, paces, pours more wine for them both. "Look, let's not fool ourselves. We're headed for dictatorship here. That fake White House in Chicago is a farce, it's so feeble the priests don't even bother with it. Did you know that our so-called president has had to take a job fixing radios to make a living? The Zorians will rule the land like the Holy Roman Empire of old if we don't do something about it."

She stares at him. "Do something? What can we do?"

He finds her passive innocence irritating and dangerous. At the same time her warmth and integrity magnetize him. Irrationally he wants to share with her his dearest dreams. He sits down again and says, "Have you ever heard of the Credos?"

"Radicals, a rebel group, they blow up military installations."

"Sometimes. What else have you heard about them?"

"Not much. We don't have any in Boston. They're mostly up in Vermont, and over in the Ohio area, I think. They live like gypsies, traveling around stealing things and making trouble."

Alex laughs curtly. "Television news."

"That's right. Is there more to it?"

"You bet."

"Tell me."

And he does.

"First of all," he says, "they're people just like you and me. Ever since they started questioning authority, and especially since they started actions about fifteen years ago, they've been quietly captured and incarcerated. The jails are full of them, all over the country, and Canada as well. And a lot were killed too. In the past their actions haven't been coordinated, and it was fairly easy to pick them off. But now they've got an organization."

112

"This doesn't sound like anything I've heard about," she says, apologetically dubious. "I only know about the atheist rogue bands that hate all authority and go around destroying property just for the fun of it."

He doesn't reply at once, only lets her own words sink in. "Come, Vita, you know where that kind of information comes from."

"Well, where does yours come from?"

"Personally?" He hesitates.

Now she's staring at him as her expression goes from puzzlement to comprehension. "You're involved with them, aren't you?"

"Vita, I do trust you. But you're part of the powers that be. Your husband is way up there, and a devoted Zorian to boot. If he ever got wind…"

"Oh, Alex, it's so dangerous what you're doing. No, don't tell me if it's risky for you. But of course I'd never say a word."

"Let me tell you just enough, then. I came here to River Bend to meet with Marcel and Miro. We'll be discussing some ideas."

"Conspiracy."

"You could call it that."

"What do these Credos want? I mean, what do you want to make happen?"

From here Alex backpedals. She knows too much already. He shrugs. "We want everything you want. But we're only talking now. Maybe nothing will ever really get accomplished, who knows."

"No more Virgin Decree? Lorna would be safe?"

"Just imagine it. Justice and equality. Democracy again."

"It sounds like a dream. I'm afraid it is a dream."

"Maybe," he sighs, "maybe."

"But it's dangerous to even imagine it. I'm scared for you."

He drains his glass and shrugs, feels suddenly very tired, stifles a yawn.

"I'm sleepy too," she concedes.

Together they move Lorna's mattress and bedding into the main room for him, set up his bed in the corner.

"Looks cozy," she says.

"It does." He kneels to open the stove door, spread the coals for a low steady burn. "Will you be warm enough?"

"Oh yes, I always am under all my blankets."

When he stands up, he's closer to her than he thought. She edges a bit backwards, looking up at him.

"Thank you for saving my life," he offers, keeping his face solemn, trying to control what his eyes are saying.

She gives him a beautiful open smile, at once shy and understanding. "Thanks for keeping me company."

He opens his arms. Surely a brotherly hug is ok. She lifts her hands and shoulders, acceptance. He engulfs her, smells and tastes the scoop between her neck and shoulder, is horrified to hear himself wail a small song of longing, presses her closer, his body blazing. Her hands are moving over his back, she's murmuring something, suddenly they are kissing, mouths one mouth, tongues one tongue. In those appalling ecstatic seconds he disappears, lost in a universe of perfect harmony indistinguishable from all the cosmos, planets, oceans, past and future.

He jumps back, dropping her. She staggers. Her face is flushed, uncomprehending. He stares at her while she catches her balance, gradually her expression registers.

"What happened?" she cries.

"No, no," he stammers, striding away to the other side of the room. "It's a mistake, I'm sorry, I'm sorry."

She's pressing her temples, not meeting his eyes. "Must be the wine."

"Must be."

"You're angry."

"I am, I'm angry. I'm sorry. It was an accident."

She's musing at him. "You know it wasn't," she counters.

"Nonsense. We're friends, that's all."

Alex doesn't know why he's so upset. He has just kissed a beautiful woman he knows he was attracted to, in an isolated house next to an inviting bed. But he has never experienced a kiss like that before. A voodoo vortex where he ceased to be. He never wants to lose himself like that again.

"Of course we are, we're friends." She's reassuring him, consoling him. "Let's forget all about it, it never happened. Okay now, shall we agree to erase it from our minds?"

"Yes of course."

But he's very much afraid it will not be that easy.

5

The next morning Vita wakes to a loud cracking sound, like thunder. She lies stiffly listening, trying to identify it. Snow still blanks out the window. It's warm under the covers but her cold nose tells her it will be a chilly trip from bed to clothes. She hears Alex stirring in the next room, and their kiss returns to her nerves like molten suffusion, an acute equal mix of desire and embarrassment. She hurries it out of her consciousness. Neither one of them needs that kind of problem.

When she opens the door, he's buttering toast, cheerfully formal.

"Good morning, Vita. I've already fed the goats. Have some tea."

She grins gratefully, matches his comradely tone. "Thanks, I will. Can you decipher that noise?"

"It's melting."

"Oh, of course. Not too fast, I hope."

"Sounds pretty fast to me. I think we'll have flooding on our hands by tomorrow."

She steals a look at him, knobby nose, bushy beard and eyebrows, big hands, long legs folded under the chair. Just a man, like any other. She feels quite heady with her escape from such a tricky situation. But still she wonders with some indignation why he had to be so negative about wanting to kiss her. Doesn't he realize how many men do?

She says almost saucily, "I hope you slept well. Was it as comfortable as it looked?"

He mumbles, "Great," chewing toast.

Within an hour the snow slides down from the windows, revealing an immaculate moonscape blown into valleys, mountains, crags, peaks, hollows, ridges, gullies, canyons.

The farmhouse from here resembles a great white whale, its spout the smoking chimney. The sky is bright, on the verge of releasing the sun.

Vita watches the heavily clad figures working on digging a path from the house to the barn. It looks as if the old snowplow is out of commission, or maybe nobody thinks using emergency fuel for it is justified even now. She thinks she spots Lorna and Sienna clearing off the porch. Two more people are on the roof, shoveling snow from the solar panels.

Vita and Alex get the back door open and clear out the soiled straw. The air is very moist, warming. The goats nose and nudge, pressing to go out, then backstepping like old ladies at sight of the icy prospect. The snow falls away from the cottage in great chunks, boulders breaking apart as they land. The sounds coming from everywhere accumulate into a tumult. Dripping, crackling, sliding, thudding, trickling. Little pools of water start to form.

After milking, they tackle the front door. The snow gets heavier by the minute as it melts, but it's also diminishing, so soon they've begun a narrow pathway that by lunchtime reaches half way to the farmhouse. Noam and Marcel meet them in the middle, with much shouting and hugging. Vita is intrigued by the warmth between Alex and Marcel, like long-lost brothers. Marcel's grave gray face is alight with happy laughter. Watching them, again she registers Alex's tall frame as supremely masculine yet graceful, both muscled and light footed. In spite of herself, for an instant she recalls the feel of his lips, with a spasm of pleasure she only half acknowledges. It's only later that she registers how comradely Noam and Alex are as well, realizing that means they already know each other. Vita is brushing aside assumptions like cobwebs. Nothing is what it seemed: neither sweet rustic

River Bend, nor government official Alex, nor simple-hearted Clove and Noam.

Everyone gathers around the big table for a cheerful late lunch that includes Vita's yogurt and sour cream. Lorna doesn't look any different, her mother notes with relief.

"Where did that man come from?" Lorna asks when they're clearing the table.

"I found him in the hay the first night of the storm. He was practically frozen."

"He's nice."

"Yes, he is. He's a diplomat, going on to Boston as soon as he can. Will Garth have to leave soon too?"

"Afraid so. Tomorrow if it's passable. He only came to warn us about the storm."

"Volunteered to come so he could see you, I suspect."

Lorna tosses her head at this invasion of her privacy, though she clearly enjoys the thought.

Vita persists, "Did you wear your new dress?"

"It's beautiful, mom." Lorna puts her arm around her mother's shoulder. "How are the goats?"

"The goats are just fine."

They hug, wordlessly acknowledging their love for each other, their forgiveness for everything and anything in the face of protecting that. Vita draws breathless strength and peace from her child in her arms.

That afternoon they all make their way to the barn to help with the horses and chickens, and repair the boats stored there. All except for Alex, Marcel, and Miro, who have disappeared for their meeting, to nobody's surprise. Garth and Lorna work side by side helping each other, anticipating each other's moves, touching when they can or dare. He certainly is a beautiful boy, thinks Vita, I don't blame her one bit. Abundant black curls, long lean face with piercing almond eyes, skin the gold-red-brown of autumn oak leaves, a laugh that takes you with it. And best of all, clearly devoted to Lorna.

Clove and Vita climb to a loft to check supplies.

"Thank God we got all the buildings up on piles a few years ago," says Clove, "we'd had enough of floods. But with no cellars, storage is harder. Let's see, how are we doing? Potatoes and apples ok, cheese good, bottled tomatoes and dried fish running low though. Frankly, I don't know how we're going to cope with having no crops now til at least May. We'll have to start planting all over again."

Clove sits down on an overturned box. She has dropped her bustling cheer like a veil, looks haggard and worried.

"What about Williamstown?" asks Vita. "Can't we get supplies there?"

"Everybody's in the same situation. What's extra will go for skyrocketing prices on the black market. And the government's not going to help, anyway we don't want them paying attention to us. And we're short of cash, but what will we barter with? We need everything we have."

Vita puts a hand on Clove's shoulder, reluctant to try words. "Plus we have to feed the animals too, you know," Clove adds. "And Noam is beside himself losing more topsoil, he just won't get the quantity or the quality he wants. He remembers when the soil was so rich…"

"At least we have plenty of water."

"But that doesn't mean drinking water. Yes the tanks are filled to the brim now, but we only have as much to drink as fuel to purify it. Otherwise we just have to trust that it's safe. We've had to do that before. Had some lovely diarrhea from it once, too." She lifts her face to probe Vita's. "Our biggest fear on that score is, other people will want our water. They will come and take it."

Vita is startled by her intensity. "What? How can they do that?"

"With guns."

In the shadowy loft, the smell of old apples and smoked fish mingled with animal odors of fur and manure, voices of friends and family buzzing below amid sounds of busy hammering and scraping, Clove quietly weeps, Vita kneeling distraught beside her.

6

Daisy jerks her hind leg and turns to glare at Vita.

"Sorry girl, did I pull too hard?"

The goat sighs, chewing her cud, and turns away. Vita chuckles at the animal's air of annoyed tolerance as if to say: the milk's got to come out, so let's all behave nicely.

The wide back door is open to the warming air. The lake of melted snow is flowing up over half the gangplank, brownish and flecked with ice floes. But the piles the cottage rests on keep it well above the watermark. The air is both heavy and fresh—mud, sodden wood, the mist of moving water. The pearl gray sky is tinting to blue, revealing a shy sun. It's early morning but there's been no glory in the sunrise, only trembling insecurity as if out of practice.

Lorna stayed one more night at the big house; Garth has to leave today. So does Alex—Noam is taking them both to Williamstown this afternoon in the repaired rowboat. Vita's thoughts are busy with sympathy for Lorna's sense of loss and distracted by the goats' needs, but she finds an image of Alex nudging her consciousness, and lets it in, remembering warmly their long comradely conversations, the way he colored from ice pale to ruddy health at her hands, his heartfelt political concern, his playful laugh and ready helpfulness. She frets over their kiss, it meant nothing of course, just a man and woman living too close too long, experimenting. Still, she wishes it hadn't happened, hopes it won't affect their friendship.

As she pours milk from pails into various containers, Vita recalls the fun of making milk beer—it had gone over well last night, everyone toasting the goats' contributions to their celebration.

"You're very popular at the moment," she tells the animals. "Keep it that way, girls. I hate to think any of you would have to be turned into meat, what with this food shortage. But the chickens all survived, so I don't think you have to worry. As long as you behave."

So she chats with them, finishing up the milking and forking fresh hay into their feed bin. One of the babies keeps butting her, hassling her for the pumpkin seeds in her pocket, and she gives in, letting it nibble from her hand, tongue tickling, moistening her palm. She's just setting up to make yogurt, when a splash brings her to the doorway, and there's Alex tying up a rickety raft.

"I hope this thing holds out or I'll be swimming," he laughs.

He pulls the rope tight and turns to stride up the plank towards her. She's laughing too, pulling off her kerchief and trying to smooth her hair, which in the damp springs out untamed.

"I knew you'd be leaving this afternoon. I'm so glad you came."

"I thought I'd say goodbye."

He stands there, his arms a little too loose at his sides as if he doesn't know what to do with them.

"Come, have some coffee."

"Like old times."

He follows her with his diffident lope, trailing but looming too, as if apologizing for his bulk. They take their accustomed seats, she on the sofa, he in the broad armchair.

"I won't bore you with thanking you again," he begins.

"No, heavens, don't. I didn't do anything special and you were a great companion. I would've been a basket case without you. Tell me, is the trip to Boston all set, all the arrangements? Have you got boats for the whole route?"

"Yes, they need me there tomorrow so I've got an express from Williamstown. I was able to contact them by radio. A military craft I'm told."

124

"Oh well then." Remembering he's an official chills her for a moment. "What did you tell them?"

"I got lost in the snow. So did a lot of other people. That's no problem."

"And it's true enough. Did your meeting with Marcel and Miro go ok?"

"Fine."

"We have each other's secrets now." She finds her own anxiety heightened by concern for his safety. "Be careful."

She gets up to refill their mugs, but Alex follows her to the stove and, hands on her shoulders, turns her towards him.

"I'd like to kiss you again," he says.

She laughs. "Why on earth? It was a passing fancy and a mistake. We both agreed on that."

She steps back away from him. But she can't let his eyes go.

He says, "I need to find out something. I need to make sure it wasn't important."

"What a ridiculous reason."

Vita thinks she's annoyed, but something in the sunlight and soft air is warming her, loosening her body. No, she realizes distractedly, groping for rational thought, it's not the sun and air, it's the prospect of his lips. He reads her face and in an instant they're embracing. His kisses go to her neck and somehow her breasts appear and offer themselves to his mouth while she pulls off his shirt. Their fever blots out everything, she only vaguely hears him moaning, "Oh God help me, it was…important…"

She cries, "Yes."

They manage to stagger to her bed. His hands know everything, inside her they have a thousand fingers. He tongues her ear, wailing, his mouth is open as he pushes into her. While they cry out, she holds on to him so tightly she feels he is herself.

Afterwards at first, while they lie still panting and locked together, Vita feels the whole world has embraced and merged with her, there's nothing alien in this world, nothing separate from the two of them, and this heaven couldn't possibly ever end.

As their breath gradually calms, she recognizes a kind of horror. Not the qualm of being unfaithful to Drake, or that Alex is even more married than she is, but the enormity of dealing with this new gargantuan emotion in her life. Why me, why this, why now? How could this happen? I'm a sensible person. What am I going to do?

Alex is pulling away. "I guess I'd better get going," he mumbles.

She doesn't release him, murmurs, "Stay a bit. You haven't been here long, nobody will wonder."

But he sits up, consulting his watch. "It's ten o'clock."

She stares up at him astounded, hurt already singeing the edges of her heart. He's acting like a one-night stand, she hears herself thinking, this meant nothing to him. She starts to tell him she's transformed, but the words shrivel in the ice of his disinterest.

At last she dares, "Didn't this mean anything to you?"

For a moment he's contrite, leans down to brush his lips to her forehead. "Of course, Vita, it was great. Thanks. You're terrific."

"Well, was it important, then, as you put it?"

"Important?" Now he's angry. "What do you mean? I told you it was great. Look, I'm in a bit of a hurry here. I've got a long day ahead. You can take a nap."

He gets up with a surly expression and hurriedly gets dressed. He goes into the other room and she hears him banging around at the stove. He returns with his mug of coffee. Stands over her. She has hardly moved, but has pulled the sheet up to cover herself. Here he is all business again, ready to take off, and here she is still naked, wet with him, stunned with pleasure, absurd. The humiliation stings her to say, "I'd like to get dressed too, if you'd please step outside." But she knows her voice trembles with tears.

He keeps looking down at her, a strange expression in his eyes. Is it regret, guilt, anger, disbelief? Whatever it is, it's certainly not affection.

"I'm sorry," he says testily. "I didn't mean to hurt you. I guess we've made another mistake."

7

April comes like a song. Floods have receded, mud almost dried up. Noam patiently begins planting anew, recruiting everyone for a few days so that making soap, wine, jam, cheese are suspended. Meals are sparse and repetitive. But the air is soft and the sunlight a perfect spring brightness, and spirits are high. No one was injured in the blizzard or its aftermath, there wasn't even much damage to buildings or roads. The news from other areas resounds with conflict, power grabs and disputes over resources, shortages and blackmarket scams, an assassination here and there, another unexplained abduction. Out west, Des Moines has taken over all of Minneapolis in a bloody blitz. But River Bend Farm is used to shrugging off these upheavals. Snuggled in a valley near the border between enclaves, where outside indifference has so far kept it safe from interference, its small contribution to resistance continues steady as an underground stream.

One Sunday there's roast chicken for dinner. This feast has as its excuse the departure the next day of Marcel and Miro, who have stayed beyond their allotted time to help plant. Clove arranged a little spiritual service that morning, with an Earth Mother figurine presiding, simple rituals of thanks, Sienna and Lorna on drums, wildflowers in their hair, and Clove intoning a chant. The makeshift altar remains on the mantelpiece and Noam invokes it before they eat.

"Sacred force, thank you for being with us during the storm and flood, and restoring our land to us. Keep us all safe and bless our crops for a good harvest. Thank you for this abundant food. Blessings on Earth."

He opens and raises his palms in gratitude and supplication, everyone following suit. Then he slices into the meat, passing the plates down the table. Vita has got used to participating in these spiritual gestures now and then, and their simplicity has dissolved the remaining threads binding her to the stringent faith of Zoria. Long ago attendance at Sunday School, sporadic as it was, emerges as a refreshing balance: her gentle father explaining that even though you can't see God, he's everywhere; her childish confusion of God with her father, tenderly taking care of her. Even the quivers of fear and guilt that ruled her for so many years have subsided. Her only regret is how much farther this shift of faith takes her from Drake, how it dilutes the little love she still has left for him. How could they possibly ever be together again?

Yet her mortifying experience with Alex has led her to vow she doesn't want to be with another man. Her heart and pride still ache from his treatment, but she's managing to think of him less and less. She pushes the images of their time together, both delicious and agonizing, over into the edges of her mind, like dust against the wall when she doesn't have time to clean.

As she gratefully munches juicy chicken and mashed potatoes and peas with butter and yogurt, she for the thousandth time breathes a prayer of her own to God, or whatever beneficent force brought her and Lorna to this safe sweet place. She only now and then recognizes a lurking terror that they'll be found. It's no longer Drake she envisions in these nightmarish instants, but the SF in full force, commandeered by Father Rose himself. She always cools to calm quickly by reasoning that one little girl can't be all that important to them.

While Vita is finishing up the dishes, she's surprised to see Marcel linger after bringing in a last tray from the dining room. He's always been friendly, but never sought her out before.

"Vita, I wonder if we could have a chat later?"

"Sure." She stacks a few more plates, wipes her hands on her apron and takes it off, smoothing her soft dress. This evening she's wearing the nicest thing she still has, a light, scooped neck dress. "Any time. Right now?"

"Let's join the others for a while yet. Can you drop by our cottage around eight?"

Lorna and Sienna are leaning on the piano as Beaseley belts out "Down in the Valley," harmonizing in their delicate sopranos. Lorna has been studying hard lately, and even giving Sienna lessons in history and arithmetic. She's getting fairly regular hand-delivered letters from Garth, which definitely has something to do with it. He sends her books now and then too, and she devours them at once, returning them with lengthy commentaries. At this moment she has donned her garland again, tiny white and yellow flowers circling her abundant hair loose around her shoulders. Her eyes and face are shining; she's singing her heart out.

Vita puts her feet up on a stool, time to relax.

When Lorna was seven they were issued their present unit in the Boston house. It was an exciting time. Drake's devotion and competence were being recognized with visible and significant privileges. Lorna was permitted to enroll in the special school for children of the elite, Vita got a good job and a full market pass, and Drake was assigned to prestigious committees. They were all so happy then, it seems a fairy tale, or rather an ironic dark comedy. Vita reels from the contrast. In those days she put the full weight of responsibility for herself and her child onto Drake's sturdy shoulders. It never occurred to her to doubt his plans or his state of mind. But she has to admit they were comparatively wonderful years, for all their ignorance and self-effacement. She felt beautiful and secure. Now she feels old and fearful. What she knows, the veil lifted, scrapes across her spirit in cutting shards. Her old self is a stranger, someone she envies.

It's graying to dusk at eight o'clock as Vita crosses to the cluster of cottages behind the farmhouse. There's little color to the sunset, its pink diluted and watery as if the air still remembers the flood. She passes the closed chicken coops emitting small cheeps and rustlings as the birds settle in for the night. Pix the dog gets up from his station in front of them to get a pat from her, accompanies her for a few yards like a dutiful butler, then returns to his post. There are no more foxes of course, but chickens still need protecting as far as the dog is concerned.

The four cottages lined up here sport shutters and curlicues from their time as housing for travelers in the age of motels. Their faded white paint is in tatters and on their stilts they look like tired moths. When Vita enters her eyes adjust to dimness, relieved by one lamp on a table. Outside the circle of light she has a vague impression of two messy beds and a pile of papers. She notes with awe one of the palm sized computers carried by important officials. Drake had been issued one for the summit, thrilled at this further sign of his status.

"We have something to tell you," Marcel says.

When she first met them, she had thought these men were very alike, both gray and close to sixty, both lean and intense. But she has learned better. For one thing, Miro has a jolly sense of humor and laughs often, generously exposing large teeth. And he has graceful articulate hands that draw pictures of words while he speaks. Marcel though gentle seems always sad, even bitter; his dark eyes droop with some perpetual sorrow. His shoulders slump in a mourning brood.

"We understand you know a little bit about us," Marcel continues. "But if you want to know more, just go ahead and ask."

They all sit at the table. Miro serves coffee in heavy mugs. Vita is glad to have something to hold onto. She shakes her head, nervously trying to figure out what they could want from her.

"We're so grateful to you for rescuing Alex Cohen," says Miro. "He said he'd had a chance to get to know you, and you can be trusted. So, you already know we're not hired hands, imported for our brilliant farming skills." He chortles heartily. "Of course, we've made ourselves useful and as it turned out Noam really needed us. But we came to River Bend mainly to meet with Cohen."

Vita fights a chill at hearing Alex's name. "When did he tell you this?" Surely not after their farewell tryst that went so awry. He would not be recommending her after that.

"Here at this table," replies Miro, misunderstanding her question. He hurries on. "Now, it seems that you have a sister."

Vita goes numb and loses oxygen. "Ellie."

Marcel leans forward in concern. "Yes, Ellie. Are you all right?"

"You mean she's alive?"

"She's alive, yes. Although we haven't seen her."

"For God's sake, tell me what happened. Is she okay? Where has she been? Where is she?"

Miro and Marcel exchange a look and she sees she must be ranting, but her voice goes on, rising to a pitch. Marcel gets up and puts a hand on her shoulder.

"Sorry, sorry. We should have prepared you better, we should've gone more slowly."

She shudders and calms a little. "It's ok. Go on."

"She was in a jail in the Albany region." Miro intones the facts. "She'd been there for years. Her official crime was desertion from the military, but we know she was also working with the Credos. We got her out with a bunch of others just last week. Unfortunately, a few of their guards were killed in the operation, so she's the object of quite a manhunt. We shouldn't have moved so fast and so carelessly, but that's Vinsky for you. At any rate, she's in a safe house now, recuperating."

"All this time, I thought she was dead."

"Lots of relatives of prisoners do."

"If only I'd known. I could have…"

"They don't give out prisoners' names," Marcel assures her. "And besides she thinks you're part of the regime, your husband and all that. She'll have been afraid to contact you."

"Is she all right?"

"Well," Marcel answers carefully. "She has a few health problems. Lungs a bit damaged. Nothing that can't be fixed with time and care."

"Does she have a doctor?"

"Well, yes, she was examined initially and prescribed medications."

"Where is she?"

Marcel clears his throat, but Miro jumps in. "We need to ask you a favor."

Marcel intervenes. "Forgive us if we're bombarding you with all this. I know it must be overwhelming. Do you want to stop for a while?"

Vita gives him a grateful small smile. "No, don't mind me. Please go on."

Miro says, "She's in Albany but she can't stay there. They've got to get her out within the next forty-eight hours. All the prisoners are hiding in the back room of a restaurant that's regularly searched. There are six of them and we want to break that up, one by one if possible. Can you take her?"

"What? Here?"

Vita is faint with the idea that she could soon be embracing Ellie, still struggling to accept that she's actually alive.

"Alex says the goats are quite comfortable," pursues Miro. "Couldn't she be hidden with them?"

Marcel says, "Don't worry about Clove and Noam. They know."

Know what? Vita feels awash in levels of intrigue she's only begun to grasp. To her embarrassment and relief, tears begin, quiet and hot on her cheeks.

"There, that's enough," Marcel says more to Miro than to her. Then he comes to pat her shoulder again. "You think about it. You need to sort it out. We know it poses an element of danger to your daughter. It's a hard decision."

He gives her a handkerchief and persuades her to move to a more comfortable chair by the stove, stirs the coals to a higher glow. She sits in the muted light, her head spinning and aching. Out the far window she can see a misted moon. After all these years, her sister. The love that Vita had so painfully wrapped and put away pours out unmarred, whole and rich, love she now can give again. The wound begins to knit, closing over.

8

Because she deserted from the military," explains Vita.

She has decided precisely on the half truths that will satisfy Lorna, keep her safe from the deeper complicity. Lorna doesn't need to know anything about the Credos.

"You mean, now you actually *want* me to move to the farm house?"

Lorna in her peppermint striped pajamas that are getting too small for her, pours milk into her tea, stirs it with an irritated rattle. Vita suddenly sees her resemblance to Ellie, that intent frown, the lift of her chin, the same stubborn shrug of shoulder. How they will love each other!

Vita smiles. "Well, I assume Sienna won't mind?"

"Not Sienna, what about Clove?"

"It's ok with Clove."

"You asked her? Wonders will never cease."

"Don't be rude."

"Sorry, Mom, and it's fantastic you found your sister."

"Your Aunt Ellie," smiles Vita, trying the sound of it.

But that night all idylls present and projected come to an end. Lorna and Vita have just settled down before bedtime with their books.

"Listen to this, Mom," says Lorna, and starts to read a passage out loud.

The sound from outside is a distant but distinct rumble. Thunder? Vita begins to recognize it but naming it is eluding her. Lorna sitting across from her is paused in mid-sentence, her book still raised. Machines, Vita realizes. She hasn't heard such a shuddering roar since her last trip to Williamsburg, when a convoy of troops passed them on the road. Lorna doesn't even place it.

"What a horrible noise," the child remarks.

Vita at the window can't at first make out specific shapes beyond fencing and trees. Even after her eyes know, she can't grasp what they're telling her. Trucks, two military trucks swathed in camouflage green and brown, coming in the exact direction of her own face. Now their gigantic headlights blind her.

The goats begin frantically bleating and bumping. Lorna comes to cling to her from behind.

"Mom, what is it? Who are they?"

Her child's voice asking for reassurance and protection, Vita's searing awareness that she can't provide either, there's nothing she can do.

But she says, "Hide. Get under your bed. Hurry!"

Once Lorna is out of sight, she boldly opens the front door. Two men get out of the front of the truck and stride towards her. From the back of the truck jump six more men, forming a line, holding rifles like scepters.

"Mrs. Gordon?"

"Why do you want to know? What are you doing tearing in here in the middle of the night?"

"Mrs. Gordon, we've come for Lorna Gordon. Don't give us any trouble." The man is not young and he looks tired. "We don't want to hurt you."

Vita stands away from the threshold, keeping outrage in her expression. "What a way to treat people," she scolds, "just wait til I tell your commander. This is an independent farm, we only have goats here, we don't mess with politics. Leave us alone. You have better things to do than harass women alone in the dark…"

But the two men are storming around the cottage, slamming into things and grunting at each other. They even shove the hysterical goats aside and stick their rifles into the hay. It's only a matter of minutes until they find Lorna, drag her out sobbing and push her into the main room and

138

towards the door. They ignore Vita's screaming. They don't say another word to her. Except at the very end when the first man turns and states simply by way of explanation, all reasonableness, "This girl is government property."

Vita clinging to his boots is kicked away, and before she can stand up Lorna is thrust into the back of the truck and it takes off. The volcanic noise and the puffs of sickening fumes paralyze her for a moment. Then she runs for the farmhouse with all her muscle and breath.

9

Alex stares at the map on the broad screen before him, riveting his eyes trying to memorize it. At the same time, one corner of his brain is frantically figuring out how to access it for the Credos. All the enclaves are identified by their military bases, ammo stockpiles, and power sources. This is exactly what they need—Vinsky in Albany, Marcel in Burlington, and Miro in Hartford. They could superimpose the map they already have of water reserves and television centers. Then the Credos would have the key to the whole northeast.

"One small problem," says Ambassador Ladd sitting at the table beside him. "The roads are clogged with refugees, we can't move those troops at more than a snail's pace. That plan doesn't count on reality."

"So?" snorts Father Rose. "Each maneuver will just have to be preceded by a stomp and sweep. It's that simple."

"Stomp and sweep?" objects Chief Barry. "But these are families with children and belongings. They'll need a few minutes warning at least, to get off the road."

He and the priest are sitting to one side at the head of the table, half facing the screen. Father Rose doesn't even bother to look at him.

Instead Rose says to the audience in terse jocularity, "We're finding it works best without warning. Gunfire has a way of motivating people."

A few polite chuckles. No more objections from anyone, including Barry.

When Alex returned to Boston over a month ago, one of the starkest changes he found was this reversed relationship of Rose and Barry. The Chief has become a scarcely acknowledged figurehead, the priest completely in charge. Even the general public knows this and seems to have accepted it.

For now anyway, everyone is obsessed and excited by the imminent arrival of the sacred Zoria herself. She is to lead a massive outdoor service on May twenty-first. Grand six-foot high posters show her in all her holy grandeur, plump hands raised in blessing; loudspeakers carry her breathy voice; the main road she will travel is undergoing cleanup and beautification; families take out their best clothing, admonish their children to be good or Zoria will know about it.

The first thing Ladd had Alex do was get himself fitted for a high-necked jacket, this indication of loyalty no longer an option. If you don't wear one, you're suspect. The colors are limited to gray or army green, so the fashion has had the disconcerting effect of making every official look like they belong to some kind of military order.

But Alex doesn't have an ounce of energy left to object. He's not sleeping well. He finally got an eview session with Gloria, but she was stony and unresponsive, and although her attendants assure him she's fine, he's worried to the point of frantic. He tried to pressure Ladd to get him assigned back to Albany right away, but that suggestion was met with disbelief.

"Cohen, don't you understand the situation? Albany is trying to impose an exorbitant water export tax, Burlington is making all kinds of noises about a forest products ban, and Hartford is threatening to secede from the alliance. All this, on top of that jail break the blasted insurgents pulled last month. We can't spare you here for one second. What's the matter with you?"

So he writes contrite emails to Gloria and hopes she gets them.

Alex's report to the Credos is weeks behind schedule, because the Nons' buildings were so devastated by the recent floods he hasn't yet been given a meeting place. On top of all that, sex with Diamond isn't as relaxing as it used to be, and she's accusing him of losing interest. He feels he hasn't had a moment's peace since he arrived. Even alone in his comfortable room, with time to unwind, he paces and curses and his head hurts.

Rose says, "Our agenda today starts with our top priority: helping Albany find the traitors who broke out of jail and the scum who harbored them, and ensuring swift punishment. We have intelligence they're headed for this area. We'll get them. Then we'll need something public to demonstrate what happens to subversives and heretics. What a glory it would be to catch them while holy Zoria is here among us. Boston could hold a grand spectacle with glorious Zoria passing judgment upon them, presiding over their divine punishment."

Rose's face is mottled maroon with excitement.

Alex works on his neutral expression, feeling faint in the greenish light of the computer screen. All ten people around the table, including the two women, are sitting at attention wearing their regulation clothes buttoned up. Alex closes his eyes briefly to escape the strong feeling of being trapped. He finds an image from his boyhood that often helps under stress: leaping into cool pond water on a hot summer's day, the sensation of velvety liquid massaging his flesh. But today it doesn't work. His armpits are sticky and he's close to trembling. He hopes no one can tell he's far from the suave, calm team player he's thought to be.

Alex knows that Vita's sister is among the escaped Credos, knows what Marcel and Miro will have asked Vita to do. What she of course will do. Being forced to think about her grates like iron on stone. It was natural for him to make a pass, why did she have to respond so passionately? She seduced him, and he resents it. Why does he resent it—it was wonderful. Well, for one thing it's damaged his relationship with Diamond; for another it's brought to an agonizing level his guilt about Gloria. It's one thing to have a bit on the side like Diamond, who fits in nicely with his political agenda and expects nothing but pleasure in return, and quite another to be expected to have strong feelings, to have his heart touched. Now here he is worrying about Vita, as if he needs another problem! He burns with such annoyance he feels it must be reflected in his face, glances uneasily around at the others.

Chief Barry is pleading, "Not a public execution. It's so barbaric. Can't we please think of something else?"

Alex wills his mind to the matter at hand. This kind of meandering about emotional stuff must stop or he'll be in trouble. He clears his throat authoritatively and hears himself say, "These rebels are making more noise than they're worth. They've got no power with the people. Whether they're executed or not won't mean much."

"That's right," Barry agrees gratefully. "We're making too big a deal out of it. Zoria rules."

Alex isn't sure he has pleased the right person, but to his relief Ladd concurs.

"Father Rose," Ladd asserts, "with all due respect, our agenda today holds some other very crucial items. I think we can all agree that recapturing the insurgents is essential, and leave it at that."

There's a general hum of approval around the table. Alex is back in stride.

"The code was easy to decipher I must say," Diamond comments. "Two o'clock tomorrow in the hut with the blue door on Orchard Road."

She greets Alex's arrival with this news from the Nons. She's the recipient because the fruit vendor's assistant in the marketplace is the contact, and she has established a routine of going there every day.

"You're so smart," says Alex. He has just run up the stairs and shrugs off his jacket. She comes into his embrace, but though he hugs her heartily, he does not kiss her. "I know that place," he continues hastily. "That's the one we had meetings in last spring. Good people."

He sits at her table and grins up at her. She doesn't show any recognition of rejection, but swings her hips at him as she serves coffee. She's looking good this afternoon, dressed in red and pink with a deep scoop at the neck for his viewing pleasure, bright black hair swept up and back to show the fine sharp line of her cheek. But he's troubled to realize he's not excited. He somewhat desperately undresses her in his mind, to no avail. This was bound to happen, he tells himself, it's that kind of affair. But he knows he could have gone on bedding Diamond for years, she's that inventive. Besides, he likes her, admires her. What's the matter with him?

Fortunately Diamond herself insists on business first.

"Look," she says, "I need to tell you a couple of things. Since I saw you Tuesday I've learned that three of the escaped prisoners are here in Boston. It was thought very clever to hide them under the cat's nose, and maybe it is. One is in the old subway tunnel at Alewife, and two are in the courthouse attic, where they store all those computers and electronics they think they're going to use again someday."

"Do you know who they are?"

"One of them is Vita Gordon's sister. She's slated to go to River Bend Farm. But there's been some hitch, I'm not sure what it is."

"What do you mean?" Alex can't conceal his alarm.

Diamond, sitting opposite him, her capable hands tightly encompassing the coffee mug, gives him a hard quizzical look. "She saved your life, you say. You stayed alone with her for a few days, you say. Just how friendly did you get?"

Alex brushes her off. "Don't be silly."

"Why are you so upset?"

"I discussed this whole thing with Marcel and Miro, advised them. I feel responsible. Tell me what the hitch is. Can't River Bend take her?"

"I don't know what it is, "Diamond responds coldly. "I told you that. Calm down."

"Well Mrs. Gordon's useful to the Credos. I can care about that, can't I? End of story. Now what else have you got?"

"Okay, Cohen, okay. So, my next piece of news is, my application to work in the TV tower has been accepted. I'll just be a flunky, the liaison between Services and the editors, but I'll be spending quite a bit of time there helping with cutting and splicing, that kind of thing. I got a really good recommendation from Barry. He likes my work. Especially the videos I've done of events and parades."

"What a break for us!" Alex glows at her in honest admiration. "What a trooper you are, my dear. When we take over the station, you'll be right there, on the inside."

He reaches across and puts his two hands over hers, presses warmly.

She continues happily, "Then you'll really adore me when you hear this. I think I've got a recruit."

"Great news. Has he or she passed the trust test?"

"He. Yep, he works in the transportation office and gave me some info nobody else would know. Look." She hurries to a drawer and pulls out a rolled up sheaf, spreads it on the table. "See, this is where a new cable is planned. It looks like it's targeted to carry all the wind power we buy from Maine directly to the palace area. He said work has started on it already."

"Unbelievable." Alex stands over the plan, his finger tracing the dotted lines. "Right under our noses, but over along the coast where nobody goes. It bypasses all the communities now dependent on that Maine power. I didn't know anything about this."

"Well, Ambassador Ladd probably doesn't know either. He's not exactly a favorite around the temple these days. To tell you the truth, I don't even think Barry's advisory circle is the real power behind the throne any more."

"That wouldn't surprise me." He adds reluctantly, "That means I'm not much of a player any more either."

Diamond turns and moves a bit closer, so her breast brushes his arm. She smiles up, asks, "Are you hungry?"

He knows he could interpret this sexually, that she expects him to. He says, "Have you got any more of that smoked trout?"

She steps back chilled. But before she can reply, he has seized her and crushed his mouth on hers. He's going to take this luscious offer if it kills him. He's roused by his own fury. He makes love to her fiercely, in combat with himself.

Afterwards, as they lie entangled in the rampage of disheveled sheets, Diamond says in a clear voice, "You're in love with her, aren't you?"

10

When Vita returns to Boston at the end of April, summer heat already blazes. The air hangs paralyzed never stirring, the sun sears from a cloudless sky whose brilliant blue flaunts weeks without rain, just when newly planted crops crave it most. There hasn't been a drop since the blizzard, which seems months ago, though the swollen lake has only recently retreated and pieces of buildings and trees are still scattered all around like child's play. A fence from nowhere slants against a wagon cut in two by a tree trunk without branches. Vita's house has lost a chunk of its roof, patched up temporarily waiting for materials and workers.

Now looking up at it she stops, on her way home from the marketplace, exhausted already in the middle of the day. Not only from the heat and the weight of groceries, no, they would be bearable. It's that she can't live one second without the torture of imagining Lorna's ordeal. Vita has been back for only four days, but she has tried to see Lorna on every single one of them. The temple guards are starting to titter as soon as they catch sight of her.

Drake won't speak to her. When she showed up at his door, he took one look and walked away, didn't return until the next morning. Then he packed his bag and moved out. The apartment is clean and neat, but with many of her favorite things gone. At first she tried stubbornly to find them, slamming through cabinets and groping under furniture. Where are the framed pictures of her parents, her sister? Drake knows how to punish her. She supposes he has erased her from his life entirely.

Vita finds some shade under a surviving tree and sits heavily. The leaves above, between her and the harsh sky, seem drooping though barely unfurled; one large branch hangs broken, exposing wounded wood. One bird perches unsinging. Up the hill the temple gleams in its cruel whiteness simulating peace, down below the pond shines mockingly, masquerading its pollution. The newly plowed and planted fields are efficient to see, but their earth is a dangerous pale dry color. The little indistinguishable Non figures toil with pails, toting water from the pond in robotic rhythm.

Leaving River Bend Farm was heart rending. Though she knew she couldn't stay there without Lorna—her soul was already flying after her daughter—already gone—that place had given them such respite, it was like a death to end it. But after all, its beauty had been a lie, hadn't it? All the love and comradeship, the feisty goats, the cozy cottage, the days of good labor and delicious food, all sham and delusion. It had only been a matter of time before the authorities found them. She should have known that.

She thinks of Lorna at age two, hair still a wispy spray, legs and arms still baby chubby, toting around her favorite doll, mostly by the leg. She was a stubborn child even then, but smart and sweet too, and Vita never less than adored her.

She gazes up at the temple and adjoining buildings. She has no idea where they're keeping her daughter. If she did, she'd be under that window every minute until they dragged her away. Yesterday had been another confrontation, when she was forcibly removed from the temple steps, as entering worshipers looked askance. She guesses she will be arrested soon. What will be the point of that? She must get hold of herself, think of a sensible plan.

Clove warned her. "You've got to keep your head, Vita. Don't do anything rash. It won't help Lorna."

Hugging Clove goodbye like leaving an island to swim back out to sea, Vita shuddered without tears. Clove's broad face beaming comfort, Clove's warm bulk smelling of chicken feathers and dough. Thinking about her and missing her, Vita juxtaposes Diamond in her mind. The two women couldn't be more different. Yet they are the only friends she has. She'll be seeing Diamond tomorrow; she looks forward to the restfulness and familiarity of her intimate home, her strength and wise perceptions.

Most importantly of all, Diamond may be able to help with Ellie. Vita has no idea where her sister's being hidden. Where will she go now that Vita can't provide refuge at River Bend? Diamond will at least have some good advice.

Now, Vita chides herself, get up and go on home. But she can't, doesn't have the will. Leaning back against the tree, she stretches her legs out, skirt over her knees. It's a pretty blue and yellow patterned skirt, with shapes of stars and little flowers. She had missed it in River Bend. At least Drake had not done away with her clothes. On the contrary, they'd been all neatly folded and stored. The sweat has dried on her face, but her hair is still damp at the temples. She smoothes it back with her palms and wipes them on the skirt. No overalls here.

Near her feet an inchworm has paused on its journey across a twig. Yellowish green, it's about the length of her smallest fingernail. All at once it raises the top half of its body, as if to better reconnoiter. This tiny creature has a life as important to it as hers is to her. The thought grasps her heart, in awe and sadness at the beauty of every living thing, its delicate complexity and fierce burn of purpose. She watches as it drops back onto all its minute feet, inches onward.

She daydreams of Lorna at age ten. That was the year, 2059, when Vita was promoted at Services in time to help process victims of a new cancer outbreak in Boston's southern area, where suddenly people of all ages were developing brain tumors. Lorna was accepted into a top class at her school, and started studying history. She came home one day all eyes, exclaiming, "I never knew there used to be airplanes for regular people! They used to fly all over the sky!"

But what Lorna was really thrilled about in those days was her volleyball team, and her stellar role in it. She had a shiny gold uniform, shorts and sleeveless top, with her number 6 emblazoned on the back. When her team won the final match one spring afternoon, she was so euphoric Vita feared she would faint. Four years ago exactly, Vita calculates, yes it was the very beginning of May. Far, far away now. Vita starts to sink into the seductive trance of yet another narcotic memory, but catches herself and gets slowly to her feet. She must put away the groceries, freshen up, and try another tactic with the priests. This time she'll go around to the office entrance and pretend to be an employee. It could possibly work; she's energized at the thought.

The first thing she notices when she comes in is that the door between the main room and the front room is closed. She's pretty sure she left it open. She splashes her face and neck with water, drinks greedily from her sparse supply. She knows what's going to happen. So she waits, fussing at the kitchen counter, starting to mix up some greens and cheese for her supper. The front room door bangs open.

"Vita," says Drake. "Come here."

She obeys, with a sinking feeling like going to an execution, but at the same time a little pale hope that she can use this situation if she's very careful.

"Hello, Drake."

The front room is pleasantly cool—he has installed the air conditioner. This is a good sign. Would he have bothered if he was just going to rant and run? She follows him in, closing the door, and stands until he motions her to a chair. He sits on Lorna's bed. He's in shirtsleeves and his hair is roughed, its gray edges prominent. How could he look so much older in just five months?

152

"Listen carefully, Vita." His tone has slightly softened, mollified by her obedience. "You have a very important decision to make. I've been given an ultimatum. Father Rose himself has ordered it. You have sinned and broken the law. Fortunately, Lorna has been rescued and brought to perform her duty as a daughter and a citizen and a dutiful child of God. But you, you may have noticed, are as yet unpunished. This cannot be allowed. It sets a very bad example, you must realize that."

Vita follows the expressions on his face with wonder. He's so sure of himself, so indignant, so morally superior, yet genuinely concerned for her, soothing, as if talking to someone contemplating suicide from a bridge. She decides not to answer right away. Find out everything that's on his mind.

Drake continues, "I know you're sorry in your heart. I can even somewhat understand why you committed this crime. I think it's possible that you'll come to see that you did a terrible harm to Lorna, you will beg her forgiveness, and mine. Vita, here is my offer." He gets up, paces, stands in front of her. "I will take you back," he says magnanimously.

Vita looks up at him with what she hopes is a grateful expression. She imagines the scenes to come—living with Drake again—and can scarcely contain her distaste. Does he see it in her eyes? He suddenly makes a fist at her and threatens, "If you don't agree, here's what will happen to you. This house is no longer your home, you'll have to find one as best you can, and you know what that means. No one will dare take you in. You will live with Nons, if you can survive that. You will be a pariah. You'll never see Lorna again."

Vita has one moment of terror. She knows he's right. Such a future spreads itself out vividly before her, twisting her gut. But she collects herself quickly. She knows how to work this situation, she's dealt with this man many times. She stands up, smoothing her blouse, pulling it tight, briefly passing her hands over her breasts and hips, adjusting her dainty skirt. She walks to the window as if at a loss for words, puffs her hair out around her face. Chooses a contrite look, turns and cocks her head at him.

"Drake, I don't think we ever will agree on this. You'll have to acknowledge that I think what I did was right."

He is relaxing his hands, his shoulders, sensing that he has won.

"I concede that, Vita. But I ask that you keep it to yourself. You are to behave as if you are a loyal wife and citizen who has clearly seen the error of her ways. You will attend re-education sessions, you will be monitored."

"I can do that," she nods. "I can do anything to make sure I stay in Lorna's life."

"And mine. In my life, too, Vita."

"Of course." She smiles at him. She's safe now and that makes her smile genuine.

Drake comes over to her, puts his hands around her face. "I will try to forgive you, I will ask God's help in trying to forgive you, Vita."

"Thank you."

He kisses her on the forehead, a patriarchal blessing, to establish the deal they've made.

"Friday evening there's a gathering at Chief Barry's, a very important social occasion. You and I will be there."

Vita reassuringly puts her hand on his arm. "I'm going to be good, Drake, I promise."

11

Alex argues, "Let's not repeat the mistake of moving too fast."

"Too fast?" Vinsky sneers and glances over him dismissively. "You've lived too long among the fancies, Cohen my man. Ask the prisoners we freed if it was too fast."

Around them the faces of the group show a mix of derision and concern, the balance depending on which Credo faction they're from. But none of them wants to argue Vinsky's point. The hut is stifling hot. The window is covered for security—too many Nons would be willing to betray them for favors—so only a faint whiff of air pants through now and then. Along with the odors of sweat and mold and dust, from the next room comes a pungent smell of cooking, not entirely pleasant, as if the food has already seen better days.

"Look, I've got to get back to Albany by next week," Vinsky pursues. "We have to finalize this plan. I say let's take out Zoria and Rose, and let the chips fall where they may after that. And believe me, folks, they will fall. Things will never be the same."

Alex retorts, appalled, "Vinsky, you can't be serious. Killing even one of them will bring down disaster. They'll arrest everyone, they'll torch all the huts, they'll declare martial law and…"

"Wait, Alex," says Lema, the scrawny gray-haired grandmother who can be counted on to inject conciliatory wisdom. She wears a red bandana faded to mottled pink wrapped around her bone sharp forehead, giving her the air of an ancient chieftain. "You have to admit liberating the prisoners was a good idea."

"But Lema," pleads Alex, "can't you see, it's already stepped up their hysteria, given them the excuse to pass even more repressive decrees. Not allowing you people to use irrigation water, for instance. You know that freeing our jailed folks was supposed to be part of the strategic plan, part of taking over the television stations, water sources—a coup. Now they're talking about public executions, about shooting refugees…"

Lema, who because of her arthritis is sitting in one of the only chairs, stirs uneasily.

Vinsky spits out, " 'You people.' Do you hear yourself? Did you hear that? He doesn't belong here. Don't pay any attention to him."

"Look, Vinsky," Alex says, springing to his feet. "Keep a respectful tongue in your mouth. Don't rile me."

Lema intervernes hastily. "Guys, guys, we can't afford this hostility among ourselves. Cut it out. Now, Alex, sit down. I want you to listen to me for a minute."

Alex glowers over smug Vinsky for an instant longer, then sits, alarmed that he lost it. He's the diplomat, he's a man of peace. He's supposed to be able to face down people like Vinsky by his mere civilized demeanor alone. Now he has descended to the rabble-rouser's level. He hasn't even got to the essentials of his report from Marcel and Miro and nobody seems to care. Their sensible step-by-step plan pales in the light of Vinsky's rash fervor.

"We know," says Lema, "that things are only going to get worse anyway, and fast. We can't rely on Chief Barry's good will any longer. The priests are taking over even before we've done anything. Anything besides sporadic subversions and getting caught for it. Now, of course we all agree that the strategic plan is the ideal way to proceed. I've studied enough history to know that this is what could work. But, dear folks, we don't have that kind of time, do we? Couldn't assassination be the answer after all? I think we should at least discuss it. In a cool, reasonable manner." She turns to Vinsky. "Let's hear what you have to say. Spell it out for us."

As Alex makes his way back through the narrow dirt streets, his head is spinning with the depth of his failure. From being central to the drama of his time, it seems that in just weeks he's been relegated to the sidelines. First he's ignored and insulted by Father Rose, and now he's been dismissed by the Nons. He has realized that his meeting with them was not delayed by accident. Vinsky arranged it, buying persuasion time before even letting Alex on the scene.

He maneuvers around a group of grimy children playing a game with sticks and stones. A barefoot woman stumbles by, carrying on her back a bundle of twigs and grass almost bigger than she is. On all sides there's destruction from the floods, every other hut in pieces, strewn around in mud-caked debris. The sounds and smells assail him, and in their cacophony and rot they tell him that Vinsky is right. He doesn't belong here, and how can he tell these people to be patient?

Despair has slowed his step, and he begins to attract attention. With effort he makes it to the back of the market, slips behind the fence and rests against it. He can see Diamond's window, but he can't move. He wants to sink down here and never get up. He feels unmanned, impotent, erased.

"What's the matter?" cries Diamond.
"I can't do it any more," Alex says.
She has come in half an hour after he arrived, bustling with cheery greetings, starting to unpack groceries from her tote bag, then suddenly realizing he hasn't moved from the

couch. He's just lolling there like a rag doll. She plunks down a cabbage and comes for a closer look.

"What's happened? You look terrible." He shrugs. She gets out the hard cider and pours him a full mug. He gulps at it. "Better?" He nods, tries a smile that ends up as an apologetic grimace.

"I'll bet I know what it is," she says. She's standing in front of him, hands on hips.

"You do?"

"It's that Vita."

"You're not going to bash me about that again, are you? I told you it didn't mean anything."

"Well you didn't just fuck her. You fucking made love to her. I can tell."

"I told you…" Alex starts to offer his palms to plead with her, then puts them instead to his head. "Diamond, I'm exhausted. Let's not talk about her right now. I need to tell you what Vinsky's trying to do…"

"I don't give a shit."

Diamond's lurch into foul language has startled him. He had thought he talked her out of her jealousy the other day, when she so outrageously accused him of being in love with Vita. He furiously denied it. She shouted and wept and finished by embracing him. What has gotten into her now? Energized by the need for a quick solution, he gets up and pours himself more cider. He walks to the other side of the room, turns and looks at her. What will bring her around? He has got to get on with business, it's urgent. Damn Vita, she's the cause of all of this nonsense.

"Diamond, she can't compare to you," he says. "You are the best."

"Prove it."

"How? Come here, I'll prove it to you."

"No, no. This. Promise me you'll never see her again."

158

"Diamond, that's so unlike you. You sound like a jealous wife. What is your problem?"

"Ha! I knew it. You do want to see her. But let me tell you something, Mr. Don Juan, you can't. She's gone back to her husband."

Alex is so astounded he can't even grasp for pretense. "What?"

The two of them stand at opposite ends of the cushioned round room, staring at each other. One in wounded triumph, the other in jarred disbelief.

He says, "You must be mistaken." He swipes vaguely at his forehead as if clearing fog. "Okay, we know Lorna was taken. Vita would return here then, okay, to be near her, try to do something. But she would not return to Drake. She can't."

Diamond laughs with brittle gaiety. "I guess you don't know your sweetie so well after all. I do. She's a slave at heart."

"You don't believe that. You told me once you thought she'd be a good Credo recruit. You're just trying to rile me, Diamond."

"I saw her today. She told me herself. She was accompanied by a new friend, who's been assigned to monitor her. Joan. What's more, she's forbidden to fraternize with little old me any more. Apparently her husband doesn't like me. Vita has agreed to resume being a good wife, and they are back together, I swear."

"Joan Kimball, that robot? Vita would hate Joan, Vita's too alive. And Drake? No, no."

"God, what I wouldn't do," moans Diamond, "to make you feel that way about me."

12

The greenhouse reception hall looks suitably glorious. No expense or effort has been spared. Zoria will be the honored guest, and of course that means Jesus Christ himself will be here. Parrots blue-green and crimson flit among palm trees, oranges and strawberries adorn plates piled high with delicate triangle paté sandwiches and crackers with caviar. Waiters in crisp white weave in and out among the lofty crowd, wafting trays with fluted glasses of champagne. Joan is beside herself with awe.

"Zoria is pregnant with Jesus, is she not?" breathes Joan. "Jesus Lord lies in her womb, does he not? I'm sure I will faint at the sight of her, won't you, Vita?"

They are sitting on a divan facing out, looking down through the glass wall of the greenhouse at the streets thronged with people on either side. The guru, the goddess, will travel along that very way in just a few minutes.

Vita thinks with something like amusement, Zoria has been pregnant for at least twelve years, that's a stretch. She's acutely aware that just two years ago, the last time the great guru graced Boston with her presence, Vita was almost as breathlessly gullible as Joan.

She replies eagerly, "Oh, yes, it will be grand," sips at her glass and munches from a little plate in her hand. She moves the taste of strawberries and caviar around in her mouth, deliciously, derisively. She's getting good at this. She no longer worries that her thoughts will betray her. Joan even seems to sincerely like her.

"Vita, you know frankly," Joan said just yesterday, "I'm sure you are really a good daughter of God. You only ran away because the devil got hold of you for a bit. You're basically a good person. I don't think you'll ever stray again."

"Oh, no, I won't," agreed Vita earnestly, thinking, "good, go tell that to your masters."

Joan says, "I'm just going to go fetch some more of those sandwiches for us, you stay right here."

Vita stands up and watches her scoot off, a tall supple figure, so blond she's almost albino, wearing a white and red dress that does not flatter her but shouts her allegiance. Vita has got used to taking orders from Joan. She stays put and glances around at all the gorgeously attired people of the elite of her community, most of the faces familiar, and swallows hard at how alien she feels. There's been so much loss since she was one of them. Does it balance the illumination of self she has gained?

The stage is adorned with white and red bunting, surrounded on three sides with Zoria's flags depicting her standard inverted cross. Vita wonders where they got the bleach for all this white, and why the flags are waving—there must be fans concealed somewhere.

Suddenly there's Alex. He's standing looking at her from across the room. Her eyes are riveted. His soft brown beard, his lanky grace, the memory of his voice and touch. Her well oiled pretense wilts. At this moment she could not pass herself off as anything other than stunned hurt. She turns her back abruptly. All this time, these months since they were together, she has schooled herself in renunciation, sometimes accusing herself and sometimes him of wildly misjudging the situation, but always coming back to the assurance that she meant nothing to him. Or rather, there probably had been the start of a true friendship, which they had managed to ruin.

She's trying to breathe normally, closing her eyes for a moment, when she hears him say, almost in her ear, "Hello, Vita."

She starts and nearly staggers. But then she turns to him.

162

"Mr. Cohen." Cooly, half playfully. That should fix him.

"Your chaperone will be back in a minute," he says. "I have to see you."

"What do you mean?"

"Ellie will be in Boston in transit very soon. I can get you to her. Just listen, don't interrupt. When Zoria enters, I'll be under that pear tree over there, the one in the corner. Meet me there."

"I can't. I have to…"

"Don't worry. Everyone will be distracted. You'll see." Then, as they both note Joan hurrying towards them, he says heartily, "The holy hall looks splendid, all decked out. I've never seen such a wonderful sight." He bows gallantly to Joan with a grin he must know is absolutely charming. "Mrs. Kimball, you're looking lovely today. How is that talented boy of yours?"

Joan is not stupid, she knows a snow job when she sees one, but she simpers willingly, "My boy is just amazing, thank you. Star of the soccer team. We'll be watching him play tomorrow. I hope you'll be there."

"Wouldn't miss it." Alex glances at Vita to make sure she's recovered her equilibrium. "Mrs. Gordon has been telling me all about her husband's recent achievements."

"Oh, yes," Vita obliges, "Drake is doing wonders."

After Alex has bid a cheery goodbye without looking at her again, Vita snatches two sandwiches in a row from the plate Joan proffers, keeping her back to the room. Out in the street the first phalanx of Zorian guards appears, riding white horses with red bridles. Then comes a band on a float, drums and trumpets prominent, faintly heard through the thick glass. Even this late in the afternoon the heat out there is grueling, but the crowd waves frantic flags, their shouts rise. And now here comes Zoria herself, enthroned on a white float resembling a cloud, her head looking like a small knob atop her gigantic body draped in red.

Father Rose summons the guests away from the window. "Come, people, chosen ones, give a proper welcome to our savior."

Then he takes his place on the stage with other priests and officials forming a V facing the spot where it seems she will appear. Drake is among them, proud and stern in his immaculate high-necked jacket, honored with a place near Rose. Chief Barry has been relegated to a lower level, but his pleasant broad face doesn't reveal any discomfort or doubt he may be feeling. Vita follows Joan for a moment, then slows. Joan doesn't notice, pushes forward, her face alight. Gradually Vita backs towards the corner. Alex was right. Everyone is intent on the imminent divinity. She puts her hand on the cool bark of the tree. He steps forward, close.

"It's good to see you," he says. "We're still friends?"

"Of course," she says impatiently. "Where's Ellie?"

"It's tonight. I'm sorry I couldn't get to you sooner. I only found out yesterday myself. I seem to be out of the loop somehow I'm afraid."

"Where's she going?"

"I don't know for sure. She might know. You can ask her."

At these words Vita swells with heady joy. I can ask her, I can talk to her. "Thank you, Alex."

He gazes down at her with glowing eyes, his hand goes slowly to her shoulder. "You're wearing the same blue dress I met you in." He fingers the fabric.

"Is she here now? What do I have to do? Just tell me, I'll do it."

The crowd's murmur burgeons into a hum of awe. Up ahead, Zoria is being lowered throne and all by some mechanism above. A heavenly descent. Trumpets sound.

164

"She'll be in the old Alewife subway station. She'll have to leave before dawn. When can you get away? Seven or eight?"

"I'll manage. Can we say eight?"

"Right."

Zoria has risen and begins to speak in a whistling wheeze.

"My children, my little ones, Jesus will bless you when I bring him into this world at last. He will forgive all your sins and you will live blissfully ever after."

Alex says quickly, "Be at the bottom of your hill at eight, where the old bleachers start, the entrance to the field. Don't worry if I'm a bit late. Try not to be recognized. But if you are, just say you had a bout of nostalgia or zeal, or something."

Vita nods, presses his arm briefly, and moves away. He disappears into the crowd.

Joan has not noticed her absence, she's standing transfixed.

"But woe unto those who fail to follow the Way," Zoria continues. "Jesus will send them all straight to hell." She rants against "unbelievers" who think humans caused environmental catastrophe, when it was clearly God, sending us a message. She continues with a litany of punishments awaiting anybody who doesn't toe the line, then a chorus of male voices sings a thrilling hymn. Vita has time to think through how she will manage her escape this evening.

The banquet is incredible. Vita has never in her life seen so much food in one place. She sits demurely beside Drake, gratified to see that he takes her submission for granted. He pats her possessively now and then, and relies on her to second his points of conversation. Zoria presiding at the head of the table is near enough that Vita can study her at leisure. She's so fat she needs a special chair. She has four chins, and each of her deeply dimpled arms is as large as a good-sized goat. She looks to be about fifty, her small features almost disappearing into crinkling flesh, crowned by an oddly bland mop of thinning brown hair. She eats hurriedly and continuously, as if her life depends on it.

Vita tries to imagine Ellie at this moment, traveling towards Boston, riding hidden in a wagon or van perhaps, frightened, exhausted. Does she know Vita is here, does she even know anything about Lorna? Will she trust her? Twenty years! The image of the prancing laughing seventeen-year-old will not give way to what Ellie must look like now. The picture that clutches Vita most tenaciously is their last encounter, over breakfast, sunlight cascading through their windows, the glinting blue lake, Ellie's bronze hair falling brightly over her mischievous smiling eyes.

Joan goes home with Vita. Drake remains for honored blessings and consultations with the powerful and redeemed inner circle. While Vita makes tea for them, Joan wanders about the rooms, commenting on details as if she's in charge, which of course in a way she is.

"I'd move that round table closer to the sink," she says, "don't you think that's more efficient? I love this little yellow pillow, why don't you put it on an armchair where it will be noticed? This shelving doesn't seem sensible. Why don't you get rid of it? I know a place where you can buy a nice little pinewood dresser instead. You can certainly afford it now. I wish I had a daughter so I could get all those perks."

As she pours boiling water over tea leaves, Vita thinks about scalding Joan. It would be a pleasure. Joan sits down in a chair along with the reassigned yellow pillow. Vita moves the designated table closer to the sink, and serves Joan's tea.

"You have such good ideas," she says. "I'll give the dresser a thought. It sounds nice."

166

"It's very pretty," Joan assures her. "I saw it the other day at the antique dealers, you know, Harvey's."

"Harvey's."

It's seven thirty. Vita contemplates tripping Joan or hitting her over the head. The woman is holding forth tirelessly and with complete self-absorption on the benefits of strict adherence to Zorian doctrine. While she's in mid-sentence, repeating, "and all you have to do is obey, it's that simple…" Vita yawns widely, gets up and stretches.

"Oh you poor dear," says Joan. "It's been an emotional day for us, hasn't it? And I must get back to my patient husband. He's so good about this wonderful new friendship of ours. He's going to be promoted to assistant chief officer of security, you know." She collects her lanky pale form, and at the door gives Vita a kiss on the cheek.

Vita almost feels sorry for her. Surely she must realize that her husband has been promised a reward because his wife is a personal spy—or does she? Can she really think Vita is her friend? Vita wants to believe that Joan is that innocent, it makes her own rebellious impulses less violent. She watches the ghostly figure fade out of sight down the stairs, closes the door and rushes to get ready. She knows she should worry about what Drake will do if he returns before she does and finds her gone. But she can't. She has become a one-thought creature, directed to action. When she slips out a few minutes later, she has exchanged her dress for dark clothes including a hooded jacket.

The sun has set when she reaches the entrance to the old bleachers. They lie mostly in ruins, jagged chunks of concrete like an archeological specimen. Half of them have been carted away for other purposes. In their place straggle weeds and spiny young trees. Some of the rock crevices spout delicate blue flowers, ironic beauty. Below, the shadowed fields stretch to the pond, which is dark except for shiny green algae trimming its edge. There's a moon, a silver curl, but too many clouds to anticipate any display of stars. Vita leans against one of the ancient pillars. She has spotted the ragman's cart standing a few yards away. Is he asleep inside? The horse seems quietly resting. Against the distant shuffle of lapping water, she hears muted human noises from the houses behind her, where some windows have begun to show lights.

A man lifts the curtain at the back of the ragman's cart. Before she can be afraid, she knows it's Alex. He comes swiftly, taking her hand without a word, pulling her to a run. In an instant they're inside the cart, in a mound of old clothes and cloth, a musty moldy smell. The ragman appears from nowhere and covers them up. A moment later the cart is moving, at a fast clip.

"So far so good," says Alex.

They're lying side by side. His face is inches away. The light is a gray slant that keeps moving as the curtain sways, so his eyes are alternately black and bright.

"The ragman?" she asks.

"Credo through and through."

"Alex, did you know they found out where we were? Lorna's being kept in the Temple. She'll be forced to…"

"Yes, I was sickened to hear it. I'm so sorry, Vita. That lovely young girl, so much promise. Can you at least get to see her, do you think?"

"I'm doing everything I can."

"Which includes going back to Drake?"

"He's my husband."

Her stoic finality sounds defensive to her, but what can it matter to him anyway?

He reaches out to touch her hair, repeating, "I'm sorry."

13

Vita clings to Ellie while both Ellie and Alex try to extricate her.

"It's after ten, Vita," Alex urges. "Don't be foolish."

Ellie says, "Go my dear, go. I want you to be safe."

Vita pulls back to gaze at her sister hungrily one more time. She's so changed, Vita didn't recognize her until she smiled. Dull hair streaked with gray, eyes haggard, forehead and cheeks striated with lines. Around her mouth no laugh lines, only downturned grooves. There's a deep scar on her neck, just under the chin. She's scrawny thin, she feels all bone in Vita's embrace. They had cried together for a long while, their voices are still thick with tears.

But there's been time for much to be said, details of their lives, remembrances of parents and growing up, small things that even made them laugh a little. Fears too, warnings, plans, hopes for the future.

"I can handle Drake," says Vita, and settles back down stubbornly on Ellie's mat. "Just a few more minutes."

Ellie sits down again beside her, entwined.

Around them the old ceramic stone of the abandoned subway platform splotched with mold damply glistens in the light of one candle, plus that of Alex's lantern. Subway maps fading into the wall trace long ago travels, ghostly history. A box of crackers and a half eaten apple tumble against a container of water and a tiny bundle of belongings, wrenching summary of Ellie's ordeal.

"I wish you weren't going so far away," says Vita. "It'll be a long time before I can get to Vermont."

"You have to rescue Lorna first."

"Ellie, you don't know…"

"How hard that will be. Of course I do. You have to try."

Vita cups the beloved face in her hands. "My little sister is stronger than I am."

"No she's not. You have a deep soul, Vita. There's power there."

Alex insists, "Vita, you have got to get out of here."

"Yes, yes, okay. Just tell me one more thing, Ellie. After the military recruiters grabbed you that day, why couldn't you get me a message? I was worried to death."

"I told you, I did, at least I thought I did. I sent an email to the library. But it was unauthorized so maybe they discovered it and deleted it before it went out. Then I tried twice more, sent notes with scouts I trusted. But something must've happened to them. Then, my unit was called up to fight on the southwestern front—you remember the Kentucky massacre?—and I decided to desert. After that, I heard you'd gone off with Drake. I couldn't risk contacting you with him around. And let's face it, your heart was all involved with him and his beliefs, would it really have been wise? I was on the run, going through all kinds of hell until I met up with the Credos." She gives a shy smile to Alex. "They are the best. They gave me a new identity. I'm Belinda the baker, don't forget. Deserter Ellie disappeared from the military radar screen years ago. As Belinda I worked with the Credos on lots of projects before I got caught. We were betrayed on a mission to take out the Albany gun factory. They were waiting for us."

Vita holds her sister close in one long last hug, eyes squeezed tight to brand the memory of the feeling on her brain. "My brave girl. I will see you again soon and we'll forget all that."

The wagon could go much faster, but it would attract attention, so Alex and Vita have to be satisfied with a leisurely clip. With every bump they roll about and into each

170

other. Vita is quiet for a long time, savoring each moment with Ellie, faint with happiness and worry. Then she thanks Alex again and again until he puts a finger on her lips. The gesture startles her with its intimacy. Her eyes widen in alarm. But though he must see her distressed response, he doesn't take his finger away, instead continues to trace the outline of her mouth.

He says slowly, "We didn't make a mistake, back in River Bend. I want you to know I think about it all the time, you in my arms."

She takes his hand away. "You were cruel. You're being cruel now."

"Ah, don't say that."

She can see his eyes, as they fade in and out with the flapping of the curtain, cloud with tears. It's more than she can stand.

"You're some kind of sadist," she says angrily. "Why are you trying to come on to me again, after what you've done? You treated me like a used handkerchief, for God's sake."

"Vita, Vita. Please. I was just so horrified by what I was feeling. I've never…I've never felt that way about any woman, even my wife. It was unbearable, to want you so much and know I couldn't have you. It was torture."

"That's not how it looked to me," she retorts. "You acted like a man who'd satisfied his lust and was moving on."

"Now that's cruel, Vita."

She doesn't reply, takes her eyes away. Every fiber in her body wants him, trembles towards him, but her heart and brain are screaming warnings. Giving in would be a disaster. She can't trust Alex not to take her and toss her away again. She can't risk this further turmoil in her life.

"Leave me alone," she says.

"I can't," he says miserably. "I want to, but I can't."

171

"Forget it. I saved your life and you got me to my sister. We're even. That's the end of it."

There's a light in the window of her apartment, and as she hurries up the hill Vita knows that Drake is already there. Waiting for her. She goes cold. This confrontation could be ugly.

He says, "Where the hell have you been?"

Standing there red-faced, sounding and looking like a caricature of a jealous husband.

She takes off her jacket, goes to the mirror by the sink and combs her hair slowly, her mind darting at possible tactics.

"Why are you always spying on me? Am I your prisoner?"

He strides over, spins her around, pushes her up against the sink, and spits out, "Tell me."

She realizes he's been drinking more than his usual amount. She tries to turn it to advantage.

"Your breath! You're drunk. That must have been quite a party."

But it's the wrong thing to say.

"Don't you mouth a single heresy to me, woman. Tell me where you've been. Right now."

"I'm sorry, Drake, I'm so sorry. Please forgive me."

"For what?"

"I didn't mean to criticize the sacred rituals, I know how magnificent they are. I just wanted to get out for some air, for a walk. It's so stuffy in here. Joan had to go home early and I felt lonely. So I thought, I'll go have a stroll and a look at the moon. I'm sorry. I just went out for a walk."

"The hell you did. Tell me where you've been." He has grabbed both her arms and is shaking her. "You slut! Have you been sneaking around?"

"No, no, how can you say that, Drake?"

172

She starts to cry and he punches her in the face. She falls on the floor, tasting blood. He stands there staring down at her. Another look comes into his face and she knows what it is. When he reaches down and pulls her to her feet, she goes limp against him. He twists her around and bends her over the table, yanks down her trousers. He crams into her and fills her with his liquid in an instant, while his noises turn from grunts to sobs. After he pulls out, he turns her around again and kisses her, his mouth smearing red with her blood.

14

Alex sits on the edge of his bed in the middle of the night, a man at a crossroads. He looks down at his now quiescent penis, which had waked him throbbing during a dream about Vita. He had given in to its urgency while still half asleep, wetting his shorts that now lie where he threw them on the floor.

He starkly studies his situation. He's obsessed with a married woman who is closely watched and in any case so angry she may never want to see him again. He has lost credibility and clout with the cause he cares passionately about; far from his former respected leadership, he's been reduced to giving unsolicited advice. His mistress no longer interests him, but she's his easiest direct link to the Credos, and turning out to be a fury in jealousy to boot. Contrary to what he's always assumed, Diamond is an unlikely candidate for a friendly parting of the ways. His relationship with his boss is good, but both he and Ambassador Ladd are becoming more and more marginalized as the priests gain ascendancy. Everything he has prided himself on is in jeopardy.

Gloria. He has always been so proud of taking good care of Gloria. Now look what he's done. She's outraged at him, cold and punitive. Since his departure she has only agreed to an eview once, early on, and she'd looked at him with supreme disdain, her replies mechanical and distant. She never answers his emails except to write, "why are you staying there in Boston, why aren't you here with me?" along with details of her maladies and the various remedies her helpers provide. Most hurtful of all, sometimes she resorts to irony: "It must be nice enjoying yourself without your poor sick wife, having a good time away from your responsibilities. Carefree as can be. Out of sight out of mind, that's the way it is with you." He deeply feels he has failed her. What's worse, her image occurs less and less frequently to his brain, violently displaced by Vita's charms. Good God, he doesn't even want to see Gloria, is aware of dreading her deciding to come to Boston. When he had sincerely begged her to, so many times. What has happened to him? He has become the shadow of the man he once was. Is he going crazy?

He's got to sort this out. What are the priorities? He gets up, lowers the temperature on the air conditioner, and looks out the window. His rooms are in one of the newer buildings on Temple Square. Just months ago, this pre-dawn view had been dark and deserted, but now the square is lit all night and SF patrols are frequent. There go two of them now, marching side by side in their gray-green uniforms with white lapels, their mini machine guns glinting. Zorian flags sprout everywhere, and larger than life posters of Zoria herself adorn any available space.

Vinsky and Rose, the maniacs on both sides, are going to get their way, at least temporarily. Escalating confrontation, pointless killing. He has to face that. But he can fight them both, even without a power base or significant support—he has to. So for the short term, he must try to keep Diamond happy, and that means not seeking out Vita, which in any case is both dangerous and hopeless. He must keep the pressure on Vinsky to cool down, and try to get the other Credos to see reason, or at least recognize some doubt about radical action. They can't be allowed to destroy themselves; they are the only hope for civilized survival. He must vigorously back up Ladd in the effort to keep peace among the enclaves, continuously pointing out diplomatic solutions and their benefits. For his own self-esteem, he can't assume he has to win, only that he has to try.

He goes back to stretch out on his bed. Lies there naked feeling vulnerable and sad. Life is not much, and too long.

176

The following week, on June 5th, all hell breaks loose.

"It's war," says Ladd as soon as Alex arrives that morning.

"Albany? Don't tell me we're forcing the Finger Lakes issue. That makes no sense. That was just posturing, surely."

"No, no, the agreement we negotiated still holds, for now. It's Hartford. They invaded our southern border just at dawn. Looks like they're after the food supplies."

"I thought they had a reasonable crop last fall."

"They were hard hit this March with the floods. Their lower valleys still can't be cultivated. Our Providence area is too much of a temptation, all our stored grains and soy especially."

"Probably want them for their ethanol plant more than to feed people. Their priests are even crazier for fuel than ours."

Ladd nods reluctantly, his white eyebrows knit in consternation. To distance himself from this suspect sympathy, he responds with patriotic fervor.

"It's a good thing we just upped military service to five years and lowered the age to sixteen," he says. "Father Rose had foresight there. Today he also revoked all deferments—for studies, apprenticeships, farming, fuel system work, all of them. We'll have a terrific fighting force."

Alex nods morosely, remembering the young faces of the recent recruits in the parade he had seen only yesterday. All decked out in new uniforms, eyes bright with bravery and ignorance. Children.

He reminds Ladd, "Hey, Rose had something to do with relations getting to the point where Hartford prefers violence to diplomacy."

The ambassador shrugs, half in admonishment. He strides over to his laptop and projects a map onto the big screen. "The attacks are here, and here. Both areas were well reconnoitered. Our defenses are weak just at those points."

"Have they actually declared war? It looks like we could treat them as skirmishes and try to get a ceasefire."

"Well, that's not what Rose wants to do. The Chief reads the war declaration soon, at ten o'clock. All televisions have been activated."

Alex slumps into a chair. At least Albany is okay, peace in his own diplomatic territory preserved for now, Gloria safe. But this stepped-up militarism can only spell a polarization that will further the methods and goals of the radicals among both Zorians and Credos. Ladd standing in front of the screen turns to Alex with more bad news.

"As you know, our drought here is in its second month, which makes almost four months in some parts of the south," Ladd says. "And sure enough, as we suspected they've got outbreaks of yellow fever in the Carolinas, spreading much faster than anticipated. So naturally the refugees fleeing north are increasing at the same rate. Drought and disease, put those two together. It's a mass exodus."

"We can't handle that."

"So now Rose wants refugees shot on sight."

Alex's stomach turns. "Carnage." Then he has an even blacker thought. "Hartford has a good supply of munitions. I'll bet Rose won't stop at turning back the invasion. He'll continue deeper into the enclave to get his hands on that ammo. He's been handed the perfect excuse."

"I'm afraid you're right."

"They'd better prepare the clinics. We'll have wounded here by tomorrow."

In front of the screen Ladd's thin worried face wavers with the map's various colors, outlines of borders. He mutters, "Thank God my son is serving out west."

178

For a moment the men's eyes meet in understanding of the enormity, then both blink and return to business.

Ladd says briskly, "Here's where we come in, Cohen. The drought's putting pressure on all the regions with drinkable water. That means our relationship with Albany is crucial, even though the price they're asking is exorbitant, on top of the transport."

"Well," says Alex, "we should've put this kind of money and manpower into cleaning up our Quabbin reservoir, back when it might have been possible to rescue it. Too late now. The sediment is laced with mercury and PCBs, it's pretty much useless. So we're going to need that desalination plant pronto. What's the prospect on that?"

"Don't know. There's a lot I don't know these days. The structure got pretty beat up by those tidal waves, and anyway I would guess it's too far out to sea by now. Besides, running it would take a ton of fuel. But look, Cohen, let's keep our sights on what we do have some say in. Let's concentrate on strengthening our ties with Albany. Kiss up to the ambassador and that obnoxious assistant of his. Our job is peace on that border. And who knows, we may need their help militarily down the road, God forbid."

"Right." Alex flips open his appointment folder. "Our next official meeting isn't til Thursday. Shall I book a lunch with them before that?"

"Something impressive, and secluded. Try to get Barry's dining room. And update me on their domestic situation, so I can commiserate with sincere concern, you know the drill."

"Got it."

When Alex goes out at lunchtime into the boiling heat, sweat starts along his back and scalp after just a few steps. As he crosses Temple Square from the administrative buildings to the main street, he notes that television screens are carrying a repeat of Chief Barry's declaration of war on Hartford. Knots of murmuring people stand in front of them. He passes the Services building where Diamond works; Vita doesn't yet have her old job back. A yellow dust swirls and drives across his face, starting a cough.

He's still coughing when he comes into Diamond's cool restful room. She's waiting there, with sandwiches and cider all prepared on the table covered with a gaily colored cloth.

"There'll be an air alert tomorrow I'll bet," she says.

He pulls her to him. "Oxygen masks. Not good for kissing."

"Not good for eating either," she laughs. "So let's eat. I made egg salad for you. It's a deal, no war talk 'til you've been satisfied."

He laughs too, relieved at her casual affection. It will be all right with her, he can handle it. With a soft paddle of her rump, he sits down in front of the little feast.

15

V ita and Drake kneel in the Temple, preparing themselves to enter the inner sanctum. They quietly chant the Zorian mantra and the familiar words of self-abasement and obedience. The elderly priest who has accompanied them kneels at a distance. There's nobody else in the cavernous marble and gilded high-vaulted space. Faint music comes from somewhere, high voices, flute and harp. A wailing nostalgic sound, constricted and piteous.

Vita's thoughts strain towards Lorna, somewhere on the other side of that white wall hung with its giant inverted cross draped in crimson cloth. She imagines she hears her child's voice, lifted along the melody behind the bars of the music trapping her. With solace and not a trace of guilt, Vita savors details of her secret sessions at her own private altar, unrecognizable as such by any one else—just a corner of Lorna's dresser, a photo of the two of them together, a ribbon, a dried flower. She has followed Noam's practice from River Bend, spiritual celebration heretical in its simplicity, its absence of abjection, its joy. She's sure that Lorna has kept that in her heart too, perhaps at this very moment, as she's being prepared to meet her parents for the first time since her capture, she too finding Noam's words and holding onto them. "Sacred force, spirit of life, be with us now, connect us to precious Earth..."

It's been two months now. Two tortured, transcendent months. Her last view of Lorna that terrible night, screaming and twisting, has faded in its cutting edge, but has transformed into a core of rage that keeps her going. The more she schools herself to appear Joan's star pupil, passive and worn down by authorities both higher and close by, the more the core burns. Sex with Drake is almost an out of body experience that she watches from above their sweating bodies. As far as she can tell, he's duped completely, partly because he so wants to be. Possibly she even may be able to ease away from Joan soon. So it's as a pilgrim both restless and patient that she now waits so near her goal, so many obstacles overcome.

When Lorna was three, she treasured a stuffed monkey named Leroy. Because they were on the road so much at that time, the toy took on superhuman meaning. If Leroy liked something, it was ok and if not, tantrums were in order. Leroy always initiated a new bed and passed judgment on it. Drake with a solemn face consulted the monkey about plans and timing. Vita made sure a place for it was provided at the table. What she remembers vividly in this moment is Lorna's plump pink arms clutched around the ragged and stained Leroy. In those days the child's hair was soft ethereal yellow exactly like corn silk. She looked like a Rubens rendering of Cupid, complete with rosebud mouth and dimpled knees. Eyes closed, Vita sees again the flushed tiny face, inhales the honeyed baby flesh. Her longing to again fully enfold her daughter like that, fiercely and unequivocally, grasps at her muscles. The memory of the child's small body warm against hers is wild with hunger.

The singing stops. Drake's devout murmurs continue, but Vita opens her eyes to the glittering candlelight, the shifting shadows beyond. The old priest is looking back at her. No doubt he knows her history, is prepared for breaches of decorum, ready to pounce. Vita's knees are hurting, her neck is stiff. But of course that's meant to put her in a mood of proper awe. Lorna probably has to do this kind of thing all day long, to the point of discomfort, pain. Vita's anger soars again, tastes bitter, sets her jaw.

At last their escort voices a final chant. He rises, taking his time. Vita and Drake follow him towards the altar, pass behind it, shadows deepening. Ahead she can see clearly only the white flash of the priest's attire. The stone statues around them may look benign properly lit, but in this eerie twilight they seem to lean forward and threaten, tensely tremble, menace. In a line, Vita between, the three of them proceed very slowly, perhaps because of their guide's age, but more likely to display reverence. A great wooden door opens, and they're in a long dim corridor, echoing and sterile. Suddenly there's an enormous portal like a bank vault's. It springs open noiselessly, but when it closes behind them the sound is violent, sonorous. Now the corridor becomes a carpeted hallway lined with portraits and smelling of incense.

They climb stairs wide, shallow, and curved, and begin passing other people. Two young priests, laughing, a bustling group of nurses, a man in the uniform of the top ranking SF. As they enter a wide high-ceilinged room, the atmosphere strikes Vita as that of a decadent monastery. Signs of worship abound—crosses of all sizes, garlanded portraits of Zoria and Father Rose, statues of saints and famous Zorians. But comfort is everywhere obliged, from plush settees and soft carpets to chandeliers and crystal bowls of fruit. The background music is pious, but lively conversation overlays it.

"This is the social room," their guide tells them proudly. "Where the priests can congregate and rest. Parents meet with their daughters here. Some of the ceremonies are held here, too. For example, should you be blessed with a fruitful daughter, the baptism will be followed by a grand celebration in this very room. Those are glorious occasions."

"We pray for it," says Drake.

The priest seats them in a booth side by side. Then he bows, mission accomplished, and disappears.

"Are we supposed to wait here?" Vita is whispering though there's no need.

"Obviously."

"Where is she?"

"Calm down, Vita. Recall where you are. This is sacred ground. Maybe you'd better repeat the mantras again."

Vita hangs her head and keeps quiet as long as she can. Then she says, "Drake, dear, do you know how long they'll let her talk with us? Can we take her out?"

"Take her out! Are you crazy? Of course not. And she wouldn't want to go anyway, would you? She's blessed to be here, you've acknowledged that yourself."

"I know. Sorry."

Vita squeezes her eyes shut for an instant, seeking equilibrium, and when she opens them, there's Lorna, led by the hand, approaching. She's in a lacy white dress with a low neck and puffy short sleeves, a narrow pink ribbon at her waist. It could be the outfit of a ten year old except that it fits snugly around her breasts and hips. Her face is very pale. She's smiling, but her smile doesn't move. Her companion, a plump woman in a nun-like blood-red gown and headscarf, motions her to sit down on the other side of the table.

Vita starts to jump up and hug her, but Drake holds her firmly in place.

"Here we are," wheezes the woman cheerily, "All set now. Aren't you a lucky girl."

"I'm a lucky girl," smiles Lorna, sitting down, clasping her hands together in front of her on the table.

Vita leans over as far as she can, grasps her child's hands, brings them to her lips. Lorna keeps smiling the same smile. Vita kisses her hands, presses them to her cheek, wets them with tears. Lorna keeps smiling.

"Well now," says Drake jovially, "don't you look pretty!"

"Thank you, dad," Lorna says.

Her voice is Lorna's but it doesn't modulate. It's almost robotic in tone. Vita begins a freezing in her spine. Something is terribly wrong.

"Well now," Drake pursues, "I can't say we don't miss you, your mother and I. But we know what an honor this is for all of us. We pray for you. I know you pray for us."

"I pray for both of you, daddy."

Doesn't Drake see it? Can he be so caught up in his self-importance, in the awe of finding himself in the inner sanctum, this elite's boys' club, that he's blind to the grotesque distortion of his daughter's personality? Vita listens to them talk, but beyond their words her gut probes for some meaning. And shortly it dawns on her. Lorna's pupils are dilated, her movements languorous. She's drugged.

Desperately Vita tries to catch her eye, grasping for some sign of awareness. But when the girl returns her look, it's with the same artificial affection, a bad actress playing the dutiful daughter. Vita is having trouble breathing. Her throat feels desert dry, as if it might close up at any moment.

She says half whispering, "Lorna, do you remember Garth?" She feels Drake tense, ignores it. "Do you remember Garth, Lorna?"

Lorna nods. Her smile wavers.

Vita pursues, while Drake under the table digs his nails into her thigh, "He's been drafted. They abolished all the exemptions. I saw him in uniform just yesterday, in a parade."

"Garth's in the military?" Lorna's monotonous tone rises ever so slightly.

"Yes, and there's a war on, Lorna," Vita goes on relentlessly. "He could be killed."

Now the film over Lorna's eyes melts for a moment and she looks at her mother with a lightning flash of comprehension. In that look in that moment, Vita finds her child again, knows she's still there intact under all the muck they've buried her in. Lorna's alarmed eyes hint tears.

Drake is beside himself. "Keep quiet, Vita! Do you want to frighten the girl? What does she care for a juvenile nobody recruit? Lorna, listen. Your mother's been under a lot of strain lately. Don't let her upset you."

After a pause, "I'm not upset, daddy."

"Good," breathes Drake. "We're both so proud of you. Don't you forget that for a minute."

Vita is grinning at Lorna with all her love and a sense of shared conspiracy. She could swear she sees Lorna reciprocate, just for an instant. It's enough. She lets Drake take over, encourages him as he waxes more and more securely pompous. He's having a grand time.

186

16

All that summer of '63, forces continue spiraling towards chaos. Alex's personal dilemmas fade in perspective. The heat, the worst that anyone remembers, is prostrating people right and left, though the fatalities are mostly Nons, so in the official view that's the least of the problems. Air pollution intensifies; the high alert black flag persists for days at a time; on the street oxygen masks are commonplace. Refugees from the south swarm the roads, a miserable looking sickly bunch, snatching food or water wherever they can. Their numbers are lessened by the heat and also the new policy of zero tolerance—every once in a while a troop of soldiers swoops in to wipe out a bunch of them—but there are so many it's impossible to kill them all or even half of them. In the end the authorities have found it easier to just herd them north as fast as possible. The wretches are prodded and pummeled along one specific route, troops with dogs guarding the fields and water sources on the way. Meanwhile, months of drought are taking their toll on all but the hardiest crops, and drinking water is rationed even for the elite for the first time in ten years. The invasion of Hartford, while successful in raiding their ammunition supplies, has not stopped the skirmishes and insurgencies that continue to send wounded to overwhelm the clinics. Corpses of refugees, heat-stroke victims, and soldiers are cremated in bundles, and the smell of smoldering decayed flesh taints the breeze. Finally, cremation has to be banned because of the choking air, so the bodies start piling up while huge pits are dug for them. It's rumored that no distinction is made in burial between the unredeemed poor and the blessed and honorable, but this cannot be confirmed.

One afternoon Alex is sitting in his Boston office mulling over correspondence from the Albany embassy. The staff there is concerned about rumors that their frontier areas are coming under the influence of the Akron enclave, where priests reign ferociously. Albany has been proud up until now of maintaining its separation of church and state, with a relatively enlightened leader, Boss Jones. Alex's correspondent is urging him to suggest aid from Chief Barry. Alex tries to think of a way to tell them discreetly that Boston's military is already strained to the limit, and that in any case Chief Barry is now at this point hardly more than a figurehead. Alex knows that anything he writes will be reviewed by Rose's staff, so getting the right wording requires a delicate balancing act.

But no matter how beautifully he crafts his diplomacy, the outlook is bleak. Without help, Albany may slowly but surely be undermined by Zorians, on the same path to priestly domination and war mongering as Boston and Hartford. Albany may well then break the water treaty. Gloria is in an unpredictable situation.

He takes a few minutes to email her again, even though he already has once today, and even though she hardly ever answers. Leaving him to stew in worry and guilt.

"Dearest Gloria, my own. I think of you constantly and miss you. I'm counting the days until we can be together again. So many events are happening to keep us apart, but everything will be ok I promise. All my love forever, your A."

Soppy crap. He's embarrassed. But she eats this honey up, she expects it. With resentment he feels a surge of the familiar yearning—if only he could reach her, he could love her well. But he never really has, so how can he be sure? She eats at his soul.

He gets up quickly and takes a turn in his small space. There's no window, but he's glad of that. He doesn't want to watch any more hysterical parades. On his wall he has maps and charts, a poster of a mountain range with unbelievable stretches of deep green trees. As he paces, gradually his brain returns to its task.

Okay, prioritize. Although the killer heat and drought and pitiful plight of the refugees weigh heavily, the only problem that concerns him directly for the moment is Akron's pressure on Albany. Although he may not be able to do much to keep Albany from turning into another Zorian stronghold, he can try to convince the Credos there to act sensibly in response. The situation is fodder for Vinsky, who's already loudly exhorting the rebels to some barbaric confrontation, no doubt about it. Alex longs for the wisdom of Marcel and Miro, someone solid to talk to. He hopes Diamond will be willing to contemplate the moral perspective when he sees her tomorrow afternoon. Though usually harsh about caution, she's smart and might admit the complexities. If only he were still friends with Vita, now that would be the perfect solution. She would know at once what he was feeling, would find fine words for it. Her image starts to heat his body, he shakes it off like a bad dream. He has work to do.

He composes a careful reply to Albany, and then contemplates trying to contact Vinsky. The man scorns him as a wimp, but he has to at least acknowledge that Alex is still in a crucial position to help the resistance. He might listen to reason. On the other hand, Alex has to admit he can't help but sympathize with fierce reaction to the specter of extreme Zorianism controlling the whole Albany region. After all, that's where his home is now, where his wife lives, where he must live as long as he has this job. Can he reach Vinsky by radio on a safe wavelength? If he can, just what will he say? He starts to craft the right words; he'll be sympathetic, present an alternate diplomatic plan.

Alex has just glimpsed the dead end in this course of action, and slumps dispiritedly in his chair, when he senses someone in the doorway, turns around. And there she is.

"Hello, Alex," Vita says. "Am I disturbing some important ambassadorial work?"

"Not at all."

His voice sounds normal. He gets up to push a chair closer for her. She sits down, with a swing of her hips that catches his throat. She's wearing some gorgeous soft vanilla colored clothes that bare her shoulders and neck and legs above the knee. Her hair is piled high into a loose golden knot but wild wisps damp with sweat curl a circle around her face. He studies her expression to see where he stands. He tries smiling broadly, but she stays serious.

"Alex, we've only known each other a few months. In that time we've collected quite a complicated history, and some resentments." She takes a small handkerchief from her little beaded purse and dabs at her upper lip. "It's so hot today," she comments abstractedly. "Alex. I hope we can let bygones be bygones, and build a brand new relationship based on our first friendship and on our shared concerns." Suddenly she lets out a chuckle and shakes her head, shifts in the chair. "Sorry. I need to come to the point, don't I?"

Alex is so charmed he can only grin like a schoolboy. Her quick mix of solemnity and spontaneity has drawn him from the beginning.

"Go ahead and preach," he says inanely.

But she doesn't register his lame response, she's all focus. "I need your help."

"About Ellie? She's on her way to Vermont, I have that on good authority."

"No, but thanks. I was pretty sure Ellie's okay. No, I mean Lorna."

"Ah. Of course. How is she? Any news?"

"I saw her yesterday."

190

Alex is stunned for a moment by vivid memories of Vita's lovely, gazelle like daughter, her little-girl giggles, her big-girl thoughtful brown eyes. Her hair in braids one day, done up in flowers another. What she must be undergoing among the priests, what must be Vita's pain.

He leans forward. "Tell me about it."

"They...they're drugging her."

Now the handkerchief goes to her eyes. It misses one tear and Alex watches it slip down her cheek, longs to touch it, longs to be there with it.

"Take it easy. Take your time."

"No, I'm sorry, I don't want to dwell on that, I'll just get all broken up. I'd like to concentrate on what I can do about it. That's the only way I can survive this."

Alex briefly tries to imagine a scenario where they rescue Lorna, and fails.

But he agrees gently, "Thinking along those lines, you don't feel so helpless."

"I've found out some details. The novices usually are in what they call training for the first few months. So Lorna should still be in that phase, she's been there two months now. But because she was a so called renegade, they may apply different rules to her. There's no way to know. As far as I can make out, training involves a lot of praying and chanting and indoctrination. The girls are drilled in the conviction that they are the virgins of God, Zoria's saintly handmaidens, blessed with being chosen to serve the holiest purpose in creating a sacred generation fathered by priests."

"All the traditional methods used by the cult to obliterate individual identity."

Vita nods. "The method works especially well with teenagers, of course. I understand that many of them really do feel honored." A look of disgust twists her soft lips. "It's so evil."

"Well, their parents acquiesce for the most part. Most are not lucky enough to have a courageous, independent minded mother like you."

She smiles at him with her eyes. "Thanks. I needed that. Okay, so the second phase involves sexual information. Some of the girls, including Lorna, have taken a preparatory course in aspects of the first phase, but this next step is new and they have some rebellions. Quite often they have to resort to aphrodisiacs as well as tranquilizers. But they keep the sex acts ritualized, at least at first, with altars and incense and all that. Until the girls are used to it. Then, apparently, the priests are allowed to take them off one on one alone, for whatever."

Vita is not meeting his eyes at this point. He wishes she would, could see how outraged and distraught he is too. Most of this information is not new to him, but then these used to be other people's daughters. Caring about Vita and Lorna makes the whole scenario sickeningly real for him.

He mutters, "The bastards."

"Describing it out loud makes it worse. I had thought it might help. Have you got any water to spare? I hate to ask, I know your supply is rationed too."

"Oh, of course," he says, dismayed he didn't think of it earlier. He reaches for the flask on his desk. "Do you mind using my cup?"

He knows she too is remembering that their saliva has mingled more than once. She actually smiles, reaches for the cup, takes a long swallow.

"Thanks. I appreciate it."

"Vita, for you…" but he stops. This is not the time.

"So," she continues. "If the girls get pregnant they're heroines, feted and spoiled like queens. If they don't, they're turned out. Most likely handed over to the military. The whole reeking thing takes a maximum of two years. By the time they're seventeen, they either return home in triumph as mothers, or put on an army uniform."

"Percentage wise, I understand it's only about twenty percent who conceive. Infertility rates keep climbing, what with estrogen mimics accumulating. Chances are, she'll escape pregnancy at any rate."

"I'm not going to let it happen either way." Vita raises her gaze to meet his and her eyes are steel. He's taken aback. That lovely azure turned the color of lead. "It's not going to happen."

"You think I can help?"

"I'm not asking you to risk your own safety. But could you manage to get hold of a guardian's outfit for me?"

He stares at her, really worried. "You don't mean you're planning to go in there, in disguise?"

"Why not?" Her tone is sharp.

"Well, you'll get caught. You'll go to jail. Jail is not pretty."

She stares back at him. "I won't get caught. And anyway, I have to try."

"But you'll be no use to Lorna in jail."

"I'm not going to jail. What's wrong with you?"

"It's a crazy plan, Vita. You don't know these people."

"I've studied the situation very carefully. I know the schedules. I have a contact inside, sort of."

"Sort of? Who is it? All right, don't tell me. Listen to me, Vita…"

At that moment the door opens.

"Hey," says a bright-faced young man with an appreciative look at Vita, "are you too busy for a slice of news, Cohen? Or I can stop back later."

Alex returns his easy grin. "Just a bit busy. I'll come get you in a minute."

After the door closes, Alex quickly assures Vita, "He's not a blabbermouth."

"But we need to have a plausible explanation. I was thinking, if anyone asks, we can say I came to see you about an honor being presented to Drake."

"But that's not my department."

"Well then how about Joan? The woman who's been babysitting me. I could be consulting you about her husband's promotion."

"Kimball. He's the guy in Treasury who's up for promotion, right? That will have to do. But it's kind of feeble. I'm not directly involved in that either."

"No one will ask." Vita plunges forward. "Now, when you've taken the uniform, how will you get it to me? Can you come by the library? That's where I'm working now."

"Not in Services?"

"Not yet. I'm earning the privilege of returning to Services, as Drake puts it. This job is only part time, and pretty routine."

"You worked in a library before, long ago, right?"

"That was a real library—books of all kinds. This is more like an archive for the authorities. But there are some interesting old magazines. I enjoy the quiet."

"Good, sure. I can stop by. When's a good time?"

"How about Wednesday afternoon?"

"I'll be there, with or without the outfit."

"I can make one, if worse comes to worse. I can sew it, it's all loose clothing anyway."

"No, the real thing is safer. I'll try my best."

She gets up. "Thank you." He stands too, holds out his hand. She takes it in both of hers. "I knew I could count on you, Alex."

194

Only after she's gone does he realize how unlikely it is that he'll be able to get his hands on the uniform of a temple guardian. He was so warmly distracted by Vita's presence and the prospect of another rendezvous with her, that he wasn't thinking straight. He consoles himself with vowing to dissuade her from her foolhardy plan, and sets his mind to figuring out an alternative that has a chance of working.

17

On Wednesday morning Vita is racing to complete a task her boss came up with at the last minute the day before. The old man fancies himself a scholar, and spends most of his time pouring over old documents in his dusty office on the first floor, but now and then he gets a specific idea for a project.

So yesterday he started fussing at close to five o'clock. "I told you, the 2020s all have to be sorted according to theme, like political theme, don't you understand. They had political parties in those days, don't you know. We need to be able to find publications according to their themes."

His favorite research topic is Washington scandals, back when it was still the center of power.

"I'm sorry, professor, I thought you wanted them sorted by month."

"Well, of course by month you foolish girl. What am I to do with you. But also by theme."

"First thing in the morning," she promised.

"My knees are really bothering me, my dear, don't you see. I can't be expected to come up all those stairs to check on you again."

"You can count on me." Smiling her most dedicated smile.

"I know I can."

His yellow teeth shone upon her benevolently.

So now she hurries her fingers through the old paper files. The *Time* magazines from 2023 are already sorted by month. The January issue is easy, as the main story is tidal waves taking out the California coastline and maps having to be redrawn; there's no category for environment, so she decides to file it under geography. In February there were four major stories: the bird flu pandemic, cancer clusters cutting wide swaths, another outbreak of mad cow disease in New England, and the president announcing an extension of his third term. According to logic this issue should be filed under medicine, but she knows the professor, so it goes under politics. In March, the big news is the drinking water shortage; she files that under social. And so on.

The magazine ceased publication altogether in 2032. It was a bad year for disease, with regular epidemics that closed down business everywhere for weeks at a time, but also there was just not enough paper, even when made from alternatives like fast-growing bamboo. For a while they made do just with electronic media, but then they couldn't get parts for the machines and anyway fuel was too wildly expensive for anybody but the elite. By then the only news features were manufactured by some faction or other and not taken seriously by anybody.

The room is not as well air conditioned as the government offices, and Vita sits dabbing at sweat, wearing the lightest of her sleeveless blouses, her shoes slipped off. Beyond is the entrance to the stacks: one windowless room with rows of publications, documents, and books deemed acceptable. Undesirable books had never been burned or even banned; they had simply been trucked to the outskirts and left to the rigors of weather. Once a few years ago by chance she had come across a moldy mountain of them, already half turned to soil, even their spines melting, words obliterated.

The two windows near her are covered with dark shades, so the light is dim. She only has one tiny solar lamp the size of an egg. Around her the shelves packed with old files and boxes of papers loom duskily.

Once in a while Vita yields to temptation and reads parts of the articles, but the advertisements fascinate her most of all: buy this car, come to this clothing sale, send your children to this summer camp. A world she remembers her father describing, lost not only in time but in believability. In 2023 she was three years old, so her parents must have been in their thirties. That was real life for them. Gasoline powered engines, ready-made clothes for all, choices for your children. All sailing merrily along on a delusion—underneath, the sands of dissolution already shifting irrevocably.

Vita contemplates the photographs of women in a variety of dresses and pants, bathing suits and bras, putting her mother's lean face and body in them, reaching back for some sense of her. Still practicing law at that time, her mother Diane would have worn suits and sensible shoes and carried a laptop, like the poised woman in this picture, doing business equally with men. But romanced by her father, she would've worn gowns, too, and lacy underwear probably. Vita gets new insight into her mother, who to her in girlhood had always seemed just out of reach, a star in a refined realm. Diane often appeared to look at her children as if she didn't quite believe they came from her own body. And in fact Ellie and Vita were both uncompromisingly blond, the obvious offspring of their Nordic father, while Diane was brown haired and small boned, next to her stolid husband a delicate incongruity.

Diane often resented her children, her home and its duties, even her husband, Vita saw now, because she was a woman dedicated to her work. The milk of human kindness didn't flow plentifully in her veins, no, but she was tough and determined and brilliant. She knew what she wanted and she didn't have enough of it. And then in later years, before her cancer, how she suffered as women's roles slowly constricted, reverting to the prejudices and taboos that still had been lurking under the surface.

Vita is saddened for her mother musing on how differently she relates to Lorna, her mother love a well of sustenance. But for the first time she sees herself as the brave and independent daughter of that brave and independent woman. She's proud of Diane in new ways, loves her in new light.

But of course, the transcendent strength of her own motherhood is also the very source of her present agonizing anxiety. She goes over her rescue plan one more time, meticulously, down to what she'll say if accosted inside the temple grounds, and which exit she'll take with Lorna who will have changed into the uniform, pretending to be escorting Vita out. It's so simple it has to work.

When Vita hears someone coming up the stairs, she assumes it's Alex. He's very early but perhaps he was able to get away sooner. She turns to the door, already feeling his presence, the pull of him, but it's not Alex. It's Diamond.

"Hi, Vita. Surprise."

"Diamond! I'm so happy to see you!" Vita jumps up to hug her friend close, leans back to gaze at her. "You look terrific. I've missed you! I hope you could tell from what they made me say that I didn't mean a word of it."

"Of course, I knew they had you basically under house arrest, with that dreadful puppet Joan."

They pull chairs up close, knees nearly touching. Vita leans forward in eager affection, noticing with chagrin a coolness in Diamond, even something like hurt accusation in her eyes. Vita has seen her in passing several times since her return, but always in a public place where she didn't dare communicate more than a polite nod.

"I'm so sorry I've seemed to be avoiding you," Vita says. "You must know it isn't on purpose. And I never even had a chance to thank you for helping us with River Bend. It was a perfect, lovely place, I want you to know that, Diamond. We were so happy there."

"But they came after you. I was a basket case when I found out. And now poor Lorna…"

"Yes, unbearable. We went to visit her last week. Oh, Diamond, I can't tell you how awful…they've got her dressed up like some little doll…"

Diamond pats her hand, shakes her head sadly, swinging elegant ebony earrings. She's dressed for work in her usual neat elegant manner, prim understated lace at her collar.

Diamond says, "I shouldn't stay long. I just really needed to see you."

"Well, I've been a perfect Zorian wife for a good two months now. It looks like they may slack off soon. Joan is already shadowing me less. Sometime in the future I may be allowed to see you sometimes. That is, if I'm still here."

"What do you mean? Where would you go?"

Now Vita pauses. Should she trust Diamond with her plan? It seems an absurd question, considering the extent that her safety and Lorna's have been in her hands in the past. Who on earth should she trust more? Yet, she has sensed a reticence in Diamond that she doesn't recognize. Her friend's sympathy seems a bit brittle somehow, her old affectionate ribbing humor absent and in its place a stock woman to woman show of concern. She tells herself it's because of the length of time since they've been close, but she heeds her doubt. She backtracks.

"Of course, I wouldn't go anywhere without Lorna. What I meant was, as soon as they let her out, we'll leave this place together, forever."

"So it's over with Drake?"

"Well," Vita responds truthfully and thoughtfully, "I don't know. I think if he ever came to his senses and stopped being an automaton, I could love him again. But that's not likely to happen."

"Is there someone else?"

Now Vita looks at Diamond with alarm. This kind of prying is not like her, and her tone is so intense it's almost menacing.

"No," Vita replies, but she knows her eyes betray her.

Diamond leans back and lets out a deep breath. "There is."

"Well, if there was, there isn't now. So it doesn't matter."

"It matters to me." Diamond gets up quickly and steps back, folding her arms and glaring down at Vita. "He's mine."

Vita's shock turns to relief. "No, no, Diamond. Believe me, I haven't had anything to do with any man connected with you. My brief fling is married, he has a wife in Albany."

"So does mine," Diamond replies with icy irony. "My lover is married and has a wife in Albany. My lover is Alex Cohen."

Vita's heart is suffocating. "You can't be serious."

Now Diamond barks a loud tight laugh. "So, you thought you were the only one?"

The room blurs and Vita recognizes the heat of tears. Through them, she stares at Diamond, willing her barbed words away. "I don't believe it," she keeps repeating.

"Of course you do. Of course you believe it. He has a way with his hands, doesn't he? And how about that little whine he gives when you put him in your mouth? Tell me, does he tease your tits too, just to craze you?"

"Stop, stop!"

"No, you stop. You leave him alone, do you hear me? He adores his wife, he always goes back to her, but I'm his little whore and that's what I want. Get out of my way, Vita Gordon."

Vita fumbles around her desk and finds her handkerchief, blows her nose. But the tears keep coming, not with sobs, only with small despairing moans. She has never before in her life felt her heart break.

Diamond continues her barrage. "We've been fucking for over a year now, all the time whenever he's in town. He told me about you, said it meant nothing to him. He was just horny, cooped up there in that shack with you, that's what he said."

Suddenly Alex looms behind her. They had not heard him on the stairs, but he clearly has heard Diamond. He strides over to her, grabs her arm.

"Shut up!"

Diamond's scowl opens to amazement and her persona changes dramatically.

"I'm only explaining to her…let go, you're hurting me," she cries. "I'm only saying what you don't dare to say. Can't you see, I had to, Alex?" He flings her away and she rubs her arm, plaintively repeating, "Can't you see?"

"Get out of here, Alex," says Vita, leaning on her desk for support.

But in his rage he's still concentrating on Diamond. "You bitch."

"I'm only telling her the truth."

"What truth? You don't know anything about it. You can't begin to know."

Diamond staggers back. Then she pulls herself up, tosses her head, and starts to unbutton her blouse, in a mesmerizing silence. Alex and Vita watch as she exposes a transparent bra and runs her hands over her breasts. Her mouth is half open, lips quivering.

"Look, Alex. How many times have you done this to me, Alex?"

He abruptly turns away. "You're torturing everybody, Diamond."

But Diamond looks archly at Vita.

Vita says, "Get out, Alex."

Alex steps towards Vita, hands outstretched. "Don't listen to her, dearest, darling Vita. She's insane with jealousy. It's you I care about, very, very much. Oh, please."

Vita looks up at him, his contorted beloved face. Their eyes lock in pain.

Diamond says, "Choose. Choose, Alex. Right now. Do you want sex whenever you want it, what I do for you, what we do. Do you want direct access to the Credos' messengers, do you want to fulfill your destiny, help save your world? Or do you want to chase after a married woman who fucks her husband at his every whim and is a prisoner under lock and key most of the time? And doesn't know a rebel from a priest and doesn't care."

Still looking at Vita, he replies, "I can't help it. I'm sorry, I choose Vita. It's over, Diamond."

Diamond says, "You'll be back. You'll come crawling back. You know I'm the one for you. What about Gloria? What about your precious wife? Just wait til your charming guilt trip kicks in. Any minute now. You don't have a heart to give to Vita, Alex Cohen. Gloria has got it, all wrapped up."

Alex reddens, turns to her. "Leave it alone, Diamond. I'm really sorry. I know this wasn't part of our bargain. Thanks for everything. You were wonderful...to work with."

Diamond flinches at these words that are more of a dismissal than anything else he could have said. Vita has begun to realize that Diamond's passion for Alex is more than physical, and he has cut her to the quick.

"Alex, you may have chosen me," Vita intervenes, "but I do have something to say about it. And I think you'd better leave."

"No, Vita," he says. "I won't."

"Never mind," says Diamond, buttoning her blouse. "I hope you lovebirds rot in hell."

And she's gone.

Vita braces for Alex's approach, getting ready to push him away, but he doesn't move. He just stands looking at her.

He says, "I love you, Vita."

She believes him. It's in his eyes, the agonized set of his shoulders, the pleading set of his jaw, the working of his hands. It's in what he just did, renouncing and alienating Diamond for good, risking making a dangerous enemy out of her. Vita believes him because she wants to.

But she says, "I don't believe you. How could you be sleeping with her, even while you were coming on to me? How two-faced can you get!"

She's sitting on her desk, exhausted and unnerved. He drops heavily into a chair, buries his head in his hands, chokes, "I don't know. I can try to explain it, but I don't blame you for hating me."

"So explain it," she says coldly.

Without looking up, he begins mumbling randomly. "I take good care of Gloria. I'm proud of that, it's important to me. So I've never looked for someone else to love, never. I only wanted the sexual release, I need that, you know, I'm human. Gloria can't make love, poor Gloria. Diamond's an active Credo agent, having an affair with her was the perfect cover. It was even suggested to us before we thought of it ourselves. I'm not going to pretend I didn't enjoy it. But it isn't even in the same universe as making love with you. That's what shocked me so, made me cruel to you. I couldn't admit to myself that I could feel that way. You changed my life. You're a new world." He looks up at her without raising his head. "I want you more than I've ever wanted anything in my life."

She shakes her head. "How could I ever trust you?"

"Trust will come. If you could only love, me, Vita."

"What good would it do for us to love each other? The world won't let us."

Then he's beside her, touching her hair. "We'll find a way."

Her hand lifts to stroke his cheek. In slow motion he pulls her up and into his arms, into a prolonged hug that feels like a promise, so that when their lips at last meet, it's a seal.

After they've kissed for a long while, he says into her neck, "Isn't there somewhere we can go?"

She takes his hand and leads him into the next room, down the corridor of stacks to a dark corner behind. Somehow his trousers are gone and he has lifted her onto him, they collapse to the floor against the wall while she rides him, crying out. In the crest before her orgasm, in the suspended instant after the wave builds and before it breaks, for an eternal micro instant while there's a colorless void where surely everything else in the world is also frozen, a space filled with suspense between building and releasing, between rising and falling, Vita knows she's in love.

For a long time afterwards, they stay locked together, aware that when they pull apart the world will be with them again. They kiss slowly, nibbling, laughing softly.

Later, dressed and returned to the office area but still unable to let go of each other, they talk about the plan to rescue Lorna. He convinces her to wait.

"There's construction planned for the northwest wing," he tells her, "there's flood damage over there." His arms are wrapped around her, both her arms circling his neck. "It should be happening within the next three weeks, tops. That's when all the routines will be changed, regular guards displaced and temporary exits arranged, that kind of thing.

Just the sort of upheaval that favors a break. I can get you a map of the setup."

Vita is in such a state of sweet relaxation she can't feel urgent about anything. But she says, "I don't think I can wait three weeks."

"When it means the difference between success and failure, you can," he urges, pressing her closer. "Besides, you'll have time to sew the outfit. I just can't figure out a way to get one."

"After that, I'll be leaving. Lorna and I will be on the run, heading for Vermont where Ellie is. I may never see you again."

"Oh yes you will. I'm coming with you."

She stiffens, but holds him close. "You can't do that. You'll lose everything."

"You are everything."

18

His words come back to haunt Alex that night. He sits on his bed lecturing himself severely. How could he have promised Vita he would leave his wife and his job and all his commitments to follow her wherever? It makes absolutely no sense. At the same time he feels in his gut that he can't do anything else. His brain and his reason have nothing to do with it. Well, three weeks is long enough to think this through more sanely. Surely he will not always be consumed so completely by this dawn of love, feeling as if the sky has opened up and swallowed him and he's in a spiraling vortex both ecstatic and terrifying where every sensation is new, as if he shed a skin, has been raw and vibrant catapulted into a fresh world.

During the rest of this week and into the next, he seeks Vita out whenever it's feasible and sometimes when it isn't, risking gossip. Since he's no longer visiting Diamond, any observer would deduce that he's pursuing Drake Gordon's lovely wife. Nobody would blame him for his good taste, but at the same time they'd wonder that he could be so rash: Drake is becoming a powerful man. On the other hand, sexual dalliance carries far less of a stigma than any suspicion of anti-government activity, so their trysts probably serve to deflect that danger at least.

The corner behind the stacks is now made cozier by a thick blanket and some small pillows. Alex and Vita call it their bower, and they manage to spend quite a lot of time there. They make love intensely, reaching heights neither of them has yet experienced, discovering worlds. Then lying half naked and spent in the shadows they nap and talk, kiss and plan. Now Alex knows all the corners of Vita's body and just exactly where and how to make her shiver and clutch him fiercely. She has learned what drives him to distraction, makes him whimper. They laugh, too, and tease, and whisper endearments: they are lovers in love. Leaving his qualms to be dealt with later, Alex gives in to a happiness he's never known, moments of pure joy when the earth seems to sing just for him.

The following Thursday, Alex is returning to his office after visiting Vita when he notices agitated crowds in front of the street televisions. People are hurrying from all directions to join them, jostling for a view. At first he hardly registers interest, he's so wrapped up in the delicious melt of his groin on the one hand, and the punishing beat of the sun on the other. New sweat sprouts to join the dried sweat of lovemaking. He wipes at it with his handkerchief and slows to see what the fuss is about. Cameras are focusing alternately on Father Rose's angry tirade and on dead bodies, interspersed with long shots of stalwart soldiers marching.

"What's going on?" he asks the man next to him.

"Hartford's driven out our troops," is the gloomy reply. "And they're on the move, attacking just outside Providence. The tables have flipped completely."

"They're after our grain silos," says Alex.

He hurries to seek out Ladd. He finds the ambassador already huddled with Chief Barry and several advisers.

"So," Barry is saying, "what we thought was a quiescent situation, with the occupation stabilized in spite of small insurgencies, has suddenly exploded. How come nobody foresaw this possibility?" His broad honest face is distraught. "We'll be hard put to find the resources to counter it, what with all the other problems. Refugees, drought, Tallahassee flu heading this way…"

Alex slips into the chair next to Ladd with a sheepish glance. Ladd, his sparse hair awry and his long pale fingers worrying a sheaf of papers, doesn't acknowledge him: this time his two-hour lunch break has not been overlooked.

Fortunately in the same instant Father Rose makes a lordly entrance, booming, "But of course we will. Of course we'll find the resources, and we will prevail!" He doesn't sit down, but stands behind his chair at the head of the table, beefy ringed hands splayed and displayed on its ornate back. His look at Barry is withering. Barry's awed and chastened nod to Rose is pitiful to see. He concedes apologetically, "Yes, of course, Father, I was just about to say that."

Ladd notes, "We got in so easily. The bastards must've reconnoitered right away."

Barry shakes his head sadly. "We thought they were running. It looked like a rout, a bunch of chickens. They must've faked it."

"That's enough," snorts Rose. "Cut the namby pamby lamentations. Dear God, you sound like a bunch of wimpy widows. Yes, our Hartford mission has taken a serious hit. Those responsible are being punished. But we're on the offensive already. General Tate has taken over as of half an hour ago. This could work in our favor."

Alex waits with a mix of misgiving and amusement to see what possible positive spin the priest can put on this crisis.

"For one thing," Rose continues, "our new recruits can get a taste of battle. Get that baby fat out of their cheeks. Then, too, it gives us carte blanche in dealing with the Hartford citizenry. No holds barred. General Tate is pulling back all troops within enemy territory and clustering them around the water and food supplies."

"But I thought we were going to negotiate," objects Barry. "They're marching on Providence. What if they seize our cache there, grain and ammo…what if they're after the geothermal plant in Attleboro…"

Rose turns to a stout bald man in military uniform. "Explain."

The man leans forward eagerly. "Their people will be starving at home. We'll make sure they can't even get water. They won't support an aggression for long."

Just then the door opens and Drake Gordon appears, hurries directly to Father Rose, hands him a slip of paper. Alex tries to keep his eyes off Drake, the man who possesses his lover. He wills Drake's broad shoulders slumped, wills his strong hands flabby, feels a surge of jealousy close to hatred. He's shocked by his murderous passion. He's supposed to be a man of peace, a diplomat, a negotiator, he's cool headed, he doesn't lose his temper. The corroding sensation of this rage seeping from his own bones chokes his sense of self.

While Rose, still standing, reads the document, Ladd pulls his lanky shoulders out of a slump, looks around the table, takes a deep breath, and says too loudly, "The new recruits have only trained six weeks. They're raw, they're all in their teens." Everyone looks uncomfortable, stealing glances at Father Rose. But Ladd continues, "Also, starving civilians is not our usual procedure…"

"Shut up, Ladd." Rose's voice is repressed. His silken bleached robes set off the reddening of his skin to the mauve that people have learned to dread. For one moment his monumental hands clutch the chair, then release. "Ambassador Ladd, we need you in Albany. Now. Cohen too."

Alex's ears are ringing with words he hopes he's misunderstood. Leaving Vita now, at their sweetest commencement! He feels the ground falling away.

Rose motions Drake to hold his chair while he sits down, then waves him away. Drake bows and leaves, first taking a few steps backwards. Why doesn't he just go all out and kneel, Alex thinks savagely.

"Ladd and Cohen will report for briefing directly after this meeting," Rose adds without looking at them. It's as if they're already gone, their opinions no longer matter.

"And now, people, it seems a bizarre thing has happened." He irritably waves the paper Drake brought. "It's been confirmed by this report that the damn Nons have sent all their children away." He glares around thunderously contemplating each face at the table. "Can anybody explain this?"

"How could that happen?" blurts the bald military man. "We guard their exits. We know where they are at all times."

"Not any more, it appears," Rose counters with a small sneer.

"Well, we did have to pull SF away for active duty..."

"They went by boat."

"Oh well then," the officer quickly assures him, "we can catch them. Our coastal crafts are faster than anything. I doubt they have fuel. They must be under sail."

"They left yesterday."

"Oh. But still..."

After a long pause, Barry asks tentatively, "Why would we want to catch them?"

"That's what's bothering me," concurs Rose. "We don't want more mouths to feed. Also the Non offspring suffer all kinds of medical problems, especially lung conditions and malnutrition—we don't want more flack in that department. It's good riddance. But that's not the puzzle. Why would they want to get rid of their children? There's a reason. I smell conspiracy."

Alex jolts out of his gloom, realizing abruptly that Credos must be involved in this situation. Vinsky! In the past Alex has heard discussion about finding sanctuary for the children if the Nons decide on some really risky revolt. But it never went anywhere. The younger mothers, especially, argued vehemently against it. But he remembers Lema arguing in favor, pointing out that elders would go with them. He pictures her holding her small grandson, a serious sturdy child always showing off his collection of shiny pebbles. If a good safe place has been identified, it does make sense. Now he's all alarm. Vinsky's contingent must be planning drastic action. Alex absolutely must reach his contact, the one Diamond is apparently no longer facilitating, to find out what's going on and to let them know he has to leave town.

"Maybe," Barry ventures, emboldened, "they're afraid we'll steal them away."

"Please God," cries Rose, stretching his arms heavenward. "May it never come to that. If we're ever so short of births we have to start adopting the unclean!"

Shortly after five o'clock Alex enters the marketplace, aware that anyone who cares knows he rarely goes there. It's dawned on him that the Nons may have been trying to reach him and Diamond blocked the effort. Maybe she's been sitting on these plans for weeks, gloating at his oblivion. But would she do that? Would she really risk the good of the rebellion for revenge? But then, she knows how little he has come to count among the radical Credos now in charge. She has always admired Vinsky.

Alex fingers a clump of garlic cloves. He decides that blueberries will be his excuse if somebody questions him. He's always professed a passion for blueberries, that should do it. Besides, it's the fruit seller's assistant he's after. He identifies the man by his white beard and limp, though he's never actually met him. Alex studies the berries with great interest, remarks to the vendor how fresh they look, orders

214

a quart. As he hoped, this gets him invited to go behind the stall to the wagon, where the assistant is working.

A few words suffice. He asks for a new intermediary for the next time he's in Boston, pinpoints the ragman as the best contact meanwhile in an emergency. The assistant acknowledges that messages have recently been sent to Alex that he didn't get. Okay, he'll now have them directed to Albany.

Alex leaves the market with a sense of relief, and a load of blueberries.

Then he rushes to Vita's office, but she has already left for the day. So she'll sleep well tonight, not knowing the cruel news he'll break to her in the morning. He's glad to prolong her happiness, but longs too for the consolation of her tears and sympathy. He realizes he has stopped short on the street, gazing into space amid busy passersby. The sickening heat has begun to relent before sunset, so more people are venturing out. Alex hurries on, but not before he sees in the sky the exact same color of Vita's eyes, a blue so deep it spirals into night.

19

The professor is scolding Vita, but she can't concentrate on his words.

"You're not half way through those files, I expected better from you, young lady. You have too many visitors. Now listen carefully. This is Friday. I want you to promise to finish the 2040s by next Tuesday. Can you do that?"

Vita looks up at him blankly. He's leaning over her as she sits at her desk. His breath smells. His large ears have loose lobes that shake as he lectures; she locks her eyes on them to focus.

All day, since saying goodbye to Alex, she's been in a state of shocked emptiness. She'd never truly entertained the idea of their parting. Her dream that they would free Lorna and flee with her together had gone unexamined, blithely foregoing any reality check. But there he was, early this morning, bounding up the stairs to her before she'd even begun work. His kisses conveyed the alarm. She kept her mouth on his, pressing his head down to her with both hands, not wanting to hear whatever words he was about to destroy her with. By the time he spoke both were out of breath.

"I have to go to Albany. I have to go," he kept repeating as she shook her head each time.

They stumbled down the corridor of stacks to their bower, made love quickly and furiously, more as a negation than any act of tenderness. Now she sits blankly and limply, conscious only of the dampness between her legs, where the last of Alex seeps.

"I'll try," she ventures.

This must be the right thing to say, because the professor straightens and sighs, "I do count on you, Vita. You're a bright girl. I wouldn't want to see you mess up."

"Oh, I won't mess up, I promise," she says eagerly in a devoted tone.

At this the professor pats her shoulder and dodders out, makes his way slowly down the stairs.

To clear her head, Vita paces, swinging her arms, taking deep breaths. Fragments of thought float into some sort of order. The pain in her heart sharpens with increased alertness. She acknowledges it, greets it as a companion she won't soon be rid of, pushes on to the problems at hand. The professor won't tackle the stairs again today, so she can take time to recover and think, then race through the next file. Drake will be out elsewhere for dinner tonight, so she'll be able to work on the uniform when she gets home; it's almost finished.

Of course she'll go ahead with the plan to free Lorna, with or without Alex. But she'd been counting on him more than she realized, for moral support and to protect them as they made their escape. Her rosy images of the three of them dashing off into the sunset mock her now. Bitterly she cuts short her yearning, it can only weaken her. It helps to recognize that Alex did have a choice. Catastrophic as it would have been to his career, and so also to his top-level access for the Credos, he could have refused the posting to Albany, defied the world for her. And he didn't.

Just before five, Joan arrives. Of course, this would be the day she'd choose to impose herself again. She's no longer Vita's official babysitter, but her zeal rebounds periodically, probably because her husband's promotion is not quite finalized.

Joan sits waiting, like a snow blown giraffe in all her long-necked whiteness, expectantly observing Vita. She exudes a distressing mix of ownership and awe, as if witness to a prized dog's exploits. And in this situation Vita does

218

feel a little like Joan's pet—fussed over, admired, exhibited, leashed.

"You're so efficient," breathes Joan. "You learned this job really fast. The professor must be thrilled."

"Oh yes he is." Vita displays her best disciple's tone. "I'm grateful." Then she adds for good measure, knowing Joan will eat it up, "I'm so glad to be of service. You've taught me how important that is."

Joan sways from the waist with self-satisfaction, makes a smug smile. "Well, you've been a good student, Vita dear. Your rehabilitation is complete, I'm proud to say."

Vita watches her own fingers flipping through paper folders, concentrating as best she can. July, August, September, all the while Joan's sibilant voice careening around the room like a malicious sprite, stinging Vita now and then with some particularly absurd pronouncement.

When they finally head out into the airless heat, it's after 5:30. Vita persuades her companion they don't need to go to the market or stop to watch the television news, but just when they're about to turn the corner off of Main Street, they run into a security cordon. Before they can wonder why, marching bands blast from a distance and they know they're in for another parade. Joan is thrilled. Vita joins her in jumping up and down and clapping her hands, all the while seared with frustration. Every delay means less time to finish the uniform and go over her rescue plans. And mostly, she needs time to cry. She's stabbed by thoughts of where Alex would be at this instant—riding in a van looking out at passing countryside, thinking of her? Thinking of his wife? She can feel the tears building, waiting until she can allow them to engulf her.

But here she is stuck standing with Joan, wedged into the fervent crowd. The peculiar trance that parades induce, especially nowadays, has begun its sway. Blaring trumpets and drums, bright colors, a sea of flags, a sea of uniforms, the roar of the people drugged with it. First come the veterans, one-armed or one-legged and disbelieving, then come the top brass, dripping with medals, then a gaggle of top priests. All of these are riding on floats fabricated from old car shells dressed up to look like heavenly clouds, drawn by horses decorated with jingle bells and ribbons. Following them are row after row of active duty troops, marching with eyes straight forward. Many of them are so young they're baby-faced—boys and girls, not men and women. She's glad to see Garth is not among them, hopes it's because his parents have managed some sort of reprieve. Now comes a monstrous float that gags her breath: in the front, three babies held by guardians, behind them on little thrones three girls dressed in red, smiling vacantly.

"The new temple mothers!" cries Joan, alternately waving both her hands at them and hugging Vita as if Vita herself had given birth.

Father Rose claims a float all his own. He poses waving and dispensing blessings, encircled by a bower of lilies. A few moments after he passes by Vita, he throws up his hands, a riot of red blooming the back of his white cassock as he tumbles out of sight. For a few eerie moments the band continues playing, while the soldiers stagger backwards to a stop, horses rear, and the crowd's cheers fall into stunned silence. Then the music drains away in dissonance and the screaming starts.

Vita is jostled to her knees, struggles up but is swept away. Some people are trying to flee while others push forward to see what's happened. Vita, glad to be rid of Joan and hoping against hope that Rose has been killed, almost welcomes the hysterical sea buffeting her back and forth. Slowly she makes her way to the wall of a building and edges along it away from the furor. She's both acutely aware of her physical self, and removed from the chaos around her. She can feel every detail of the wall with her fingers, the grooves and bumps, her heart is banging her chest, her knee blazes from a scrape. But the scene before her isn't part of the experience. Her one idea is escape, this wall her accomplice. She watches as a man falls, picks himself up, falls again; several people run over him. He rolls out of the way, to curl beside her moaning. She finds herself wondering why his nose is bleeding if he was stomped on the back, but the answer doesn't really interest her. She finds deep satisfaction in every inch of progress she makes along the wall, caressing its surface, pressing into it as the sole tangible reality. Only when she can begin to run does she allow back the thrilling concept that Father Rose is dead.

Two hours later, Vita is more or less calmly sewing in her front room, airconditioner whining, while leftover stew waits on the table. In a few minutes she'll slice up some tomatoes and onion for a salad. September's bounty is substantially reduced this year because so many crops have died of thirst, but she and Drake are still eating well. As she rounds off the last seam, she goes over the rescue scene as if it's already happened: taking off the outfit and helping Lorna put it on, the two of them sauntering towards the exit Alex identified as the safest bet because of construction. In the dusk she and Lorna arriving at the ragman's wagon waiting behind a fountain in the lower temple gardens. While the wagon sets off at a trot they change their clothes, donning rags, thrusting the other clothes under the pile, intermittently embracing each other and crying joyfully.

Vita tries on the finished product, admiring in the bedroom mirror her bulky resemblance to the temple guardians, figure and face hidden in thick folds of blood red fabric. She looks so shudderingly real she wishes she had time to sew two of them, but she doesn't and this will have to do. She has scheduled their flight for this coming Wednesday, right after dinner when the girls are in transit from one duty to another. It's just the right time for daylight to be dimming as well. Vita wraps up the uniform tightly and replaces it in the bag, covers it with material that couldn't possibly interest Drake or even Joan, shoves it back under the bed.

Then, imagining Alex approaching Albany, she's getting ready to let the sobs come, when odd heavy thuds sound on her stairway. She stops to listen as she steps out of the bedroom. The door slams open. Drake rushes in, followed by three big SF men.

Drake grabs both her arms and shouts, "What have you done with her?"

"Who?" she says stupidly. And then crying out, "Has something happened to Lorna?"

Drake is still shaking her. "Where is she?"

"Let her talk," says one of the men, a burly wheezing fellow without eyebrows.

Drake drops her arms but doesn't step back, studies her face up close. In his eyes horror, fury, murder. "Don't lie."

But Vita is only dimly aware that these people are threatening her. She's trying not to let her knees buckle. "What's the matter? For God's sake tell me."

The man lacking eyebrows helps her to the sofa. "Tell us what happened, Mrs. Gordon. It will go better for you."

"What do you mean?"

"Where were you this afternoon? Where were you at 6:40?"

"I was at work. Then we saw the parade. Joan Kimball and I. Father Rose got shot. Then I came home."

After more interrogation, it's clear they're beginning to doubt their assumption. Drake suddenly droops from rage to grief, falls into a chair and buries his face in his hands. "We're ruined, ruined. She's gone."

222

"Gone?" Vita repeats like a tolling bell, wild hope beginning to dawn. Could this mean that Lorna has somehow got away?

No-eyebrows says, "If it's ok with you, sir, we'll check with Mrs. Kimball. That's an easy story to corroborate. But I have to admit, it looks like your wife had nothing to do with it."

Drake nods, not even bothering to stand up or try to look official. After the SF men have gone, he moans, "I'll be a laughing stock. I'll be demoted. I'll never live it down. We'll lose this apartment. How could she do this to us?"

Vita contemplates him with pity and scorn. This self-centered wreck is her stalwart husband? She gets out the wine and pours herself a hefty mug. Her heart is singing. Off and on she worries how Lorna managed it, whether she'll escape safely, how frightened she may be feeling at this instant. But Vita knows her child. Lorna will be smart and crafty, and she will soar in her freedom.

Part III

1

Wrapped in the cumbersome guardian outfit, Vita huddles in the back of the jolting van. They've passed through Boston's town center so she dares peer out the grimy window at the huts and fields, soy crops yellowed with drought, corn dried on its stalks, soil whitely parched. The crowds of slower vehicles have thinned somewhat, and the refugees and other pedestrians have moved to a side path, so the van picks up some speed.

Vita's on her way to River Bend, and the thrill of it weaves comfort through her calculations. She and Alex had planned to go there first with Lorna, on their way to Vermont to join Ellie. She's counting on Lorna going there too—where else could she go—though Noam and Clove won't have let her stay long, because the authorities will hit on that same possibility. Hopefully Lorna's already come and gone, and Vita will follow as soon as she finds out where, and makes sure she herself can't be followed. Unless Joan springs another surprise visit to her office, nobody will miss her today until Drake comes home later on tonight. Besides, what are the chances the authorities will care any more? Her value lay in Lorna and Drake. Now Lorna has disappeared and Drake is in disrepute because of it. If Drake takes it on himself to pursue her, she can handle it. She shakes off fear like an old skin.

There's a sickening smell of animal waste, the van must be fueled with it. Vita takes a drag on her canteen, glad she's not hungry. She can save the apples and cheese she brought until later. They won't reach Northampton before dusk at this rate. She doesn't know how she'll get to the farm from there, has resigned herself to finding some kind of lodging for the night. It will be great to get out of the uniform, painful in this heat, though invaluable as her ticket to both preferential treatment and anonymity. The van has some meager semblance of air conditioning that goes on and off unpredictably. Sweat coats her body. She continuously pats her wet face with a small handkerchief, envying the man next to her his hefty bandana.

On the road, three bicycles carrying a family keep pace with them for a while. A mother and young child on one, the child perched atop a bundle in the front basket; the father sitting between two bags of belongings so huge he's dwarfed; and a boy about ten pedaling behind. The boy is soaked through and looks exhausted, as if his bike might topple any minute. But the expression on his little dust coated face is fierce with focused effort and determination.

The woman looks up and meets Vita's eyes. Her expression of cold hatred is a shock. But of course, what she sees is a well-nourished temple guardian riding in an air conditioned machine, protected by power, secure in her status. While her own people toil along with nothing, and nowhere to go. These are probably not even Nons, they don't look abject enough; they're from the south and have been on the road for weeks if not months. Where could they be going? Where does their hope lie? Possibly the New Hampshire settlements or the Maine territories, or even Canada. The Canadian border is tentatively open again, now that everyone isn't trying to flee there. The recent freak snow events as far south as Atlanta, have made people realize that the earth's warming means nothing predictable except increasing extremes.

In any case, the young mother's hate shows what was behind the attempt to kill Father Rose. Too bad it didn't work. The bullet went into his shoulder and out the back. Vita has seen the television images glorifying him more than ever. He wears his arm in a sling and bares the wounds, parading them like stigmata. The assassination attempt has only meant an excuse for a crackdown. It's a good thing

228

the Nons sent their children to safety, because as they must have predicted, their pitiful shacks and vegetable gardens are being raided and hacked to pieces. Those that can have scattered to the winds, the others have been rounded up and crowded into pens. Chief Barry is pleading for their lives. Vita pities him. Boston is so far from the benign and hopeful enclave he founded twenty years ago. Like everything else, it survives now only through coercion and violence. But the Nons are doubtless too necessary as laborers for them to be eliminated.

Vita only briefly allows awareness that Lorna, like Ellie, is on the run in no better circumstances than this brave family, and possibly worse. She can't afford such dark thoughts. Instead, she closes her eyes and imagines her daughter and sister together in a vague sweet green place where nothing can hurt them. She dozes off and wakes abruptly to shouts.

"Out, out!" The van has stopped and the driver stands gesticulating at the passengers. "Get out. Fire."

Vita jumps up, clutching her carrying case close to her chest. The man beside her is already making for the door. No sign of fire, but there's a faint ashy odor in the air.

Descending into the crippling heat, Vita stumbles and is steadied by the driver, who explains reverently, "Don't worry, sacred lady, it's only wildfires west of Worcester. Burning for days now. You'll have to do a detour. We've got a wagon almost ready. Go on over into the shade there."

What he has indicated is a broad, half-dead oak with leaves shriveling brown at the edges. The benches are taken but someone obsequiously gives up their seat for her. She drinks from her canteen and tries not to faint.

When they arrive in Sturbridge, it's almost dark, though the September heat has not abated, only settled into an airless pall. This wagon goes no further, and there won't be another until morning. The passengers are being given directions to the nearest refugee camp, three miles out of town, but the driver says to Vita, "You'll find a room at the inn, sacred lady, no problem. Just this way." He escorts her down a labyrinth of streets onto the veranda of an old hotel. Shabby with creaking steps and smelling of mold, the building still somehow retains suggestion of glory days. She gives the driver a generous tip, hoping that's the appropriate thing to do.

Her room is tiny, but she has it to herself. She's grateful for the water—a small pitcher for drinking and a pail for washing—brought to her by a squat mournful woman who apologizes, "You'll have to use the outhouse. We still have the lovely old toilets, but not enough water for flushing. Not for a long while now, those were the old days. I have kids who don't even remember it." She goes away mumbling, in a sort of dazed pride that she does remember, has known a better life. Vita has brought her own little slice of soap, so she bathes quite satisfactorily, then sitting naked on the bed devours all the food she brought. Before falling asleep she lulls herself with memories of Alex, skirting the pain, gathering the pleasures like flowers. Already she hordes them, knowing they must continue to serve her for many a lonely day.

Very early in the morning, when dawn has just begun to color, Vita looks out the window to see a little vegetable garden, in the dim cooled light appearing serene and wholesome. She puts on her now dry and aired garment, finds her way down creaky broad stairs. A tall wooden fence broken in several places surrounds the garden. In one corner an old toolbox serves as a bench where she sits. Here close up she's confronted with the truth of the matter: it's been a long time since this was a blooming place. The blackberry

230

bushes are bare, green tomatoes have shrunk on the vine, and those shriveled clumps are what once promised to be lettuce. The soil at her feet is powder, and when she jabs it with her toe, it puffs up like smoke.

But she's swept into memories of Cayuga Lake, where she and her sister tended a plot much like this. In her mind's eye she sees lush vines drooping green crescents of beans, bright curling lettuce heads and darker chards, carrots and radishes with their orange and red caps pushing through, red and reddening tomatoes hanging like apples, blackberry bush heavy with fruit, strawberry patch sporting plump crimson heads. She and Ellie squat on their haunches in the rich damp earth, weeding and chattering, faces smeared with berry juice. Their father is carrying stones from a pile to fashion a low wall. He picks up rocks as if they were toys, his bare chest running with sweat. But he stops to congratulate them, admire their work. He was always doing that, cheering them on even when he himself was consumed with some other task or worry.

She must be eleven in this recollection of him, because she remembers that soon afterwards came reports of the unprecedented hurricanes and tsunamis on the eastern seaboard, when old Boston was swept by tidal waves. Her father explained that Boston was where the rebel Americans beat the British rulers. He said that it was a great city and would survive. But Vita saw the images on television—houses flooded to their roofs, cars floating, trees scattered like sticks, people with tragic faces like in the movies, and she knew in her stomach that the historic city was gone forever.

Here in this ghost garden the only things that seem to have survived are one yellowing clump of chives and some rhubarb with leaves like elephants' ears still green. Vita is hungry enough to break off a piece and chew on it, as slowly as she can to dispel the sour taste, twirling the juice on her tongue. She's fantastically grateful, as if this stringy bitter fruit has been gifted just for her sensation, just for her edge of hunger and hope and reminiscence at this moment of morning illusion. When she gets back to her room, the pitcher of water has been replenished and there's also an offering of bread with cream cheese and a few dried plums. It's a good thing I'm so sacred, she chuckles to herself, eating it all, feeling voluptuous. On her way out she gives the mournful woman a generous sum. But she chides herself. She must spend her money wisely. Besides the amount in her purse, she has sewn some into her underwear, but who knows how and when she may need it?

At the bus depot her mood turns somber. The wildfires are heading west, blocking their route to Northampton, so the wagon can't leave until the next day. Vita threads her way back towards the inn through crowds of ragged and often barefoot people, many of whom just seem to be wandering about. If they are not dazed or drooping their heads, they stare at her with either anger or pious fear, both expressions that deepen her discouragement. As long as she's wearing these clothes, she's doomed to getting help only from those that embrace the powerful she's come to condemn.

In the middle of the night Vita is wakened by a volcanic noise of running and yelling that shakes the window. When her door is smashed open, she's still in bed naked, sheet pulled to her chin. She screams but the sound is hardly audible amid all the other cries. The three masked men tell her to get dressed, and prepare to watch, but one of them shoves the other two out the door and waits, back turned.

"Please don't take me back to Boston," she begs, once wrapped in her voluminous outfit, heartened by his show of respect.

He grabs her arm, pulls her out into the hall. "We're not taking you anywhere. We just want your valuables. We don't care what you rotten Zorians do. Your days are numbered anyhow."

Vita is swept along the hallway and down the stairs with the other guests, who are in various states of undress and outrage.

"You won't get away with this," one man is shouting at his captors. He's wearing half an SF uniform, trousers with the jacket missing.

One of them cuffs him hard across the head and laughs, "Fucking priest asshole scum. We'll kill you all, just wait."

The SF officer's cheek bleeds down his white undershirt, splashing burgundy spots.

Most of the intruders are a sorry looking bunch, undernourished and unwashed, though they all sport some kind of blue band around one arm, whether ribbon or torn cloth. But some of them, clearly the leaders, are neatly dressed, their sky-blue armbands carefully cut, face masks of such a dark knitted material they could well be the folks going about their civic duties by day. The guests are herded out onto the wide hotel veranda. After they're all seated on the floor as ordered, a swashbuckling little man appears to stand before them. He's the boss and he doesn't need to say so. In spite of his runt-like shape and stumpy neck, he has an air of smug authority that silences everyone.

He looks down at his captives, his beady eyes through the mask slits a mix of scorn and satisfaction.

"Well, well," he says, "so this is the cream of the crop, the so-called elite. Pretty pitiful, I must say. Now listen, folks." When a woman starts to sob, he gives her a quick kick. His boot hits her thigh with an audible smack. "Shut up. Nobody's going to get hurt, not unless they give us any trouble. You're going to give us all your money, and anything else of value. You know what's valuable, don't make us have to tell you. Take it all out and put it on the floor in front of you. Now. And don't worry, if you left it in your room, we have it already."

In another minute the row of cowering people has little piles in front of them, and the intruders are already gathering them into sacks. Vita now notices that some are women, though well disguised in unisex clothing, hair cupped under caps. She has realized that these must be rebels, Nons and Credos, on some kind of rampage that seems extremely risky. But what have they got to lose after all? Has Ellie taken part in raids like this? Vita longs to jump up and declare her allegiance to their cause, but she fears they won't believe her, and the other guests will, so she'll lose both ways.

She just hopes they get away before some kind of armed force arrives. And they do. Suddenly they're gone, melted away. The whole operation hasn't taken more than half an hour. Slowly realizing they're free, the now impoverished guests stagger to their feet with loud rages and lamentations.

Back in her room, Vita doesn't bother to pick her mattress up off the floor, just falls onto it. Now almost all her money is gone. She hopes she can steal more rhubarb in the morning.

2

"Look, do you want to win or what?"

Vinsky's getting belligerent, has jumped to his feet, pacing around Alex's living room as if it's his own stage. Alex is seething. Vinsky has had the gall to come to his door at this late hour, close to eleven o'clock when Gloria has finally gotten to sleep. Alex was peacefully skimming over tedious minor reports, feeling pleasantly drowsy, when the perfunctory knock sounded. Before he even stepped back to let Vinsky in, he warned, "Keep your voice down. Please. My wife…" The fear of waking Gloria is making him more docile and at the same time more tense than such presumption ordinarily would. He would have preferred to say, "What the hell are you doing here?" It's risky for him to be visiting Alex so openly, even though they both have foolproof covers. Vinsky's is the model traveling salesman, which suits him perfectly.

Vinsky nodded and sat down politely but kept to the edge of the chair, powerful thighs poised. Alex is impressed as always with the strength coiled in that short round body, the ferocious focus in that meaty face.

"Cohen," he began reasonably enough, "You and I are at an impasse. That clash at the meeting today, we just can't let this go on. I thought we could talk it over."

"Well, good," Alex responded, not believing him. "Would you like something to drink? I have wine, also some very good water."

"Water, thanks."

Alex got mugs of water for them both. His mind was racing around for the best approach here. Clearly, in making this highly unusual move, Vinsky is calculating on succeeding. But why does he care that much? The meeting this afternoon ended with a majority in favor of considering Vinsky's plan.

Excitement was palpable in the musty basement room, along with, Alex has to admit, a flare of hope and confidence lately on the wane among the Credos.

He replies carefully, "Of course I want to win."

Vinsky paces, pumping his short muscled arms dramatically.

"Cohen, you just don't get it, do you? We've got as far as we can playing nice. Just look at what's happened in the last five years. Boston's gone from being a decent place to live to a fucking religious dictatorship. The Zorians are taking over Hartford and Akron too, and they're busy undermining Albany and Burlington as we speak. You know all this. You've seen it. Back when you joined the Credos in the 50s, we all thought we had plenty of time. We even thought we were making progress."

"We did make progress. We've built a strong movement …"

"Okay, okay. And our methods, sabotage, and robbery for redistribution, that kind of thing, they did work for a while. Disabled most of the oil refineries, closed the plastics and pesticide factories, got food and clothing to the needy. Our operatives within the system influenced policies enough so it seemed we were drawing out democracy a little farther. But, admit it, all that time we were fooling ourselves about the big picture. The air's a little cleaner, there's less mercury and atrazine in the water, a few kids didn't die, but so what? All that time Zoria was marching on."

Alex stands up facing him. He's much taller, and that feels good. Still, he keeps his voice low and conciliatory.

"Vinsky, you're right about a lot of things. But you've got a gloom and doom scenario. Chief Barry's a disappointment, granted, but Albany for one certainly is capable of resisting the priests—Boss Jones is tough. And the Nons have been politicized to the point where they can help themselves more. Our long term goal of taking over the media and the military is getting closer. People like Ambassador Ladd…"

"Oh please, spare me, don't start on your folk heroes again. We heard all that from you this afternoon. It's Boy Scout drivel." Vinsky walks away and back again, glares up at Alex like a pitbull facing down a St. Bernard. "Don't you understand what's happening, what's already happened? Rose's assassination was bungled, okay, but that's only the beginning. The Nons are on the march. With the Credos help, the money and valuables they're collecting are buying us guns. Why, just a few days ago we raided a hotel in Sturbridge that netted us a bundle, cash and watches, rings, gadgets, stuff like that. At this rate we won't even have to take over the military. We'll be an army."

"Now that's a Robin Hood fantasy," counters Alex. "These people have no training and many of them are half starved. You're hallucinating. You're just going to get them all killed."

"They would not, do not, agree with you."

This remark stays in the air as both men stare at each other. Alex hears the truth of it. A chill begins across his chest.

Gloria startles them both. She's standing in the doorway draped in her white nightgown, moaning. The men look at each other, Vinsky's eyes questioning, how much does this woman know, and Alex's answering, she knows nothing so be careful.

"Well," Vinsky says heartily, "this must be your charming wife. Perhaps she can help resolve our little dispute about the quality of the grapes I ordered for you."

But his acting job is lost on Gloria, who hasn't registered anything except the distress of a stranger in her home. Alex goes over to put his arm around her.

"Dearest, this is my friend Vinsky from the market company."

"Why is he here? I was asleep. Oh, Alex I'll never get to sleep again now! Make him go away."

Alex takes her shoulders and tries to turn her around with soothing words, but she wrestles away from him with a little hurt cry. Her gown falls from one shoulder and drapes almost revealing her breast. She's the picture of wounded womanhood, or no, more like a violated child.

"How can you?" she accuses.

Vinsky's plump face is the picture of amazement. Alex is torn between protective guilt, and anger at the absurdity of her behavior from the other man's point of view. As usual, guilt wins out.

"Of course, dearest. He's just leaving."

"If I could only," she says rolling her eyes in appeal, "have some of that powder, you know, the kind that puts me right to sleep. You never let me have it."

"Now, Gloria, you know that's only for special times. It's not good for you."

"This is a special time," she cries, her voice rising, "this is a very special time. It's all your fault. I was already asleep. This horrible little man came to my home, on purpose to torment me. Oh, Alex, what is he going to do? What's he going to do to me?"

She looks tragic and beautiful, a Greek heroine on the brink of disaster. Her disheveled hair cascades in velvet shadows around her white drawn face. How can he resist? Besides, he's embarrassed, has to put an end to Vinsky's witnessing this. He concurs reassuringly, and with promise of the sedative, gets her back to bed. He unlocks the cabinet where it's kept and mixes it for her. She gulps it greedily. She's got what she wants.

238

When he returns to the living room, Vinsky's sitting with an expression on his pudding face that can only be called pity. Whether it's for him or for his wife he's not sure. Probably for them both.

"Sorry," Alex says. "Where were we?"

Vinsky's tone is flat, superior. "Your faith in our movement is wishy-washy, Cohen, I can see that. Maybe you and I won't be able to see eye to eye, after all. Maybe we should just agree on that."

"You ran through all our successes yourself a minute ago."

"That's history. This is now. Now we have to get something done. No more talk."

"Talk is what I do," Alex says with more discouragement than he wants to reveal.

He's tired, he's embarrassed, he's sad. He feels as if his commitment to the Credo cause all these four years plus was nothing more than an exercise. "I'm not ready for this," he confesses, "I'm not cut out for it."

"Now we're getting somewhere," says Vinsky with surprising satisfaction. "Let's hear it, Cohen. You have to make a decision. Do you want to drop out or are you willing to go the whole nine yards? There's no more room for fence sitters."

"Now just a minute. You know very well what I've helped accomplish. That's not fair."

His complaint sits in silence. Vinsky takes a drink from his mug and looks around the room. He's palpably waiting for Alex to hear his own words. Alex does, and gets up to walk to the mantelpiece to stare at Gloria's gnomes. She makes them out of clay and paints them. There they sit in a row, somewhere around three inches high, with uniformly red hats and black shoes. Their faces look a little like Vinsky's, squashed and belligerent.

How did it come to this? He has never felt so disqualified, so diminished. A man like Vinsky making him feel inferior, when just a year ago he was at the top of his form, respected in both camps, vital to both, working with Barry and Ladd to strengthen and democratize the northeastern alliance, while backing Credo efforts to undermine the vestiges of the polluting corporate powers. Proud in the conviction he was making a difference, working for a better future. Was he deluded? Was it all for nothing?

He tries to be angry. "What do you want me to do," he says, turning on Vinsky, "blow my cover and pick up a laser gun? A lot of damn good that would do. Or do you just want me to shrivel up and disappear?"

"What we want you to do," says Vinsky calmly, "is stop objecting to our plans. Help us get on with it, instead of badmouthing our methods." He does not stand, has learned the disadvantage of that, but he pushes further to the edge of his chair, looking up at Alex with porcine eyes squinted to slits. "We still need you, Cohen, you're still a main man."

Alex hates that Vinsky has seen through to his cowering self-esteem. He hates even more that he's grateful for the compliment. As a last resort he summons up the image of Marcel and Miro, the time he met with them at River Bend, the three of them plotting in that cottage so proudly, so sure they were the vanguard of a new world. Right. Three old guys irrelevant to the brutish forces at work all around them on both sides. I'm only forty-three, he thinks, they're pushing sixty—have I been fiddling with the old guard while reality passed me by?

"Try me," he says.

"Zoria."

Alex sits down heavily. He knows what's coming. Assassinating Zoria has been on Vinsky's agenda for a long time. Now at last he's got the Credos listening.

Vinsky goes on, "Zoria's having a field day with these wildfires. The drought's bad enough—you know, God's wrath and all that. But the fires are biblical, proof that Jesus is on his way. She just had a big rally out in Akron, you know about that. Thousands of converts. This has got to stop, fast. Fortunately, the Nons are swaggering right about now. We've got money and it's to their credit, we've bought guns and they're learning to use them." His small eyes sparkle smugly. "Yes, Cohen, we are going to train the Nons. We've got one training camp set up already, we weren't sure we should tell you about that, who knows what kind of fuss you would've made. These people are eating enough for the first time in their lives. They taste freedom, they taste blood."

Alex shakes his head. "Killing. What you're talking about is a whole rampage of killing. That's what we've come to?"

"Somebody has to win," retorts Vinsky. "And it has to be us."

3

Vita struggles with the baby's diaper, which she has just cut out from the material of her guardian outfit. Other women are busy nearby fashioning shirts and shorts from the rest of it. Splashes of the red cloth run across ragged laps, slide through hardened hands, get held up against chests, ripple under needle and thread, this red the only real color among faded clothes and weathered faces. The child is not crying, only staring at her fixedly with huge wise eyes. He seems to know that now he'll be cleaner and his rash will get a rest. There's only one safety pin, so the other side has to be fastened with string. At last she succeeds, and holds him up for display. A few people return her smile.

"Here," says the baby's mother, "this is for you." She hands Vita a sleeveless smock. "It's sorta skimpy but you got to admit it'll be cooler."

Vita thanks her and puts it on, belting it with a piece of tattered rope. The garment ends above her knees, but she's grateful for anything at all. When she decided to share her cloth with the group, she hardly had hopes for even this. Actually, to be truthful, the generous act was decided for her. They simply all stared her down.

The group is gathered under a bridge by a river halfway between Sturbridge and Williamstown. It's been a terrible few days since she got back on the road. One thing after another. First, the hotel manageress had disappeared along with fresh water and food. Come to think of it, she'd been nowhere in sight during the raid: perhaps she was in cahoots? At any rate, her absence left Vita free to help herself to the rhubarb that morning, but others had beat her to it and there were only a few stalks left. A bitter breakfast.

Then, the fire had cut a swath from Worcester to Springfield where it still smoldered, so the wagon she took refused to go any further than the outskirts of a town called Ludlow. Vita probably could have persuaded the driver with ample money, but she'd already drawn from her hidden stash and had very little left. While she was sitting in a cave of shade with others waiting out the cruelest heat of the day, someone gave her half a sandwich. It was soggy and the meat was dubious, but she couldn't remember anything ever tasting that good. At about three o'clock, the group began collecting their belongings. Most of them ignored her. Finally a woman approached and bent over to touch her shoulder.

"Sacred lady, you can't stay here. You won't find another ride in this place. Come with us."

Her accent was lilting, southern, so these people must have been traveling for weeks or even months.

"Where to?"

"You'll find help in Ludlow, sure. Priests and police."

"I don't want priests and police." Vita in alarm clambered to her feet.

The woman looked at her askance and then narrowed her eyes. "You're not really a sacred lady, are you?"

"No," blurted Vita, "I'm not."

"Running away, are you?" The woman's face was calculating. "What from?" When Vita didn't answer and started away down to the road, the woman yelled out, "Hey, guess what, this here's no guardian, this here's a runaway."

The others, some dozen of them, a few with bicycles, one family with a wheelbarrow, turned to stare. Instead of greeting her, they seemed to resent that she'd been fooling them. When Vita joined them they all turned away, avoiding her just as before. She straggled along behind, frantic with thirst and immediately soaked with sweat. The bicycles moved on ahead and vanished. Yellow dust swirled with every breath of air. All around were wilted fields and trees, the lost colors of late September uniformly browned.

At dusk they began looking for a refugee camp they'd heard was nearby. But when they found it the place was not only packed full, but reeking of human waste. So they moved on, reaching the river just after dark, gathering under the bridge beside the wall of a concrete support. Vita slept fitfully in a far corner, visited periodically by rats that boldly sniffed her for signs of anything edible. Dawn revealed mountainous piles of rusted steel nearby, gruesome and ghostly in the trembling gray light. An enormous old junkyard, a graveyard for ancient automobiles, the empty windows of the orange-brown shells like a hydra of staring dead eyes. How could there ever have been so many cars?

Vita dozed again and was roused by bustle, cheery cries, a laugh or two. She was so depressed and miserable she thought everyone must have gone insane. But instead they were all busy, even the children. Men were hauling auto carcasses from the dump to fashion shelters; women surrounded two huge pots over a fire (the pots too were shaped from the old metal); from one wafted a delicious smell. Two kids appeared with a sack of shriveled potatoes, a girl was chopping leaves of some sort, an elderly man struggled towards the fire with an armful of sticks and twigs, a boy was cheerfully hammering a loaf of rock-hard bread and tossing the pieces into the cooking pot. Vita crept close.

"Can I help?" she tried.

One woman gestured to the potatoes. "Wash 'em."

One pot contained a thickening soup, the other boiling water. Vita hurried to locate a container and scooped water into it. Before scrubbing the potatoes, she took several gulps of the water. She knew that boiling it wouldn't get rid of every contaminant, but she just had to hope for the best, she was so desperately thirsty. Only after they had all feasted, did she find out that the meat in the tasty soup was rat. By then her stomach was so grateful she didn't care.

As everyone sat around eating, she told them some of her story: her daughter had escaped from the temple and she'd set out in disguise trying to find her. They listened with interest, even sympathy. Then they began to look meaningfully at her outfit.

"We need new clothes for the children," one man stated flatly.

That was how Vita found herself volunteering hers, exchanging sacred robes for skimpy refugee garb. In her small carrying case she had packed a change of underwear, a toothbrush, a light jacket, and a favorite dress of Lorna's. She couldn't have carried any larger bag without looking suspicious, but she wonders at the folly of using space to bring clothes for Lorna. The crazed state she'd been in as she fled Boston had been what propelled her to action, but at the same left little room for foresight. Later she bathes with great satisfaction in the grimy river with some of the other women. She offers to share her slice of soap, but they prefer their chunk of beeswax soap that kicks up a fragrant lather.

Apparently it has been decided to stay here for a while. No one consults her, nor does she identify any particular leader. But it seems to be the communal will. She can understand why. The old car shells make wonderful homes, the river is an endless water supply, and nearby fields, abandoned to drought, still can yield useful nourishment.

Vita is wildly anxious to get to River Bend. But it's another fifty miles or so, and she realizes that she needs the protection and resourcefulness of a group. That afternoon she's weighing her options, at an impasse, while helping wash laundry and string it up on lines to flap in the gritty breeze, when a blast of chilled air hits her back. Sunlight blanks into gray and she looks up to see a gigantic dark cloud, moving swiftly like a living thing. Her cries of alarm and warning mingle with the others, the sounds swept up and swirled in the suddenly leaping wind. Everyone runs for shelter—against the bridge wall or into the car shells. Vita finds herself huddling with a small child just inside what must have been the carriage of a truck, turned upside down. They can see out the hole of the window that the rain has already begun. Thunder blares. The clothes she'd been hanging on the line writhe in tortured twists.

Of course the rain is welcome. It's been four months since they saw any. But the ferocity of its coming keeps them all in suspense. There's no rejoicing yet, no trust in nature's purpose. Sure enough, within the next hour, as the rain pours sheets, the air turns very cold. Everyone pulls away from the openings and huddles together in the middle. Even so, rain sprays in at them. The child Vita is holding starts to cry, a little girl of about six, with tawny brown skin and lovely long lashes lacing enormous black eyes. The mother, holding the baby Vita made the diaper for, puts a blanket over them, crooning, "Violet, it's ok, honey."

"She's all right," Vita says, hugging her close, "aren't you, Violet? Don't worry now, rain helps the vegetables grow."

But she wants to cry herself when the rain turns to snow. Lightning streaks the dark air, followed by cracking thunder. Flashes of blinding lurid light, then ragged explosions. White flakes coat the shore. For a time nothing can be seen through the swirling curtain. Vita holds the trembling child, and finds courage in comforting her.

When the storm ends, as abruptly as it started, the day has dipped to evening. As the people slowly emerge, the clouds disperse into a rosy sunset. In its mocking cherry light, they discover that mudslides have swept away their pots and fireplace, all the clothes from the line, and some of the conveyances. Icy mud mountains are heaped in the river. A body from somewhere downriver floats quietly by. It's wearing a dress, a purple dress, and its splayed legs are flaunting white.

A man says, "Gather round, folks. We need to sing."

Despair lurks in every face. But they come to stand in a circle. One then two harmonicas begin a haunting sweet sound. Everyone sings, voices growing stronger. "For the beauty of the earth, for the splendor of the skies, for the love that from our birth, over and around us lies." Vita joins in as best she can, the sound of her own voice amazing her with its force.

The air warms again as twilight falls. But there will be no fire in this sodden mess. Hunger is not mentioned.

4

In Albany, some 150 miles northwest of Ludlow, the snow squall stops abruptly at eight o'clock. From the window of Ambassador Ladd's office on the fourth floor, Alex looks down on the sheen of frost coating everything, people beginning to venture out and resume going about their business, slipping on the icy street. There's not much visible damage, but that makes all the more bizarre a rust colored door blown from somewhere cracked in half and wrapped around a post. Gloria has summoned him several times by eview—her fear of thunder is terrible to witness. But this time he has not rushed home to comfort her. He's trying to convince Ladd to send him back to Boston. This is difficult for several reasons, but mostly because he's not telling the truth. He needs to go to River Bend. He's sure that Vita must be there.

Only yesterday Alex found out that Lorna has escaped from the temple. At first the authorities hesitated to publicize her flight because it reflected so badly on them. But when it became clear they wouldn't find her right away, they decided to blast it as treason to be severely punished. So Lorna's lovely face flashes across television screens, with voiceovers condemning her, offering rewards for her capture. "Wayward girl rejects Affirmation," "Heresy in the Temple," "God's wrath pursues defiant initiate," "When you see this corrupt girl, contact the SF at once, on pain of your soul." The Albany public is quite intrigued with the story, it's the scandal du jour, and many who follow the Zorian way from sheer apathy admire her courage.

At first Alex assumed Vita was behind the escape, but when it became clear she wasn't, his sense of her reaction— her relief and her loss—was a physical pain, so acutely did he want to embrace her, stroke her hair, kiss her tears. He's convinced that she'll leave Drake now, and try to follow

Lorna. It's possible Lorna will have fled to River Bend, and likely Vita will draw the same conclusion, or at least go there first for help. He wonders if she's tried to contact him. They don't have any secure way to communicate, so he hopes not. In the past she could have been seen as yearning for him as lover, but now that she's on the run he doesn't want to be suspected of helping her.

Alex feels Vita in every muscle of his body, even now as he argues with his boss.

"Look," he tries again, turning from the window. Ladd is leaning on his elbows at his desk, looking up at him tiredly. "I can do a lot of damage control being there on the spot. Meet with the Chief, sound out Rose. Okay, I know we have all the facts here, but there's a difference. It's an advantage being on the spot."

"Ordinarily I would agree with you, Cohen. You know I'm a strong advocate of face to face negotiating. But we have our orders. We're supposed to concentrate all our efforts on getting help here for the Hartford conflict. We've got that whole confab set up for tomorrow, we could finally be making progress."

"Hey." Alex tries to keep exasperation out of his voice. "You know Albany's only stalling. They're negotiating with Akron as we speak. They've shifted their loyalty already. Boss Jones has his eye on the west. He wants to make a deal with Des Moines."

"We can't let that stop us from trying!"

Alex wishes he didn't like Ladd so much. Compared to Vinsky, he's sterling, a man of peace, integrity, a straight arrow, thoughtful, and with the courage of his convictions at least as strong as Vinsky's. What a pity he's on the wrong side.

Alex looks out the window again. Rosy fading sunlight glints the already melting ice in a fairy show of pink and gold.

Passersby aren't wearing hats or coats, so it's already warm again. Rivulets along the street will be torrents soon.

When he turns back to Ladd, he's stabbed with guilt. The poor man wants to go home to his family. He has a wonderful wife, children. He should be sitting down to dinner. He doesn't deserve to be hounded like this.

"I'm sorry," Alex says. "It's time to go home."

Ladd stands up heavily, comes to stand closer to Alex. His snowy eyebrows contort in a puzzled frown. "What is it? What's wrong, Cohen?"

Alex is startled. He has forgotten that Ladd knows him as well as he knows Ladd. The bond between them has been forged through years of intensive brainstorming, mutual effort, mutual support. In fact, this man is his friend. What would happen if he told him about Vita?

He falters, "What do you mean?"

Ladd puts a hand on his shoulder, rests it there while he says, "Tell me."

Alex looks away. "It's nothing."

Ladd leans against his desk, legs extended. "Tell me. Is it your home situation?"

Alex pulls himself up, ready to defend his wife, then his shoulders slump. Of course, Ladd knows all about Gloria. "It's ok." But it's a concession more than a denial. Ladd folds his arms and waits. "Well, there is this woman."

Alex hears his voice say the words without willing to, but the shock is far less than the relief. He's never told anyone about Vita, and putting the feelings into words is like a salve. As he goes on, the room darkens around them. Ladd's face is fatherly and sympathetic in the gloom. The poetry of his confession amazes Alex. He realizes all at once that he's never really been in love before.

The carrier pigeons are singing lullabies. Their cages on the rooftop are marked with the names of cities, and one of them is Williamstown. Alex peers at the four cloud-gray birds preening within, one in particular with a lavender sheen on its breast.

"Handsome fellow, isn't he?" quips the boy who cares for them. "Name's Waldo."

Alex hesitates. He's got this far, persuading Ladd to let him go to Boston, then tracking down this semi-legal operation. He's due to leave in a week, and here's his only hope of alerting the folks at River Bend, Vita hopefully among them. Noam does have a radio, but he rarely operates it and anyway the airwaves aren't completely secure. The problem is, Alex's contact in Williamstown is an old one. He's not sure the woman is still in charge of the pigeons there, or even if she's still a Credo. He's very nervous about taking this chance. He has worded the note as obtusely as he can. "A to V via Clove," it reads, "coming through." Of course if Vita gets it she will know what it means, but there are too many ifs for comfort.

Alex leans down to address the bird. "Is Waldo ready for a trip?"

Waldo returns his stare with a bright red eye. The boy swaggers a bit and gives a conspiratorial chuckle. He knows Alex would not be here with all this money handy if something were not quite on the up and up.

"He wants to go home. He's ready all right. He's got a lady friend in Williamstown. Just like you maybe."

Alex grins. How right the boy is! "Thanks, Waldo," he coos.

"Good weather, he'll be there by sunset tomorrow."

"Done." Alex hands him the wad of money, then the tiny slip of paper, watching as the message is wrapped and tied to

252

the bird's leg. Waldo flaps his shimmering wings and speaks mysteries in his soft gurgle.

5

Vita takes an apple slice from a small bowl on her lap and chews it carefully. It's the first solid food besides crackers that she's tried for two days.

Clove knitting in a rocking chair watches her, cocks her head. "Okay?"

"Delicious."

"I think you're fine now. You haven't thrown up for six hours at least."

"And I'm famished. That's a good sign."

"At first we were so afraid you had that Tallahassee flu that's rampaging up from the south. They say it starts with the same turning your insides out. But thank God, you just probably drank some bad water. So. We'll do vegetable broth next, and by tonight I bet you can join us for supper."

"What are we having?" asks Vita with such relish they both laugh.

"How does roasted eggplant sound?"

"Oh, Clove, what would I do without you?"

"Stop it."

Vita chews more apple, gazing out the window. The sun flashes back and forth from behind small white clouds scudding in a steady wind. The window is wide open, flowered curtains tossing. The air smells familiar, sweet. She can glimpse the cottage where she and Lorna stayed, now occupied by a family of four and only one goat, Daisy. All the others have been sold or eaten. It's been a bitter six months for the farm since Vita left. Even before the drought took hold, Noam started showing the symptoms of Parkinson's disease, from the pesticides he worked with as a young farmer in the 20s.

"He thinks it's the end of the world," Clove exclaimed when first telling Vita. "This sickness setting in, then the corn drying up, his heart is broken. He sits in a corner all day in a permanent funk. Every time his hand shakes he curses. He won't try to do anything."

Vita arrived at River Bend one evening on a makeshift stretcher, retching continuously. The men who brought her were surly about going out of their way until Clove served them hard cider and freshly baked bread. Then they swaggered over their good deed and went away happy.

Whether it was the river water or some suspicious meat she ate a few days after the freak snowstorm, Vita's stomach rebelled so violently her companions were afraid they'd have to leave her behind when they decided to move on. But Violet's mother refused to abandon her, so she was carted along, extra baggage the group could ill afford to burden themselves with. At least they didn't have to feed her.

"I can't wait til I start being of use around here," says Vita, regretfully licking the last taste of apple from her fingers. "When can you put me to work? I guess you don't need a goat person any more. How about the chickens?"

"We've got about half of them still. We were able to keep the layers. You can feed them, freshen the hay, collect eggs."

"Good. What else?"

"Just kitchen work like you did before. Is that ok?"

"Anything!"

"You have to realize, Vita, things are not the way they used to be. We're in a bad way here."

"I know you've had to cut back on everything, but you're safe and cozy still, aren't you?"

"Not exactly. Our fresh water supply used to be adequate, with our enormous tank and all. But people knew about it and were jealous, and now, at the same time there's so much less, we have to share it. If we hadn't agreed, it would've been vigilantes in the night for sure. That's hard on us and on the animals too of course. The horses especially are always thirsty, poor guys. The river the farm is named after—you remember the stream by your old cottage—it's dried up. It's only an empty trench now."

"I don't suppose the snow storm helped?"

"Oh, for a few hours it ran with a furious little gush, but that was gone the next day." Clove continues knitting as she talks, her puffy red hands nimble, not missing a beat even when she raises her eyes to Vita's for emphasis. Now she smiles. "The water tank filled petty well, though. We were happy about that."

"How about the crops? It's October, harvest time."

"Water. You forget we've had no water to grow food. The root vegetables are ok, but everything else is mostly gone."

Vita huddles down into the covers. She does not want to imagine River Bend as anything but bravely thriving.

"What we're doing now," continues Clove reassuringly, "is setting up a greenhouse. It's been hard to get the glass, but as soon as it's done we can grow stuff during the winter. Not much, but enough for us."

"Meaning, you and Noam, Beasley and Sienna?"

"And you, of course. And visitors now and then. Though we may have to dismantle one of the cottages for fuel. We'll be ok."

"You'll be ok, River Bend will always be ok. But I can't stay here."

Out the window Vita watches Daisy trot from under the cottage into the yard and start chomping on stubble. She flashes a bright memory of living there with Lorna, that short fairy tale peaceful time. Clove has already told her that Lorna didn't come here after all when she escaped. Vita embraces an image she has lovingly formed of Lorna, dressed for the road, brave and free, that insulting temple outfit tossed away in contempt.

"You'll stay here til you're well," Clove states firmly.

Sienna comes bustling into the room, apron wound about her, gushing, "You ate it all up! Want more?"

Little Sienna is announcing her teens with breasts and hips that seem to have been slapped onto her beanpole form by some manic sculptor. But she still acts like the child she is.

Vita and Clove both laugh fondly. Vita says, "I'm still hungry, that's for sure."

"Sienna honey, can you fetch some broth?"

"Sure, Mom."

But the girl hovers, blurting, "Have you heard anything about Lorna?"

Vita shakes her head sadly. "Nothing. I have no idea where she is."

"But," Clove insists, "that only means they haven't caught her. Granddad just checked the radio, and there's no news. Except for war and famine, of course," she adds wryly.

6

The day Alex arrives at River Bend is freshly brisk, with a sky so dazzling blue it rivals the sun. The wagon lets him off at the brow of the hill and he stands for a moment looking down. Here he finally is, and he's unsteady with the weight of it.

It's been a hectic couple of weeks since he persuaded Ladd to let him come. Just as he'd been about to leave, Gloria had a bout of hysteria that sent him reeling with worry and guilt, meaning many long hours of tending her, lengthy protestations of devotion. Then orders came from Boston (meaning Father Rose) that Boss Jones was to be presented with an ultimatum demanding that he join an alliance against Hartford. Alex and the ambassador had a hard time mitigating this aggressive stance, arguing successfully that Boss Jones has his own priests to protect him. In fact, this crisis fortuitously provided the best available excuse for Alex to pass through River Bend: he's scheduled to meet with Chief Barry and Father Rose in a few days, to explain the situation in detail.

After they received the message duly delivered by the carrier pigeon, Clove and Vita got word to Alex that she was definitely here, and would wait for him. So his eyes caressing the valley below, the house and cottages, bulk of barn, even the too yellow fields, are full of Vita's form, full of the very idea of Vita, her spirit as much as every nook and cranny of her. These few days that he has fought to steal with her rise like a heaven, as if there were no other life to live. All the while he tells himself he's compromising nothing by taking this brief gift, he knows he could be heading for something he may not be able to control. Possibly he already is out of control.

Along the road behind him the sounds of shuffling feet, horse hooves, creaking wheels, clank and rancid odor of makeshift fuels. The latest outrage by authorities in numerous enclaves involves requisitioning soybeans to manufacture ethanol for military vehicles. This has become one of Father Rose's favorite new projects. Precious soy, the hardy nutritious crop that has meant a mainstay of survival for so many. If the Boston Nons had not already risen up, that would have done it. But Alex doesn't turn around. He's already forgotten the miserable sights he saw on his way here. He takes a step forward. Slowly at first, then almost running, he follows the path down.

In the barnyard Vita pumps just enough water into a pail to wash her face and hands. She doesn't use soap so she can then give the same water to the big old hound Pix, who avidly gulps it up. Then he settles back on his haunches rewarding her with worshipful brown eyes, a smile on his wet black lips. They've finished their afternoon rounds at the hen house and a basket with warm fresh eggs sits nearby. It's almost time to get to the kitchen to start preparing the evening meal.

The autumn sunlight aslant has lost its cruel summer edge, and a capering breeze dances the dust. Vita turns, pushing hair back from her damp face.

Alex is there.

In one wild breath she opens her arms. His mouth is on hers for a long time. They don't try for words. Their sounds are acute with longing. His feel and smell intoxicating, his lips a lifeline. Her hands over and over make sure he's really here, press him, clutch him to her. He buries her into him, murmuring, whimpering. She staggers, he has to hold her up. There's no strength in her legs except to fold with his. She feels his tears.

In her next conscious moment, they're sitting on a wooden bench under the willow tree, still embracing. They have been saying things like I love you, you look so beautiful, I missed you so much, I can't believe you're here, I love you. After another small while, he says, "Where are you staying?"

"Upstairs in the main house, one of those little rooms under the roof."

"Do you suppose we could go there now?"

She laughs at his suggestive grin, kisses it. "Yes. Let's go there now."

Sienna is sweeping the porch and Vita calls in passing, "Please tell your mom I might be late, Alex is here."

On the second flight of stairs, Alex's hands are already pulling off her shorts. They fall onto her bed still half dressed. This coupling is fast and ferocious, like starving, like desperate feasting. She bucks at him in violent insistence, not letting him go even long enough to take off his shirt. She waits only to feed him her breasts, then must consummate, must have him, must pull him in, must own him, must drown.

Afterwards, she's a little dismayed at the intensity and bestiality of it. It was so hungry and mindless you couldn't really call it making love.

Getting naked, they curl together, and finally talk a little. Then Alex naps while Vita gazes at him, and beyond him at the sun's last shards in the paling sky. She already wants him again, and when he wakes their kisses this time are deep and leisurely, their caresses thorough, their moans complete.

In colorless morning light Alex is wakened by the forgotten sound of the cock crowing. For a second his sleep fuzzed brain wonders at the woman half beneath him. He has not slept side by side with anyone except Diamond for years. Then he sees and registers Vita, feasts his eyes, closes them to better sense every inch of her pressed against him. He knows a happiness in these moments that has no taint of regret or fear. The kind of full fit into the world he vaguely recalls from childhood, when the world was only his mother and his mother was unquestioningly safe and forever.

Nude with covers cast aside, air breathing through the half open window the same temperature as their bodies. Her lovely hair, the color of honey or perhaps champagne, is wreathed over his arm, her face slightly flushed. She's woven in with him, her gold tanned limbs, one leg over one of his, her hand near his groin open. Very gently so as not to wake her he puts his palm on hers.

Why shouldn't he keep this? This is so clearly the woman meant for him, the one he has always wanted without knowing it. Can he really leave her again, follow all his responsibilities to Boston and back to Albany? It chills his blood to think of it. But how can he not? Everything he stands for, his own opinion of himself, what he sees when he looks in the mirror, are at stake.

At lunchtime Alex and Vita take sandwiches to the bench under the willow tree.

She says, "How was your morning?"

She's wearing a sleeveless light green top that pulls at her breasts and bares part of her waist above the shorts. Her hair is tucked loosely up from her neck, curls of it escaping.

"I brought my little laptop along and Noam is in heaven. He hasn't had a computer for years but he's remembering all the moves. Too bad fuel is so scarce we can only run it an hour or two a day."

"But that's great. What fun for Noam. Any important news getting broadcast?"

"No. Same old same old."

"Don't tell me. I know. All bad."

"All bad."

He reaches up to brush a crumb from the corner of her mouth. She puts her tongue out to the spot, and he has to kiss it.

She says, "You're really here."

"It's all a dream." But his face is serious.

"Can't you stay?"

He sees in her face the pride this question is costing her. He knows she expects his no. He puts down his sandwich and takes hers away too, holds both her hands.

"What would happen if I stay?"

"What do you mean? You know. You'd have to give up everything."

"Not everything. I'd have you!"

"But your job, your wife. Your work for the Credos."

"I could still help the Credos. I just wouldn't be in a position to convey government information. But they need that less now, they're on a different tack. A violent, chaotic tack I'm afraid. I could join them, just the rank and file, try to influence them that way."

He hears his conversational voice, as if he's making sense.

"Alex, what about Gloria? You can't abandon your wife."

He looks out over the barnyard to the hillside, her words stabbing. Why should it be any better to abandon you, he wants to reply. But he says instead, crisply, "I see your point. It would be a terrible thing to do."

There's a long silence. Vita bites at her sandwich again, wipes sweat from her forehead. It's getting very hot even here in the shade.

"That's that then," she says, dusting off her fingers in apparent nonchalance. "So, I guess we're in for another heat wave. What do you think?"

"I think you're cruel, Vita. Don't you see the gut wrenching dilemma I'm in?"

"Oh, my dearest dear, oh I'm so sorry." She puts her hand contritely to his cheek, strokes it, strokes his hair. "I wouldn't hurt you for the world. Let's talk about it seriously, then, if that's what you want to do."

He kisses her wrist, twines his fingers with hers. "Please yes, let's just try words on it, talk it out. See where we end up."

She nods, affectionate and doubtful.

"Here's one way of looking at it. One way, that's all." He starts out hesitant, then eagerness takes over. "Let's say I contact Ladd first, tell him I can't continue on to meet with Rose. And I'm quitting my post, won't be coming back to Albany. I don't need to tell him why, he'll know. I think he'll be willing to arrange for Gloria to keep her benefits, medical, the apartment, all that. Yes, that will work. Then, I get in touch with Gloria's favorite health aide, a very nice woman, and get her to break the news. There will be a horrible scene, of course." He stops, to control his voice. "Gloria will think the world has ended. But, I think, I think she'll get over it."

"Would you need to tell her about me? Couldn't you just say you need to get away or something?"

"Something, yes. I won't tell her about us. It would only craze her more."

"Oh Alex, then you can come with me to visit Ellie in Vermont. I found out she's settled on an island in a lake. Lake Willoughby, the same one where Marcel lives. After that you can come with me when I find out where Lorna is. We'll go to her together."

"Marcel, great. I'm anxious to talk to Marcel. I could get in with the Credos at that juncture, perfect. You and me on an island. I love it."

"You don't look that happy about it," she says slowly. "You should see your face."

"It's hard to believe I can have what I really want." He looks out at the yard, chickens bustling and pecking, Pix stretched in the shade opening one eye from time to time, over on the house porch Sienna shaking out rugs. "I can't get used to the idea."

"I'm not asking you to do it, Alex. Think about what it means."

"I know. Truthfully, I am worried. About Gloria. I'm not sure she'll be able to keep the apartment. I'll need to negotiate that very carefully."

"Your whole life turned upside down. Is love worth it?"

"Is love worth it? You tell me."

"You've got two more days here. Let's leave it for now. Let it slide, see how you feel tomorrow."

"Come here. Ah, you taste like mustard…"

A frantic cry from Sienna, who's racing across from the house.

"Vita, Vita!"

She stands panting in front of them. "Lorna! There's a message from Lorna!"

"Where?" screams Vita.

Sienna is writhing in a puppy dance of excitement and impatience. "Computer. On the computer!"

Vita is already gone, rocketing towards the house like a bullet, Sienna following. By the time Alex gets there, everybody is knotted around Noam at the laptop.

"I had it just a minute ago," he's saying in his slow croaky voice. "I've lost it."

Faces turn to Alex, they move aside so he can lean over Noam.

"Good work," Alex tells him.

"But I've lost it!"

Noam's hands on the keys are trembling more than usual, like feathers fighting a breeze.

"It's on a memory disk," Clove is explaining, holding Vita steady. "We got it weeks ago. We didn't think anything of it, such a tiny little thing smaller than my thumb, and the package all battered. But it was from Lorna. Wait til you see!"

"Try that minus button again," Alex is instructing, "that one up there."

"But that's just the one…"

And there it is, a full-screen image of Lorna—and Garth. Lorna is dressed like a boy, wearing a jacket too big for her, her hair chopped off. They look very young and very tired.

"Can you activate it?" urges Alex. "Click on play."

A chair has been brought for Vita. She's so pale he's afraid she's going to topple over. As Alex coaches, Noam is able to play the disk from the beginning. It's simple and short.

Lorna says, "Hi, Sienna and everybody. Please get this message to my parents. Tell them we're safe. Tell them please not to try and find us. If you see this, Mom, believe me, it's important to leave us alone. It's safer that way. Don't worry, I'm fine. Dad, sorry for any problems. I just had to do this. I love you both. I'll be in touch if I can."

Garth's arm is around her as she talks. He looks concerned and protective. In the background are rusted metal cases, serpentine disconnected cords, a pile of ancient electrical equipment, lamps, toasters. It could be someone's basement, it could be anywhere. The message is dated October 10th, three weeks ago.

At Vita's insistence, they play it over and over again. Finally Vita's silent tears turn to howls, and Clove pulls her away, takes her to another room.

"Better turn it off," says Alex.

Noam is reluctant. He's high with his newfound empowerment. "We could check the news again," he says hopefully.

But Beaseley remarks, "We need that fuel for cooking."

After the screen has gone dark, they stare at it stupidly for a few seconds.

"Good news," croaks Noam. "She's okay."

"But it's hard for Vita," says Alex. "It's a kind of goodbye."

A few hours later Vita and Alex are walking slowly along the dry stream bed. On the way they stopped to visit Daisy, and now Vita smiling puts her face to her arm to breathe the goat smell again.

"Daisy remembered me."

"She did. She nudged you most affectionately."

They've been holding hands but now Vita lets go and clambers up a small hill where the orchard begins. The apple trees are stripped of fruit, leaves tinged with yellow. There's a cidery odor to the air, sweetening the smells of dried grass and dust. Late afternoon has brought a quick breeze that freshens through the heat.

"Clove says the apple harvest was almost normal," reports Vita, "because the drought started after they'd developed. But these trees look a bit forlorn."

She caresses the bark with her fingers, puts her arms around the trunk.

"You're going to miss her," Alex says.

"I can't stand it," she concedes, her cheek against the bark. "My child. My heart is dying."

Alex embraces her embracing the tree, splays his body over hers. "That can't happen, remember I need your heart," he says into her hair. "Listen. She's fine, she's with Garth, he's a rock that kid, he's probably the one who got her out. And you will see her again, we just don't know when."

She tells him she loves him, and he remembers this always, the press of her softness all along the length of him, his hands covering her hands on the rough warm bark of the scented tree.

7

The November heat wave begins its third day. It had been too hot the night before, so with earliest light Vita and Alex make love in a fresh breeze from the window. When she wakes from her after-doze, sky going rose and the slip of sun above the trees still benign—small and one-dimensional like a paper wafer—Vita feels sated, full, at one with her soul and the universe. Sound asleep, Alex has rolled over on his back, one arm crooked above his head, the other arm still under her. She swims her eyes over his form, the shadows and hollows, the tan line on his arm between brown and pale, the muscles of his neck, the hairs on his legs, the nest of underarm hair silky, the blank white of his belly just traced with a furry line, belly button to groin. His penis flops resting, its raging purpose temporarily stilled. She moves to place her thigh over it, its soft yield, just another little piece of flesh. Tentatively she slowly circles her leg until she feels it stir, tenderly lets it be. These joys are no longer stolen, these joys are hers now and into a future.

Because finally, it's been decided. She and Alex will be leaving in a few days for Vermont. He just has to send those two fateful messages. He's going to do it today, he's only waiting because he wants to make sure they're private and don't get seen by other people first.

Vita is impatient to find Ellie, besides harboring a wild dim hope that Lorna has gone to the same place. She also vaguely admits to herself that getting on the road with Alex will have the finality of commitment from him, will seal their bond. In all this her happiness has an edge to it, a tense and irritating pulse. She can't open to it fully, doesn't quite trust it, there's too much darkness still in range.

She has honed an image of Lorna that she constantly nourishes just behind her eyes. In this picture her daughter is not wearing that mockery of a child's outfit from the temple, nor the bulky shabby gear of the eview. No, she's in the dress Vita bought for her in Williamstown, the one she loved and wore here for Garth. Vita recalls with bitter amusement how nervous she was then about Lorna's developing womanhood. How ironic.

Vita needs action now, and her heart is pulling towards Ellie. Their last encounter was so rushed, and tense with risk. And before that, Vita has to descend into many years of memory to find the last time they were together. Digging in the garden, cooking, reading, swimming, confiding, giggling, their parents still a dependable presence. Ellie now a ghost of that pretty little sister. How wonderful it will be to see her free and getting healthy, and to share her with Alex. They'll grow very fond of each other, Vita is sure, because she loves them both so much.

She lifts on her elbow to study his face. His nose, chin, beard, the seashell of his ear, his mouth slightly open, his lips. Is that a bruise? Did she kiss him too hard? Probably. He opens his ocean green eyes, in them complete peace, smiles. She pokes her tongue into his ear, feels him grow beneath her thigh.

Good morning, they both say. This is the first day of the rest of our lives.

They wash each other at the basin, laughing, kissing, nibbling, running wet around the room like kids.

Pulling on her shirt, she asks, "So is Beaseley ok with driving us to Williamstown?"

"Noam wants to do it. He insists he can still drive a wagon."

"Sure he can. He can do lots of things. Parkinson's doesn't have to be incapacitating. I think he's coming to terms with it, thanks to you. He's really perked up since you got him hooked on the computer, and offered to leave

it here. Clove is so grateful. You're everybody's hero."
He roars a laugh and squeezes her waist with both hands.
"I wish."

His thumbs caress her belly and she catches her breath.

"You're mine," she says, opening her mouth to his.

Pix the hound dog is waiting for Vita by the hen house,
a little impatiently, though still reverently of course.

"Forgive me, Pix, I had to feel up my lover. A good reason
for being late, don't you think?"

Pix wags his outsized tail. When the door is opened the
birds rush out, fluffing their feathers like ladies puffing up
their hair. Their voices are a throaty caw of demand and
energetic proclamation. It's morning, they've done their egg
jobs, now it's time for food, fresh air, and intimidating each
other. The cock, a gorgeous red-brown luminous beacon
among them, struts with all the pompous arrogance expected
of him.

Vita tosses them their dried corn, freshens their water,
and searches in the dim light for eggs. The straw is still warm
where they've slept. She finds five, then six. Omelets! And
there are mushrooms from yesterday. With onions, she can
hustle up a special treat for breakfast.

In the kitchen there's a delicious chicory coffee smell.
Clove is slicing bread, Sienna gathering plates. But when
they see her, they stop, Clove knife in air, Sienna with a
plate half way out of the cabinet. Something is wrong. Vita
stands there, wide eyes asking them. Clove puts down the
knife and comes to put an arm around her.

"Vita, Alex just got a message."

Clove turns her like a child and leads her into the living
room. Noam is at the computer. Alex is not there.

"I don't understand," Vita says weakly. "What's
happened?"

Noam moves aside so she can see the screen. It's a message from Ambassador Ladd. No picture, just the numbing words. "To Alex Cohen Re urgent: Serious bad news about your wife Gloria. She has tried to take her life. Sleeping powder. Stable for now. Forget Boston mission. Best you come home at once."

Vita climbs the stairs like a zombie. Alex is frantically stuffing his backpack. She stays in the doorway watching. He sees her but he looks away.

"I have to go," he mumbles.

Vita sees the rumpled bed, the patches of water still lingering on the floor, the cutting shards of her dream. She's bleeding as surely as if her flesh has been pierced.

He's in such a hurry that the pack bulges out, he hasn't even bothered to fold anything. His face is pale and set, and when he turns to her his eyes are agonized.

"She tried to kill herself," he says, repeats it, mostly to himself. "She wants to die. It's all my fault. What have I done!"

Vita has no words, she stretches out her hands, a plea. He stops for a moment, looking at her.

He says, "I love you, Vita. I will always love you."

But his voice is strained, automatic, as if his brain has left it behind.

She drops her hands. "Will you come back?"

"Come back? How can I? She will take her own life, her poor life. How can you ask that of me, Vita?" He shoulders his pack. "I've got to go."

She moves aside as he goes out, not looking at her, thunders down the stairs.

She thinks she hears him say he's sorry, but she's not sure.

8

Lake Willoughby looks leaden on this dawning June morning. The water and sky are the same even shade of clammy gray. Fog dulls the outline of the steep crags on both sides, so even the air is gray. No waves, no clouds, no wind. The brooding day is already sultry even at its birth.

Vita is sitting in front of Tati's cottage with a mug of mint tea, listening for the sounds of her waking. She's been living here with the old woman ever since arriving at Tully Island almost five months ago. Though she has settled into a routine peaceful life, sadness sits like a stone on her heart. It turns out that Ellie, Lorna, and Garth had in fact all come to Tully briefly, but left long before she arrived, heading for the Green Mountains rebel camp.

Of course, it's a consolation that everyone here has met them and tolerates her questions and reminiscences, but to have missed her family when she came so far with such hopes of shining reunion is a bitter barb. The prospect of finding them sustained her through so many arduous days, she came to believe in it as certainly as faith. The repertoire of delicious images she fabricated—varied poses of the same ecstatic moments—Lorna and her Aunt Ellie, Vita and Lorna, Ellie and Vita—were desperate, she now notes with sour irony, created all the more frantically to ward off her suffering over Alex. His abrupt departure from River Bend still cuts, won't heal, no matter how much she lectures herself. She's been through every phase, from anger to numbness, and now she tries not to think of him at all. But he still catches up with her in dreams.

Before she sees it, she hears the bird singing, a clear fluting series of notes, a sound so sharp and exact it rivals the air. Then she spots it as it alights on a branch, contemplating her. A chickadee, she thinks, pleased to remember. Yes, the black cap and short beak, stout white and gray body that her father pointed out. He knew all the birds' names, and there were so many back then. The creature hops about, eyeing something over her shoulder. She carefully turns her head to see a shallow bowl of water, over next to Tati's brave clump of white daisies. That's what he wants, but he doesn't trust her or isn't desperate enough. She stays very still. Soon others join him in a stuttering array along the branch, singing earnestly as if to embolden each other, or perhaps they're discussing the pros and cons of the desired action. At any rate, in another moment the leader has flashed past her and is sipping from the bowl, then jumping in, splashing his wings, wiggling and dipping. It's too much for the rest of them, they swoop down as one and take turns sipping and splashing and dancing. Their little bodies are puffed with damp. They're having a glorious time.

Edging the lake a yellowish green band of algae sits immobile. The water has receded so that between the normal shore of sand and rocks, and the algae, there's a swath of dried mud sprouting haphazard land plants. But Lake Willoughby is extremely deep; no one imagines that it will ever stop providing its bounty. And the calm wise dark cliffs loom on either side as far as you can see, reassuringly eternal, emerging from the fog of dawn like the creation.

Tati is stirring. Vita waits too long, hears a thump. The old woman has fallen again. She's supposed to call Vita to help her out of bed, but she almost never does.

"Are you ok?" Vita squats beside her. "You didn't bang your shoulder again I hope?"

Tati looks up ruefully, in a heap there on the floor in her nightgown, knobby purple-veined legs splayed. The flesh under her arms hangs like rumpled cloth. She works a small smile.

"No harm done. Sorry."

"Let's get you up. Slowly, now."

Vita settles her on the edge of the bed with the clothes she'll need, and leaves her to dress herself. It will take her twenty minutes, but she's insulted if anyone offers to help.

In the kitchen Vita brews Tati's tea and spreads slices of bread with honey. She's become fond of the feisty old woman, admires her spirit and her still very keen mind. Above all, she loves to listen to the tales of life early in the century when Tati was young and the earth still in balance. Tati puts on a whispery fairy tale voice and Vita can picture her as she was then, fresh glowing skin and athletic slimness, striding with her friends or lovers, laughing, struggling, dreaming; and she can picture the amazing places she describes, long since gone, Cape Cod, old Boston, New York City.

When Vita first arrived, in driving sleet, she was cold, weak, and disoriented. Tati took her in, tended her with motherly care, even though her eyesight is going and she moves with little shuffles of her feet. The journey from River Bend had been exhausting, what with scarce food, robbers on the road, refugee hoards at every resting place, and most depressing of all, clutches of bloody retreating rebels after the battle at Worcester. Nobody had actually believed that the Credos and Nons, numerous though they were, could ever vanquish the well-armed Zorians. But there had been flares of hope.

Now the rebels have retreated to the mountains, and things are worse than ever. Zorians have a stranglehold on every major center in the northeast, and no longer bother with long declarations about sacred duties before they jail subversion suspects or grab virgins for rites, raid soy plots for fuel or fence off water sources. Vita hates to think of the hardships her sister and daughter face in those mountains. She can only fiercely cling to her image of Lorna safe—surely

Ellie will make sure she's safe—and her conviction they both will return to her soon. But she's beginning to think she's waited as long as she can. Next month she'll travel to join them in the rebel camp if she doesn't hear more promising news. Meanwhile, she tries to picture them in a cozy little tent amid wildflowers.

Tati and Vita munch their bread sitting in front of the house, watching sunlight struggle through foggy sky to glint fiercely off the water. Another scorching day. Vita already feels sweat prickling her forehead. Tati is quiet and Vita studies her profile. Eighty-five years are etched there, a web of spidery lines that pucker around her small mouth. She wears her thinning long gray hair in an S shaped bun.

At last Tati says musingly, "You're good to me, Vita Gordon." She turns her face with a brilliant smile. One of her bottom teeth is missing, but it has a mischievous, rakish effect. "And you're good for me. Not since my man Dom died, not since then have I had such a friend. We can talk, you and me."

With Tati, it's not necessary to respond right away, and Vita doesn't, instead thinking over the words. Tati has that influence, staunching automatic chat, making and encouraging statements that startle. Vita has found it easy to confide in her.

"Thanks, yes we can. Especially about our daughters. That's been so helpful."

"My poor darling Crea has come alive again thanks to you. And I'm so happy to learn more about Lorna. What a girl I thought to myself even when I first met her, so pretty in her thoughtful way, and sharp, and kind. You're right to be so proud. Don't worry, you'll see her again soon. Too bad she and her young man left before you got here. But they just would keep going, such stubborn kids, so full of idealism and energy. Fighting the Zorians was all they could talk about,

276

especially after the Worcester bloodbath. And your sister, too, a firebrand, can't stay put for long."

"I thought they'd all be here."

"Tough for you. I could see what a shock right away. But they'll be back. They really liked it here, I know."

"She's just a child, Tati."

"Hey no, don't think of it that way. Remember I told you what my granddaughter Fair went through? Abducted at fifteen, same age. She never got over it. But it made her stronger, oh, it made her strong! Fair is molten steel."

"Fair is a healer, too. She's gentle and caring."

"She's the only doctor we've got now. My Dom was a real medical doctor, she apprenticed with him. And she uses a lot of herbal remedies, too. She learned those from a book her husband had from his mother."

"Lorna's so beautiful and so intelligent. Well, you could see that of course. She did very well in school. You should have seen her reciting poetry, she's a wonderful performer. No, no, I just can't picture her in some kind of uniform, pointing a gun! Living outdoors, not eating right…"

"Get used to it, you can't protect her any more, not in this kind of world. Hey, when I was fifteen I was nothing but a teenager. And I went to college, and then I went to graduate school! Imagine that."

Vita licks honey from her fingertips. All it takes to get Tati reminiscing is a dreamy, "What was it like?"

Tati's feet are propped up on a stool. She smoothes her skirt and rubs her knees. "We had summers on Cape Cod—I told you about that peninsula that used to jut out into the ocean from Boston—and my father took me and my brother sailing. Sailing on the wide and splendid sea, the salty wind like the taste of life itself. We had predictable seasons then. The summers were sweet, not brutal like now. We went swimming in the ocean, too. Try to imagine a curving shore of sand, with windblown dunes and waving long grass, roaring surf crowned with white froth, as far as your eye could see."

"The ocean pounds at buildings now. I don't think I've ever seen a real seashore."

"You haven't. I'm glad I'm that old. But I remember when I started to realize. The summer we got married, in June, it rained for six weeks straight, lots of flooding, and then right away we got a heat wave. Wetter and wetter, and hotter and hotter. That's what scientists had been warning about and now my husband and I and a lot of other people began to see it. Maybe because of that first monster hurricane, the one that had smashed up the southeast some months before. The first one to actually destroy civilization in its wake. Americans had some kind of epiphany over that, or at least a dawning of understanding what this climate change thing could mean. But of course all they did was dinky little things like buying low-fuel cars and cleaning up coal factories. They didn't make any real changes. So it continued."

"Until it was too late."

"Until it was too late. And then, just when people were really waking up to what they'd done, Zoria came along and persuaded them it was God's will."

Vita recalls the face of Father Rose, the florid jowls fervid in exhortations to the flock. "Do you think the priests really believe all that stuff they say?"

"Yes, more's the pity. Of course they're often aware when they're manipulating people or facts, but it's all for a higher, sacred cause. Though I'm sure there are cynics among them. Power is a funny thing."

Vita finds herself saying, "That's what Drake had over me, power."

"And he got it in the same way, too—making you feel weak and helpless, or playing on those feelings you already

278

had about yourself. To the point where his beliefs were automatically yours."

"Because they made me feel safe. He made me feel safe."

Tati massages her knees, turns her kind intelligent eyes fully on Vita. "I do think from what you've told me that he also really did love you."

"You think so?"

"Probably very much, poor man."

Vita gazes at the hazed horizon, up at the chickadees still conferring in the old pine tree, and knows it's true. The idea of Drake's love for her no longer chills or jabs, but murmurs acceptance of the past, of her own foolishness as well as his delusions. There was a kind of heroism in his stalwart truth to his convictions. "I'm sort of glad he has his beliefs. They mean so much to him."

The two women sit in a thoughtful silence. Sounds are birdsong and shouts from the distant docks. Then around the corner of the lake slowly comes an unwieldy shape.

"Look," Vita cries, "what on earth is that bizarre floating contraption?"

"Oh," laughs Tati, "don't worry, there's a boat under that pile of tires. The foraging folks are back from their trip, they made good time. Those old tires, Vita, we use them for everything from houses to bridges and docks. Packed with dirt they're immovable. Just look at my house, it looks lopsided but it's solid as a rock…Hey, there's Miles, next to the mast."

They wave energetically, and are rewarded with yells of greeting from the odd-looking craft. Perched on top of the pile are several of the younger men, Bro among them. Bro has recently joined some of the classes Vita teaches, history and composition. Though nineteen, he'd had no formal schooling for almost ten years. He jumps up, teetering, and seesaws his arms dramatically.

"He's going to fall off," laughs Vita.

Her laughter wells from her heart, warming it, and like singing wraps her while reaching out to embrace the world, her world, with all its wounds and scabs, where mornings still come, birds still celebrate, and tongues are still caressed with honey.

9

On this same morning in June, Alex sits brooding over the corpse of his wife. He's been here all night, huddled in a chair next to the makeshift casket, not crying any more, just staring at her. He had to pay a fortune in bribes to get in here, the underground storage area where the bodies are lined up waiting. They all have died of the Tallahassee flu, which has just passed like lightning through the Albany enclave. Alex knows he's risking contamination, but at this point death seems an attractive release.

She looks beautiful, his Gloria. All the pain that writhed in her haunted features has melted away. Her soul shines out in smooth translucent skin. She's dressed in the nightgown Alex handed the nurse after she'd washed Gloria—vanishing the new and old blood, the vomit, the smells—the one with the low laced neckline. The one she was wearing that night when Vinsky came to their home to confront him, and she had awakened and presented such a vision of lovely vulnerability.

Alex can't stop his hand. He watches it in horror and awe while of its own accord it hovers over her, descends to her breast, pushes aside the filmy material. Cold, cold. But, he muses, no colder than it was in life. He palms the whole breast, caresses the nipple. Instead of martyred revulsion from her, he gets silence, acquiescent silence. Does he feel his body responding? Doesn't this awful deed have some awful scientific name, necrophilia or something? Shouldn't he be ashamed, shouldn't he be punished? But his hand stays, gradually warming her flesh a little, and he feels a tremendous peace flow through him, as if something loosens that has coiled hurt for a long time. Then in a leisurely way, trance-like, with the other hand he pulls up the gown and contemplates her sex, lying richly dark between her beautiful white thighs. How alive she seems right there, the tiny black curls untouched by agony or death, the way they must have curled all those years he never was allowed to touch them. But they too are cold, so he warms them, and pushes a finger down a little, far enough to feel the lips part. There he sits, one hand on her breast, the other between her legs, feeling himself warm with the warmth he is giving her. Sits for a long time, mind blank but heart gorged with life and forgiveness.

When he hears a stirring in the next room, he tenderly withdraws his hands and presses his face into her neck. He's roused by the guard roughly shaking his shoulder. The man is wearing protective gear including a surgical mask, so only his small pencil sharp eyes are showing. Alex could bribe him again, but he feels so tired he can barely stand. He stretches, nods, gazes down at his wife one last time. "Goodbye, Gloria, my love," he says aloud, lowers his head and hurries away.

అ∽శ

Now Alex is consumed with action. In a frenzy, he's focused and driven all the minutes of his days. The flu passes on towards the west, leaving thousands of victims hurriedly buried together, the lingering stench of corpses stifling the already unbreathable air. The air is so foul that people going outdoors continue wearing their oxygen masks even after the danger of disease has passed.

The Worcester massacre has galvanized the rebels. Officially they are routed, have run off to the hills never to be seen again. But in fact, Alex knows, the camps in the Green Mountains are every day reinforced by the arrival of more men and women, many who have nothing more to lose, but also many who are enraged and energized. Alex has sought out and been accepted by the new Credo leaders, including Vinsky. He simply presented himself in almost inarticulate confrontation, saying, "I'm ready now." Vinsky cocked his head up at him with a grin ready for mockery. But, looking more closely, instead he abruptly said, "Cohen, you'll co-captain the communication brigade. Get going." So, Alex has realized with fiery satisfaction, his face is as different as his heart.

The rebels meet regularly in the basement of Albany's old City Hall, believed to be abandoned. While in the streets loudspeakers blare religious tunes and wheezing admonishments by Zoria, they huddle around a table of maps, their carrier pigeons primed for flight to various destinations already marked for coups: Boston, Hartford, Burlington, Albany. Media stations will be taken over, prisons liberated, temples raided, and major Zorian forces lured to an ambush, all on a date they're still debating. Some want to strike soon, before the worst heat of summer, others urge waiting for autumn to provide more time to plan, train troops, and commandeer munitions.

Two weeks after Gloria's death, Alex returns to the office. Ladd of course has assumed that he stayed away in mourning. He greets Alex affectionately but somewhat vaguely. He looks pale and nervous; his family escaped the ravages of the flu, but his immediate boss and several other top officials succumbed. As Alex passed through the corridor, the atmosphere among the remaining staff was tightly anxious.

"I must confess, Cohen, I have this gut feeling the insurgents are just biding their time." Ladd is sitting at his desk aimlessly rifling through papers. "I'm not sure what to do about that. I'm not sure what to do, at all."

Alex brushes aside his first guilty impulse. Ladd is a fine and upright man, but he's not much of a player on this new stage, and he seems to know it. It's not productive to indulge regret about abandoning him.

Alex tries to dissemble his feverish focus, take on the beaten aura of grief, but it's a huge effort. Good thing Ladd is so distracted. Alex needs to use his computer to send some messages that are bland enough to escape investigation, especially to his pals in the Boston enclave. Then he'll be gone. Already his heart is in the hills, and his brain is shut off completely from anything outside the coming fight. The loss of Gloria at the same time frees and consumes him.

"You may be right, Ambassador," he replies as dolefully as he can, "you never know what those crafty insurgents will get up to next."

☜❀☞

Alex's military training was more than twenty years ago, when he fulfilled his compulsory service, so they assign him to a barracks tent with other older guys. The youngest men, some as young as sixteen, are the best source of information on tactics and arms, because they're the ones fresh from military conscription. Many escaped their training fields bringing their weapons and ammunition with them. But guns are still in short supply, so everything from knives to bows and arrows are being used. This time, they all agree, they won't risk direct confrontation with the Zorians equipped with the latest technology; they will "hit, duck, and run," their new motto.

Women are encamped here, too, of course, women and girls, laboring, marching, rehearsing raids over and over, alongside the men. The weather is breezy up here in the mountains, there are clean waterfalls, and enough food is smuggled in from farms below. This life is not any harder than what most of them have already known.

Alex has been practicing with a bowie knife for a week. He has learned well how to jab it into a person and twist just the right degree to immediately incapacitate, at the same time using a knee and an elbow to stymie any further resistance.

His teacher is Brad, the young pigeon keeper who helped him send his message to Vita just months ago—it seems eons. The boy has been conspiring with the Credos for four years already, ever since he was twelve years old and his parents were swept away in a hurricane. He knows why he's fighting, too.

"Those priests take everything for themselves. They want to keep on burning fuel to kill the air, just look at their military trucks. If it was up to them, the rest of us would just be slaves and the planet would totally die. And all their talk about God. They don't know what God is. My dad taught me about God, so I know what's what and they can't tell me any different."

They are sitting on makeshift stools outside Alex's tent after supper, whittling branches for arrows. The sweltering day has cooled but the air is still thick with stale humidity. They are shirtless, and Brad has wound a dirt-gray cloth around his temples to catch the sweat. He has a handsome open face, but an odd rhythmic way of jerking his head, much like the pigeons he tends in such a fond and brotherly way.

"Good for you," replies Alex. But he's careful not to sound patronizing. Brad cherishes his view of himself as instructor. "Is this one sharp enough, do you think?"

"Why don't you take off a little more over here, see?"

"Ok, that seems right. Say, what's Waldo up to these days?"

"Oh, he's home in Williamstown. But not for long. They'll be bringing him here soon. We got a shipment of birds from Hartford yesterday too. They're resting up for the big day."

"What's your opinion on the action date?"

"Oh, man, asap you know. Why wait?"

Spoken like a true teenager, chuckles Alex to himself. But he too is primed to go, restless, eager to taste danger and racing adrenaline, even blood and pain. He wants to feel punished, martyred, exalted. He wildly hopes he'll be killed in action. No more wretched diplomacy, no more pitiful fine points and negotiations, no more disguises and deceptions, no more guilt, no more self-hatred, no more ghost of Gloria. Training fiercely all day every day, his body is becoming sinewy, his face leathery with sun. He gives over his physical being without reservation. He has very few thoughts at all.

"So," he says, as eagerly as Brad, "in a couple of weeks? Say the beginning of July or thereabouts? The heat will be brutal, but we can take it better than they can."

"Sounds good. That'll be my vote."

Alex nods vigorously. He looks around briefly at the tents and makeshift shelters scattered over the rocky fields, where wildflowers in yellow and blue clumps survive the tramp of feet, buttered by fading sunlight. Even though this time after dinner is designated for rest, dozens of people are on the move, bustling about, shouting here and there, carrying and carting stuff, electric with resolve. Far below in the valley, dusk is diluting colors into shades of gray.

He and Brad collect their arrows and stash them in a box, points down. Then they freshen their mugs of coffee and lean back.

"My girlfriend back in Albany," says Brad, "she's really worried about this Affirmation thing they have in Boston. With the priests getting so powerful now in our Albany enclave, it looks like they'll try to start up the same program. She's fifteen. They'll take her away."

His fresh boy's face clouds down like a man's.

286

"You'd have to help her escape," Alex offers. "You can do that. I knew a girl once who did that."

Brad straightens up brightly, wants to hear the story. So Alex tells it, slowly at first, almost casually, as observer only.

"Her name's Lorna. She's the daughter of one of these big shots, but that didn't help her. In fact, that's why the priests wanted her, classy elite and all that. And her father was all for it, sacred duty, that whole crap. But not her mother. Oh no." He gazes at a far point in the valley, where the buildings of a darkening town are losing their shapes to the night. "Her mother was determined, real guts. She took Lorna to a farm where they could hide out. It worked fine for a while, but Brad I have to tell you the truth. The authorities finally found them."

Brad's open face pales with alarm.

"But," Alex hastens on, "don't worry, it turned out okay. She got out of the temple, she's escaped now once and for all."

"Wait. You mean she had to go live with those priests?"

"Well, yes, I'm afraid so, for a while."

"Man, how can you call that a happy ending? Those bastards rape girls. They don't care. They call it religion. Baloney. It's perverts and rape."

Brad jumps up and flails his arms at Alex. His thin chest, sporting only a light V of hair, heaves in fury. He's close to tears.

"It is," concedes Alex, "I'm not denying that."

He watches the young man's passion, almost enviously. Time was, he cared that wildly. At Brad's age it was his mother he wanted to defend, from the cruelties large and small of his domineering father, and from the creeping debility of her vague illness. What agonies of helpless rage he went through! Later, it was Gloria he was driven to soothe and protect, with the same blind fervor, the same reverent tenacity, the same awful gnawing sense that whatever he could do was never enough.

Brad goes on ranting and pacing and flailing, until he's out of breath. Then he stops and stares down at Alex.

"What is your problem, man," he pants, "how can you be so calm about it?"

Alex starts to say, well I'm not sixteen, but bites his tongue. "I do care, Brad. I'm thrilled that she's free now."

Brad sits down again slowly, takes a good look at Alex's face. "Your wife just died, I know. Big downer. But who was it you sent that message to that time?" Alex remembers perfectly well, but frowns quizzically.

Brad persists, "Waldo took the message to Williamstown. You said it was for a lady."

"I don't think I actually said that."

"But it was."

Now Alex is very annoyed. He's remembering Vita with all the power of keeping her repressed and hidden away all this time. She shines across his mind an infinite presence, all golden and peach, all sensual and sad. He has kept her at bay, but Brad's insistence has loosed her, and she will not be scattered back to the shadows.

"Damn!" he says.

Brad smirks.

"Shit and damn!" spits Alex, sitting forward over his knees, head in hands. "Leave her out of it, will you."

"No. Why should I? You obviously care about her a lot."

"Yes," Alex mumbles. "I loved her once."

"Once?"

"Okay, kid, if you want to hear it so badly, I still do."

In the boy's eyes he sees a whole mirror of sympathies, as if Brad can know what he's been through, as if those innocent eyes can read the writhing convolutions of his soul.

"That's not a bad thing," Brad says simply.

"I don't deserve her."

"So you're into punishing yourself?"

"I don't deserve her."

"What are you, some kind of criminal? Of course you deserve her. You deserve to be happy."

Alex stares at him. What a thing to say. He brushes aside the words like a web, but they keep floating at the edges of his mind.

10

Summer Solstice. Tully celebrates with a feast that evening. Long tables decked with colorful cloths are set up under shady trees to one side of the docks. As the sun starts to wane, loosening its sodden grip on the air, activity increases, children bringing flowers, boys bringing chairs, girls draping banners, men and women carrying dishes out from the main house kitchen. Dismissing her class early, Vita helps pour water and wine.

Small white clouds whisk through the sky herded by a brisk wind, obscuring the descending sun for an instant, then letting it flash gold, so that everything seems to be moving in and out of a speckled spiraling of light. The lake whips up whitecaps and the water gushes loudly at the shore.

Vita sits next to Tati and her granddaughter Fair, with Fair's son Orion and husband Miles. At the head of their table Marcel presides, flanked by Bro, his sister Kiva, her husband and their small daughter. Behind them all, young Yelp the dog makes the rounds using all his soulful wiles to con a treat. Yelp's round brown eyes reflect depths of comprehension from his ancestors' ingenious herding techniques, and glow with affection for muddling humans and gullible goats. He's brown and white in imaginative patterns, with perky tufts in his pointed ears. Vita caresses his silky head when he tries her in turn, but tells him no, he has to wait for his dinner.

The feast is a welcome break from the usual soybeans and cabbage or nameless stew and dandelion greens. Treats include marinated tofu, grilled trout, lettuce and tomato salad, feta cheese, cornbread, yogurt, and blueberry pie. Stella, chef extraordinaire—who, plump shiny pink with blond hair frosted white, resembles one of her own pastries—has a special surprise for the children, honeyed apple cider.

Orion asks for a third cup.

"Hey," laughs his mother, "you were too full to eat any more salad, remember."

He squirms guiltily. "But it's *so* good." His little freckled face is piteous with yearning.

"Compromise," smiles Fair, pouring him a small amount. "Now tell us what you learned in school today."

Orion nods, licking sweet liquid luxuriously from his lips. "Machines."

"What about them?"

Tati interjects, "You mean how machines burned a hole in the ozone layer?"

"And how people didn't understand," Vita explains, "In history today we were covering the turn of the century. Orion is very interested in that time, aren't you, Orion?"

"I want to know why." He appeals bleakly to his mother, as if she could surely solve the tragic puzzle. "Why did it take them so long? They knew. Why didn't they get it?"

"Didn't want to," Tati responds. "I remember that. We didn't want to understand, Orion. We worried about just about everything else."

"Elections," Orion says. "They could vote for the government then, like we do in Tully. So if they could vote, why didn't they try to fix it?"

"Eventually they did," Vita replies.

"I remember that too," Tati muses bitterly. "When it was too late. We'd passed the point where we could control it. The point of no return. And there were no more elections then, anyway."

"They did stop, though." Vita wants to give Orion some redeeming factors. "They stopped burning fossil fuels, even coal, around the late 2040s. Right, Tati?"

"Only because they were so hard to get by then." Tati grimaces. "In the end it took too much fuel to get at the fuels. Pretty ironic. Finally, people had to change the way they lived. We were forced to. We never did it willingly. Lemmings, all of us. Blind and foolish."

"Tanks," says Orion. "Tanks and military trucks still use gasoline." He makes fists. "I think they're crazy."

Vita is a bit dismayed at the success of her lesson. What good will it do poor little Orion to know how the world was wrecked?

She slices into her juicy pie topped with yogurt, the creamy white pinking from the blueberries, looks over the heads of the islanders to the main house and the plump hills behind. In the dancing light of alternating clouds and sun, in the exhilarating cool wind from the water, in the buzz of contented voices, Vita gets a surging sense of anchored well-being. This feels like the last sane place on earth. She conjures the day—soon she is sure—when Lorna and Garth and Ellie all return to share it. She can begin happiness.

Yet she knows that danger dogs Tully every day. For instance, though the Tallahassee flu has not come this far north, towns only fifty miles to the south have been hit; the drought that ended in January was followed by three months of heavy constant rain, interspersed with two brutal blizzards, creating mud rivers, uprooting half the apple orchard, and flattening homes; trees, long dry and suddenly soaked and so more vulnerable to insects, were further damaged by ice. Though Marcel and Miles have devised an elaborate water purifying system, they still have to worry about mercury and other persistent pollutants in the food and cancer continues a heartbreaking killer. Potential invaders show up on the horizon at regular intervals, and no one knows what will happen if they are armed and demand to stay here—there are now 120 people living on Tully and there's no more room unless the food supply can somehow be increased; many of the strongest young men and women leave periodically to join the rebels—it's getting harder to persuade them to stay to help with the strenuous jobs, and most importantly to protect the island. And though the crops are fine so far this year, everyone knows only too well that any kind of weather can strike at any time and throw the whole agricultural cycle out of whack.

Tati has told Vita that about eight years ago there was a battle here, when some destitute people landed and tried to take over. The invaders, weak and poorly armed, were easily beaten, though not until after too much blood was spilled. A truce was called, and the remaining newcomers were allowed to settle on the other side of the island, where, it turned out, the boulders that made it poor farming were perfect for creating substantial dwellings. Excellent foragers, they were able to identify kinds of mushrooms, berries, and roots that nobody had dared eat before. And so, before long, they were part of the community. But fear of this happening again, or worse, Zorian authorities discovering Tully's secrets (including the fact that the infamous Credo Marcel is based here), has made the islanders arm themselves with guns, disguise their homes and food supply, and develop elaborate plans for protection and resistance just in case. Tati has bemoaned more than once what she calls the island's militarization.

But Tully relies on subterfuge and camouflage as first defense. On the January day when Vita arrived—seasick, soaked through, freezing—and got her first glimpse of Tully, she despaired. There were hardly any signs of human habitation. All she could see as their boat approached through the driving ice curtain were a few huddled rubbery humps that hardly seemed manmade. The ramshackle old mansion on the hill looked like a wreck. Every new structure is hidden in some way so it's not visible from the water; the major crop area is in the middle of the island behind a tall fence trained with vines. Other food is actually grown underground, with slabs of solar panels at ground level forming a giant greenhouse. The rain cisterns and water purifiers are disguised as mossy hillocks. Nobody on the outside guesses Tully's riches or imagines that so many people in this remote place live peacefully without hunger, even educating their children.

Vita's months at River Bend Farm have given her insight into Tully's success. Here everything is tightly knit, tightly woven. River Bend is not only very visible prey, it has survived primarily through the will of one family, and relies on reactively traditional avenues. River Bend is—has been—an idyllic fallback into abandoned ways. Tully's route is into the future—shrinking into itself, toughening from the inside out, digesting every failure into muscle, unafraid to explore new possibilities no matter how exotic or even risky, forcefully focused in some way that's not the forte of individuals but of a universal spirit with a life of its own. Vita is awed by this. It's as if the countless shards of shattered hopes that line all the routes she has taken or observed, unaccountably reshape here, re-form into the kind of positive force people had forgotten could exist.

True, Tully is lucky in its leaders. Miles and Marcel, Tati and Fair, for example, are great souls—passionate about fairness, fierce and clear—but they themselves acknowledge their debt to autocratic decrees in times of crisis. No, Vita decides, it must be something in Tully Island itself, which by its very nature looks to her like a beacon forward in otherwise menacing blank darkness.

Fair lightly kisses Orion and goes to join the other musicians on the rocky ledge that serves as a stage. She's a striking young woman, small and wiry with curly carrot red hair, and she plies her fiddle with both passion and humor. A drum and two harmonicas complete the band. They belt out a foot stomping rendition of the island favorite, "Walk of Life." Stella, wearing a blouse displaying hefty cleavage in a blur of lace—frosting on angel food cake—sings in a sweet, scratchy voice.

> *"And after all the violence and double talk*
> *There's just a song in all the trouble and the strife*
> *You do the walk, you do the walk of life."*

Orion is restlessly whispering to Miles, "I want to play my harmonica too, Mom said I could."

Miles reassures him. "Soon, in a little while, Orie. Don't worry, you'll get your chance."

Now couples are making their way to the dance space over by the docks, and Marcel looks quizzically at Vita. She smiles, he's taking her hand, they join in. He moves stiffly and conservatively, as one would expect from morose Marcel who is nearly sixty to boot, but he's also clearly having a good time. Vita has always liked and admired Marcel, from the time she first met him at River Bend, when he told her so carefully that Ellie was alive and free. Here, he has been a good friend, a companion even. Sometimes he comes for dinner at Tati's house, and Vita tells many stories about her family, and listens long to memories of Crea, Tati's daughter and Marcel's beloved wife, who died of leukemia six years ago now. "Six years, eleven days, and eight hours," they tell her, often in unison.

Grinning, Marcel says, "You're the dancer in the family."

"You're right, Ellie doesn't care for it. But Lorna likes dancing, and she has a beautiful voice. She loves to sing."

"Yes," he says, "she sang for us a few times, really exquisite. When she comes back, we'll get her to join the band." Vita laughs happily, pulls away in a twirl, and he obliges without moving more than his arm. "I'm not very good at this."

"You're fine. I'm just showing off."

Like most of the women, she's wearing a skirt in honor of the occasion, with a sleeveless pale pink blouse that Tati gave her. It's more delicate and intricate, with ruffles and tiny buttons, than most clothes these days, and now, seeing Marcel's eyes lingering, she remembers that it used to belong to his wife. She starts to ask if he minds, then stops. He mourns Crea in so many ways still, let him have part of his tears as celebration.

Soon after they return to the table, Fair calls Marcel to the stage.

"Refill your wine cups, folks," urges Fair with her little Irish smirk. "To toast some words from our fearless leader, to give us energy for more festivities."

Marcel obliges, but his smile is brief.

"It fills my heart to see you all here," he says, looking out over the crowd. "We've been through so much, and every time we survive, being together and celebrating together becomes more precious. The names of the dead and absent are on our lips and in our prayers. Let's have a moment of silence to remember them, and be with them. Send your love and strength to our friends in the Green Mountains, getting ready to confront the powerful, a great day of justice and hope."

For a time there is absolutely no sound except the insistent wash of the lake, a clang of masts, occasional birdcall. Even the children are still. Vita bows her head and holds her daughter and sister vivid in her mind's eye, caressing them with all her love, willing them well and at peace, willing them back to her.

Marcel continues, "The nightmare of Earth's illness goes on and on. We ourselves will never see the end of it. But I assure you, friends, healing is on its way. We're fighting now so our great-grandchildren may have a future in a renewed world, a planet healthy and balanced again. Where all people, sharing equally, live simply in respect and harmony with the rest of life."

Marcel touches again on the approaching coup and conflict, the suffering of so many now and to come, and sounds subdued warnings about Tully's vulnerability, but he ends with a gesture of open arms.

"Enjoy this evening. Welcome the Solstice, the shortest night of the year." Somebody hands him a cup of wine and he holds it aloft. "Drink up! Celebrate! Tomorrow will come too soon!"

During wild applause, the music starts again. This time the stage is filled with children and their instruments, everything from Orion's harmonica and different sized drums to homemade tambourines, a bass formed with a stick and string, and containers filled with stones. They belt out what is eventually recognizable as "Turkey in the Straw."

Vita is clapping her hands when she feels a light touch on her shoulder. It's Bro, come to ask her to dance. Now this is a turn of events she hadn't anticipated. Bro is twenty-three years her junior, and her pupil no less. She's been aware that he looks at her sometimes in a very manly way, but then students do often have little crushes on teachers and it doesn't mean anything.

In this spirit, she jumps up and he catches her hand as they head for the dance area. Bro becomes a whirligig, all shoulders and hips, arms and legs boneless rubber, almost epileptic in his enthusiasm. Vita stops laughing as she has to catch her breath to keep up with him. She closes her eyes the more to feel her whole body responding to the wild music in the soft cool wind.

298

During a long break while the tables are cleared, Vita does a stint in the kitchen. She knows the routine, from saving rinsing water for plants to composting everything. Nothing is thrown away. Even the used soapy water does final duty in the outhouses. Then she takes Tati home, slowly as the sun finally is setting, reddening sky and water. She tucks the old woman into bed.

"Ah," sighs Tati, lying back on her pillow. "That's what I call a party, don't you think, Vita my dear?" Vita murmurs yes. "Best solstice I ever had. Wonderful people, our Tully."

Vita waits for a while outside, making sure Tati's on her way to sleep, then she wanders back toward the festivities, trying to decide if she's tired. She stands on the hill beside a tree, gazing down. Little solar lamps line the stage and dock, the lake has darkened to nothingness. The music, once more in the hands of adults, is a sensual rendition of some kind of Cajun tune.

All at once, she's startled to find Bro beside her.

He grins sheepishly. "I was waiting for you."

He's tall and skinny, with cinnamon colored hair and eyes that almost match. In this light, this close, his eyes look lion yellow. She looks up at him, not smiling. This is not proper student-teacher behavior, is it? He looks so innocent, she can't decide.

"Why?"

"I want to dance with you again."

"That's ok, but you didn't need to follow me home."

"I didn't. I just waited here."

She starts to relax, smiles indulgently. But then he takes a step closer. Her back is against the tree. He reaches out and touches her hair, just lightly. "You are beautiful."

"Whoa." She recoils and pushes him away. "This is not a good idea, Bro. Please go away."

He's not moving and he's not smiling but his face is the picture of hurt and admiration. "I don't want to go away."

"You talk like such a child," she says.

That does it. He reddens angrily. "I'm no child," he mutters. "And you know it."

"Tell you what," she negotiates, "you go on back to the dance and maybe I'll be down later."

"Promise?"

"No."

He peers into her face but sees no encouragement there, turns abruptly and is gone.

Vita sits slowly down, nestling to the tree. She watches as Bro chooses one of the girls and starts his gyrating dance with her. A sudden wave of some wonderful odor bathes her senses. Honeysuckle, she thinks, though she has no idea if that's what it is. The word sounds right for the smell. Unwanted, Alex surges into her heart, as if he's physically there, embracing her. She fights the image and the feeling but it's no use. She experiences such a yearning for him it's dizzying, jolting, screaming sharp, melting and molten. She summons her anger. How he hurt her! How he deceived her! How he lied, how cruelly he abandoned her! She tries to conjure the pain but his mouth on hers is the only sensation she gets.

Miles is on the stage and now he starts to sing. Vita has heard him before, but never has his voice seemed so angelic, transcendent. The deep timbre folds into the honeyed odor, into the heat of Alex's presence. Vita pictures herself returning to the cottage, quietly listening outside Tati's door, making her way through the pantry to the little alcove that serves as her bedroom, undressing, climbing into bed. Lying there.

Instead, she feels her feet taking her down the hill, her hips already swaying to the music.

꙳

A few days later, there's a great commotion down by the docks, but Vita refuses to release her pupils until she's made sure they understand their homework.

"Now, class, I know you're all dying of curiosity to find out what's going on. So am I. It's almost time anyway, so I'm going to let you go in just a minute. Dina, can you tell me what the assignment is?"

"Read the rest of chapter twelve," pipes the child dutifully.

"That's right. And then?"

Dina is stymied. Bro looks bored and restless. Vita has had a hard time relating to him authoritatively ever since their warm embraces at the Solstice celebration. After their troubling encounter under the tree, she'd thrown scruples and angry memories to the winds, abandoned herself mindlessly to sensual starlit dancing with him. He'd actually come close to kissing her. Correction, she had come close to letting him kiss her—much worse. She still remembers the brush of his lips on her chin as she turned her face away, the muscle and smell of him, as silly with wine they danced happily for hours. No matter how stern she's been towards him since, the damage is done.

More shouts from outside. Clearly something unusual is happening.

Vita gives up and says quickly, "Make sure you understand it well enough to tell me the story in your own words. See you tomorrow."

Pandemonium is followed in a flash by an empty classroom. Even Bro doesn't linger. She goes to the window. A large sailboat is being pulled to shore by two canoes. The sails are furled and someone standing in the prow is waving.

Vita freezes, not daring to hope. Then she's off and running, joining everyone else on the shore.

"It's Ellie," they all tell her. "It's your sister."

In another moment, they're holding each other. Ellie feels frail in her arms, skin and bones.

"Is Lorna with you?"

"No, Vita, I'm so sorry. She and Garth are still in camp, they couldn't come."

"Is she ok?"

"She's ok, Vita."

They're guided through the crowd into the main house, where Ellie is plied with food and water. She takes off her backpack, peers inside, sets it carefully down beside her. She looks gaunt and exhausted, keeps up a dry cough. Her brown hair with its gray wings is cut short like a cap around her lined face unused to smiles. She gulps water, nibbles at some bread.

"Oh Ellie, I'm so happy to see you." Vita can hardly stop touching her. "Now you can rest. I'll take care of you." She turns to Marcel. "She needs to lie down. Shall I take her home with me?"

He puts his hand on Vita's shoulder, calming. "Sure, we can set up a cot in your room if you want."

Ellie gives a dry chuckle. "I may be your little sister but I'm not that helpless."

Vita laughs, relieved and delighted. Ellie's herself, after all. Ellie takes another swig of water, wipes her mouth and face with the back of her hand.

"Vita, I've got something to tell you."

At once Marcel turns to the crowd milling around them, says quietly, "Time to scram, folks."

Everyone leaves, reluctantly. Vita leans closer to her sister, beginning alarm.

"What is it, Ellie?"

"It's hard to know how to start. But I need to make sure first that you understand Lorna is fine. She's just a little weak…"

"Oh God what do you mean, has she been sick?"

"Not sick, Vita."

Ellie bends down to lift the flap of her backpack. In it is a tiny human creature. It has a tuft of tawny hair, and a rosebud mouth in an obliviously sleeping miniature face.

"A baby? Oh, Ellie, what are you doing with a baby?"

"It's your granddaughter, Vita. Her name is Terra."

Vita stares and stares at her sister and the creature. The meaning of the words keeps escaping her. How can this be? She feels very faint but she also feels like laughing.

"I don't believe you," she says. Her voice sounds hollow.

Ellie is reaching across the table to stroke her arm, hold her hand. "It's going to take a while, I know," she says gently. "How could we even imagine."

"But what happened? Could Garth be that stupid? Does this mean that…" Ellie waits while Vita figures it out. Slowly Vita says coldly, "The father is a priest. The father is a priest. Oh my dear God."

And she starts to silently sob, breaks down completely into wails. Soon the baby wakes and screams along with her, the cave of its red mini mouth hurling a barrage of shattering shrieks. Marcel hurries in. Ellie holds Vita.

"I hate it! I hate it!" Vita is moaning. "Oh, take it away. Oh, my darling Lorna, what have they done to you?"

11

The coup is set for July 10, five days from now. Alex has been promoted to full captain, with a squad of thirty people under his command. Vinsky himself made the announcement on his recent visit to the camp here in the Green Mountains. Nobody was surprised. Ever since arriving, Alex has been a pillar of fortitude and resolve, as well as a focused and courageous strategist. He never seems to sleep, yet is always sharp and intent; he thinks like an arrow. His fierce sunburned face looks as if it hasn't relaxed for a long time. He can joke with his troops when it's appropriate, but each of them knows he expects perfection. And he gets it.

This morning he's inspecting the detention facility they've set up for the Zorians they expect to capture. There's room for a few hundred comfortably, five hundred packed full. Alex expects capacity.

"Get those cots out of here," he orders. "The prisoners each get one blanket, that's it. And the water ration is minimal, you've got that, right?"

Brad beside him nods, then while Alex stares at him, salutes. "Yes, sir."

"Get the cots over to the medical tent pronto, that's where they belong. Now let's have a look at those solitary holes you dug. Scumbags don't need to stand up. I just want them deep enough to put a lid on the bastards. Maybe a breathing hole." He chuckles without mirth. "I want a special one saved for Mr. Rose."

It's early yet, and as they head across the dusty terrain the air still holds a breathable freshness. There's been no rain since April, but during the months-long flooding before that, they had the foresight to fill every kind of container from barrels to old furnace boilers and gasoline tanks. So though it looks like another drought is happening, there's plenty of water available, at least so far. Supplies are plentiful, too. When Vinsky arrived last week, he brought with him miraculous wagons full of food that travels well, like salted fish, dried and pickled fruits, and root vegetables, as well as first aid kits and loads of ammunition. Nobody troubled to ask him where this bounty came from. His marauders and their surgical strikes are well known by now.

"Captain Cohen," Vinsky gloated. They were pacing in front of Alex's tent in an early evening breeze. "Well you certainly came round, didn't you? Didn't think you had it in you, to tell you the truth."

Neither did I, thinks Alex. He has left his old familiar self behind somewhere. Maybe the guy who always strove for peaceful solutions is lying in the coffin with Gloria. Or maybe he's only been temporarily abandoned in the burning prospect of a real showdown at last, the rage and revenge of the people. Or maybe the old Alex is only hiding behind this fierce façade that protects him from thinking too much. In any case, war has taken him in its grasp, and he welcomes the consuming fire.

Alex doesn't bother to respond to Vinsky's jibe. He remarks instead, "I need a supply of hats. What've you got?"

"Hats we have, though probably not enough. You'll be issued maybe two dozen, max. You'll have to make do."

"We'll manage. Tell me, how about our cell in Boston? Last I heard they were weak in the television takeover area. I know most of those people. They should be good, if they've got the right leadership."

"They're all set. You know that dynamo Diamond, I believe," replies Vinsky, with only a trace of a leer. "She's done a terrific job. It looks good right now."

Alex notes a fleeting image of Diamond naked, but it's stale, faded, it floats away without his having to dismiss it.

306

He says, "She's got the expertise. She's got backbone. I'm glad to hear she's in charge."

"You bet. In fact, she's the pick to lead the takeover. I chose her myself ten minutes into our briefing. She's a maniac. She must be a tornado in bed. More power to you."

Alex briefly grins with obliging camaraderie, but responds, "Now what about the big plan? Are they taking the bait?"

"That's my great news, Cohen. The Zorians are on the march. They're directing everything they have to the confrontation in Keene. We've got them exactly where we want them."

Alex breathes a sigh of satisfaction, almost smiles. "Our plants and double agents worked. The stupid bastards bought it."

"Yep, the priest toadies are convinced we're planning a showdown in Keene on the 10th. Which we are, but not the kind they think. They must feel so smug. Their army marching down the valley to certain victory. Armed to the teeth, glorious in nice clean red and white uniforms. Flags, fancy upside down crosses, drums, trumpets, the works. Piece of cake to wipe out our motley crew once and for all." Vinsky laughs loudly, his tiny eyes dissolved in flesh. "We'll cut 'em to shreds."

Alex slaps him on the back in comradely glee. But then Vinsky holds up a warning finger and motions him inside the tent. "I must tell you, Cohen—captain—there's one possible problem."

As they hunch over a small table, Vinsky confides darkly, "They may have planes."

"What! There haven't been airplanes for years. They're all junked. There's no fuel for them anyway."

"So we assumed. But our scouts have spotted a secret airstrip and teams working at night. They've got biodiesel. Three planes could be operational."

"All it takes is one," says Alex gloomily. "They'll be able to see what we're doing here. They'll be able to track our fake retreat."

"You'll have cover. You'll know what to do."

"That's how we've been training," agrees Alex. "Guerilla tactics. Not easy prey for planes. We can outwit them, we can hide like foxes."

"Right. If you hear planes, go into scatter mode right away. Don't wait for the signal. And you know, maybe they won't get the machines up and running in time anyway. Just a word to the wise."

Alex and Vinsky then cemented their newfound comradeship with several mugs of excellent whiskey, courtesy of some petty official who was grateful (and lucky) to get away with his life.

Now Alex is peering down into black pits barely big enough for a man to crouch in. "Looks good," he says to Brad.

They both know that's a high compliment.

Alex orders Brad to pick another man and the three of them huddle in Alex's tent.

"Now here's what I want you to do," he tells them. "We've got ourselves a couple of their uniforms. Back pack 'em and stick together. When the signal comes to scatter, head for your appointed rendezvous. Then the two of you will put on the jackets, stand up so you can be seen, and signal the Zorians, lure them into the narrowest part of the valley."

Both the young faces light up with this conspiracy. Brad's pal is a wiry, tan-colored, good-looking man not much more than nineteen or twenty. Something pricks Alex's memory and he asks his name again.

"Garth."

Alex knows that name. At first he resists pursuing it. This is no time for the entanglement of emotions. But as the men are leaving he can't help saying to Garth, "I think you know my friends Vita and Lorna Gordon. How are they?"

Garth's mouth drops and he begins an exclamation he quickly represses.

"Yes, sir."

"Go on."

"Well, sir, Lorna is here with me. She's in the medic tent."

"Medic tent! Is she hurt, wounded?"

"No, sir. Just not well. She'll be ok."

"I'll go visit her. How about her mother?"

"We think she's up north, Lake Willoughby. Marcel's headquarters."

"Yes, I know about that place. Good news. Come on, let's go see Lorna now."

He sends the puzzled Brad to excuse his presence at a meeting.

The medical tent is vast and for now almost empty. But a hundred cots in close rows await the calamities to come. Lorna is in the women's section, in one corner sectioned off by a tarp. She recognizes Alex at once.

"Lorna," he says, taking her hand, "welcome to our camp. How are you feeling?"

Her face is thinned and pale, she has lost all the vigor and shine of girlhood. But she's still beautiful, perhaps more than ever now, with the edge of womanhood on her and a new sadness in the shape of her mouth. Her hand in his is feverish.

"Alex! How wonderful to see you." Her voice is the same, and he hears her mother in it. But she doesn't raise her head from the pillow. "I'm better now, thanks."

"What happened?"

Lorna looks off into space. "I don't know."

Alex doesn't press her. "Any news from your mom?"

"Yes, thanks. She's in Vermont with my Aunt Ellie."

"Great. So you can join them as soon as you're well."

Lorna shakes her head on the pillow. "No. I must fight. I want to kill every priest in the world."

Alex is taken aback by the sweet child's bloodthirsty words, but then he remembers her time in the temple, has a glimmer of understanding.

"We can help you with that," he says cheerfully. "That's what we're here for."

Lorna's eyes seek out Garth, her face lit with love, and Alex sees how it is. He astounds Garth by giving him permission to stay for a while.

For the rest of the day Alex fights a mesmerizing image of Vita, standing on a shore waving to him. Her dress is filmy, almost transparent, her soft hair loose in a breeze. Her face, her mouth, the warm flexible shape of her. She tortures him, distracts his brain, fires his body. He had thought all that was cooled, or rather he had not thought about it at all. He's furious.

He decides he can't afford to visit Lorna again. But he vows to keep close tabs on her health, and sends special orders to the medics to keep him updated.

Two days later in an overcast dawn, Alex sets out on the march towards Keene. His squad is one of many adding up to nearly four hundred fighters leaving from this camp. Stalwart and eager as they look, he knows they make a poor show compared to the terrifying Biblical array they face—a hoard of uniforms armed to the teeth, flags, trumpets, drums, trucks full of supplies, and even tanks, led by priests in flowing white robes carrying Zoria's perverted cross. The Credos have exactly four rickety trucks, which run on a hybrid of solar and ethanol, a few dozen bicycles, two wagons pulled by stocky farm horses. No drums or trumpets here: they must all be light footed for the clever maneuver. Their plan is as old as warfare. Lure the enemy into ambush.

Alex is exhilarated, his fear energizing. He pictures his comrades in all the enclave centers poised for the final action, alerted by carrier pigeons to the very hour and minute they must move to take over. He knows this will work. Already he sees his cowed prisoners, Vinsky's victorious face on television, the temples and prisons liberated, the Nons getting their children back, that foul hypocrite Rose on his knees. He dreams that Earth still has a chance to heal, fantasizes that his heroism will help bring its return to balance and abundance.

Around noon he first notices the peculiar color of the sky. They have stopped for lunch. The troops sit along the side of the road wherever they can find shade, munching, chatting, passing canteens. Some are taking cat naps, heads on backpacks. Alex swallows water, hands it on, squints up again. Surely that is not how the sky should look. Those clouds are ringed with black and behind them the color can only be described as vomit yellow. Even the gray air is yellowish. He's starting to wonder if he shouldn't confer with the colonel and the other captains, when the wind picks up, whips dust into spirals. Forbidden to use his radio in case the signal can be traced, he sends Brad up ahead on a bike to request permission to cut the break short. Word comes back to get moving fast. They continue their march at a quicker pace, heads bowed into the wind, faces masked by bandanas or whatever against the pelting dust.

Within an hour the temperature has dropped at least thirty degrees, and the rain begins. Ear-splitting thunder, lightning bolts slashing blinding swaths across the whole length of sky. At least the rain settles the dust, and for a while it's a relief to be cool. They make good progress, arriving at the remains of the old turnpike bridges heading into Springfield before

311

the two o'clock deadline. The troops are soaked through and tired, but in good spirits. Alex notes the potential shelter of the pile of collapsed concrete. He seeks out the colonel.

"We've been on the go for eight hours now, sir. How about we wait out the storm here?"

"I don't like the looks of it," concurs the colonel.

And so it happens that just when the wind begins knocking people over and the rain turns to hail the size of baseballs, Alex and his troops are finding nooks and caves and crannies within the giant ruins of the bridges. By the time the snow comes, around five o'clock, most of them are fairly well protected. What they can't have prepared for is the cold. Who would have thought they would need blankets or coats? Who would have thought they would long for fires? So, fully armed, well stocked with food and water, sporting sun hats, they suffer acutely through the night. Many get frostbite. Some in the shallower caves die from exposure.

Days later they learn that the blizzard caught the Zorian force in a wide field, as they continued to march into the snow trusting in God's plan. It became legend that the thaw revealed them frozen in various poses still in military formation, still in their beautiful uniforms, like the stone soldiers of ancient tombs.

12

That same afternoon, Vita is walking in the woods. As soon as her class was dismissed she slipped away, to this grove where she has come several times before. The trees all around are stately pines, long trunks like Greek columns ending in a vast dark canopy, no underbrush, only a soft carpet of browned pine needles, moss. It's quiet and smells deeply and sweetly of pine and earth. She sits down against a tree. A bird is singing just above and she answers its call. It looks like a mourning dove. Fawn brown paling to tan, long fanciful feather tail. She hasn't seen or heard a mourning dove since the days on Cayuga Lake. Tully seems magic that way. Things she had thought long lost have survived here, honeybees, lilies, chickadees, fireflies. The trees themselves are not as damaged as elsewhere. She knows they're weakened by drought, flooding, bark beetles, battering winds, but many still stand, symbols of defiance, trust.

The bird's grieving tones suit her mood. Ever since Ellie arrived bringing that horrible infant, her soul has been in darkness. She can't even enjoy her sister's company, and in any case Ellie is shocked at her revulsion towards her grandchild. As is everyone else. Why can't they understand? Some degraded man raped her daughter, her child, her baby, her darling. Forced her at fifteen to go through pregnancy, made her weak and ill, wrecked her innocence forever. Why should the product be anything less than anathema to her? But even Tati begs her to relent.

"I can imagine how you feel," Tati says, "of course you hate the priest. But this is your child's child. Poor little Terra hasn't done anything wrong."

"No, you can't imagine how I feel," Vita always retorts. "Your granddaughter is Fair, the result of a love relationship

313

between your mature daughter and her loving husband. You have no idea."

"The baby needs you."

"I hope it dies. It should never have been born."

A brisk breeze starts, welcome in the heat that stifles even in this sanctuary. Vita rubs her arms, nestles against the mossy bark, hungry for comforting. If Bro were here right now she'd open her arms to him, hold him tight. But in a sharp sting his body turns into Alex's. It's Alex who is enfolding her, his familiar smell, his voice just the way he always gasped when he first pushed into her, his weight. The subdued memory claws through her careful construct of defenses, raw as ever. Tears start, she hears herself sobbing. She howls into the stately forest. Its peace mocks her.

Alex is gone. Lorna is gone. Lorna will never be the same. Vita remembers the last time she saw her, all dolled up in that atrocious little-girl outfit, like a mannequin, like a robot. But even then she still had fight in her, Vita could see it in her eyes. Now what must she be like? Lying somewhere sick and confused, traumatized, bitter. I have lost my child, she mourns, I have lost my life's blood.

Lorna is gone. Alex is gone. He loves his wife more than me after all, her life is more important to him than mine. He went away coldly, he broke his promise, he broke me. All I have left is my self in pieces.

Vita doesn't notice the moody and darkening sky, the tree canopy hides it. Only when the breeze turns into a crazed wind whipping up the pine carpet, and the air abruptly cools to icy, does she stand up wondering. Then all at once she knows she should run.

It's Yelp who finds her, knocked to the ground and unconscious under pelting fist-sized hail. Miles and Bro are close behind, calling her name. The hail has begun to pile

314

up over her, she's almost invisible. But Yelp sniffs her out and sets up such a yowling that the men are there in an instant. This rescue becomes part of Tully lore. But it's a long time before Vita can confess even to herself that she did not run, that instead she stood still under the attack, opening her palms and bowing her head, accepting the bruises, cuts and blood, giving into the blows as they felled her.

᠗᠗

"The major problem is our crops," Marcel reports, standing on the veranda few days later. "Almost all the boats are ok, we hauled them far enough up on shore.

The goats survived pretty well in that cavern, we just lost one kid. We've got damage to some homes, and a good chunk of the west dock is gone, but otherwise our emergency plans went into gear fast and focused. Nobody got seriously hurt. Congrats again to everybody. Our practice drills did the job." He clears his throat and looks around at the group, gathered in front of the old mansion. "But we couldn't get most of the fields covered in time. We lost almost all the tomatoes, I'm afraid."

The crowd is quiet, only turning to glance at one another in recognition of this hardship.

"They froze," interjects Miles. "Won't they keep anyway?"

"We can try to dry them," agrees Marcel. "But tomatoes don't like to be frozen."

"The berries were frozen, too," says Stella, "but I think we can make jam out of them."

"And wine," someone chuckles.

"Great," says Marcel. "And remember, all our crops underground are just fine as always. And our root cellars are well stocked. We'll be getting sick of cabbage and beets this winter!"

"The carrots are going to be ok too," someone says. "All the root vegetables will be ok."

"That's right. And a lot of the corn and apples look fine too." Marcel pauses, smiles. "Now let's give special recognition to Miles and Bro, and valiant Yelp too of course, who saved our Vita." Loud applause. "And now she wants to say a few words."

He helps her as she falters up the steps, her forehead and one leg still bandaged. At first her voice is so low they have to urge her to speak louder. She looks out at all the familiar faces smiling up at her. The gleaming lake, the soaring cliffs that embrace the sky. "I'm so happy to be alive," she repeats, and means it.

☜☞

"I always wanted a good death," says Tati.

"Gran…" Fair starts.

"Don't lie to me about it, sweetheart. Sweetpea, as your dear mom used to say. I'm as tough as you, you know. This is the end of my journey."

Vita sits on one side of Tati's bed, Fair on the other. It's a mercifully cool day toward the end of October. The old woman is propped up on pillows, free of pain, looking shrunken but at the same time serene.

Fair swipes at tears. "Gran, we don't want to lose you. What will we do?"

Vita says, "Tati, we'll be here as long as you need us. Is there any other way we can help?"

"Fair's a good healer, she's given me all the treatments I'll need in this world." After a pause while she draws a difficult

316

breath, Tati adds dreamily, "I wonder if there's a heaven after all, and I'll see my Crea, and my Leon, and my Dom, and my stupid, stupid dear old dad…"

"A spirit world, Gran, no doubt about it. Your spirit won't ever die."

Fair gets up to adjust the pillows, pull the bottom sheet tighter, smooth back Tati's thin hair from her temples.

Tati queries, "Have you made my stone yet?"

Fair's face crumples, she shakes her head. "I couldn't bear it."

"I want my stone made," Tati insists, "I want to see it. A smooth white stone, if you can find one. With my name inscribed by Stella who does it so beautifully."

From the back room comes a tiny wailing, little Terra waking from her nap.

Vita gets up and Tati calls after her, "Bring the child in here, please."

Vita pauses in the doorway of her room. Terra in her cradle stops flailing and yelling, gives her a radiant smile.

"Hello, little one," Vita says. "Do you need a new diaper?" While she changes the baby, she says, "I'm trying to love you. I'm really trying."

Terra gurgles and smiles and looks around as if at a new world. Everything that stirs or glints is an adventure for her, sunbeams and rain.

Before picking her up, Vita cautions her, "But I hate your father. I hate him in you. Beware of me, little one. I'm not the doting grandma you think."

In her arms, Terra's weight fits snug against her chest, sweet powdered baby smell, pudgy rosy flesh. She's healthy now, a healthy child should be a blessing from any point of view, there are so few nowadays. Vita closes her eyes, presses her lips to the velvet cheek. Her longing for Lorna has calmed. She knows now she'll never have her little girl back. All she can hope is that one day she'll hold and kiss the woman she's become. There have been a few messages from Lorna and Garth, all brisk and positive and saying nothing.

Tati says, "Let me touch her. Give me her little hand."

Vita's heart brands the farewell tableau: the old woman lying between the two young women, holding with her blue-veined bony hand the tiny fingers of the cooing child.

That evening Orion delivers the palm-sized gravestone, elegantly etched with Tati's name within a heart shape. He insists on brushing Tati's hair, tenderly, bravely, with no tears. A clutch of visitors gathers outside the front door, talking in a low murmur that coalesces like a moan, while the placid lake reddens, goes dark, and glitters again with colorless light from an enormous moon. Ellie commandeers the situation, allowing only one person at a time to pass very briefly by the bed, and producing snacks for everyone.

Tati has a difficult night. Vita and Fair take turns sitting with her. Towards dawn, Tati asks to see her stone again, puts it on her chest with her hand clasped over it. Then she asks for Terra, who goes back to sleep in the crook of her aged arm. And it's this way that she takes her last breaths, hard and lengthy but a bit like the croon of the mourning dove.

The morning after Tati's funeral, Ellie and Vita are sitting at the kitchen table finishing breakfast, Terra reclining in her little cushioned infant chair, fashioned of wood and shaped like a sleigh.

"Now listen," says Ellie abruptly, "You're not going to like this, and I'm sorry."

Her face under its cap of sharp spare hair still has a skeletal look, but it's fuller now, and her leathery tan has almost a healthy glow.

"Marcel got a message a few days ago," she goes on, her sinewy hands gripping her cup. "We didn't want to bother you while Tati was going, of course you needed to be wrapped up in that. But I'll be leaving Tully very soon."

Vita loses breath, cries, "Why? You don't want to leave, you can't!"

She has dropped the bottle she was holding for Terra, and the child starts a tragic wail.

"Hey, you can see I'm restless here. You know me. I've got to get back to the action." Ellie gets up and guides Terra's thumb into her mouth. Then she stands over Vita. "Look, there's such an opportunity now! Nearly two thousand Zorian troops froze to death. We never got our ambush at Keene, but we got something much better. Boston and Burlington are free."

"Ellie, you can't be serious. It's dangerous, you must rest, you're not well."

"I'm as well as I'll ever be, Vita dear. My poor body's not going to recover any further from its punishments. Besides, I've got the health of my mind to think of too."

"I don't believe this. You want to go back and punish yourself some more?"

"Vita." Her sister grasps her shoulder with a face full of urgency and pity. "Don't you get it? We're so near victory. I want to be part of that with my last breath. What's the matter with you?"

"I need you, we need you here."

"No, you don't. Terra needs you here. That's the only legitimate need going on besides getting rid of the priests once and for all. Then maybe the planet will have a glimmer of hope, or at least we'll go out with dignity."

As usual Ellie's ironic tone alienates her sister; it's as if difficult subjects dipped in bitterness and sarcasm are easier to swallow. She takes Ellie's hand from her shoulder, pressing it affectionately but not looking at her. Then she gets up and goes to the little window looking out on the side yard. The clothesline is draped with diapers side by side with Tati's sheets, motionless in the tepid air. Just beyond, apple trees gleam with red fruit. She blinks back taunting tears. How well does she know this woman, whom she loves deeply but can't really grasp over the chasm of years they were separated, the drastically different tracks their lives have taken? This person she mourned as dead for so long. She listens forlornly to the raspy voice behind her, roughened by the perpetual cough.

"Listen, Vita, half the northeast is in the hands of the Credos now. Good things are happening." Ellie is pacing, gesturing. Vita turns to focus on her words, watching with helpless worry the bony lope, the too lean shoulders. "Marcel's message said the temple girls are free, Vita. Imagine that. They're starting to lead normal lives. That at least should interest you."

"Oh Ellie, how wonderful! Free." Vita has a joyful moment picturing the young girls running ecstatically out of their prison. But then she slowly says, "Normal? I don't think so."

"Vita, people survive terrible things."

Vita looks into the telling eyes of her sister, where memory of horrors will always lurk. "Yes. I hope so. I'm sorry, Ellie."

"I'll find Lorna. We'll get word to you regularly. One day hopefully we'll be able to come back here, settle down. When the state of the world permits." She stands still with folded arms, legs apart, a soldierly sprite. "But I have to tell you, Vita, right now my plan is to die with my boots on."

"Well then, I'm coming with you. I want to come with you. We'll find Lorna together."

"Who'll take care of Terra?"

"Fair. I'm sure she would."

"How much help can you be to Lorna? She won't appreciate your showing up. We'll have to take care of you."

"She loves me, she must want to see me."

"Is that why her every message begs you to stay put?"

The sisters stand looking at each other. Ellie's sharp haggard face is defiant and loving. Standing very straight, her clothes loose over pure bone and muscle, she resembles some battle-worn stalwart in a historic painting. Slowly they move into a long hug.

"I'm proud of you, Ellie, you're a better person than me. You always have been."

Ellie steps back with a grin. "Now that's not a bit true. I would've been a rotten mother, for example. And you'll be a passable grandmother, when you get yourself together."

Vita looks at Terra, shakes her head. "I still don't feel anything. Or, no, what I feel is so conflicting—affection and anger. More like a chill."

"You'll come around, I'm sure of it."

"I'm trying really hard," Vita says still shaking her head, frowning at the baby, who lets her thumb go in a glowing smile. "The poor thing, nobody loves her and she doesn't know it yet."

"Oh," shrugs Ellie, planting a peremptory kiss on the tiny head, "somebody will. And I think it's going to be you." She grins at Vita's grim expression, continues briskly. "So, sis, we've got maybe another week together. Vinsky's on his way here, should arrive any day. When he leaves again, I'm going with him. Bro wants to come too, and I don't think Marcel can stop him this time."

"Oh no, not Bro leaving too...we need people to defend us here, people like him who can fight."

"True. Well maybe we can persuade some of the guys coming with Vinsky to stay. At any rate, you and I should have a little goodbye party, get some extra wine tonight and do some serious reminiscing about Cayuga Lake. Mom and Dad. That boy we both adored, and our evil math teacher, oh and the dogs. Remember Shadow, that charismatic old mutt..."

"He could charm you out of your first bite of food," chimes in Vita, finding a small laugh at the memory.

And so it happens that when Vinsky's boats arrive early that evening, one full of supplies and one carrying a dozen injured, the sisters are busy in Tati's little kitchen preparing a festive meal just for the two of them. When they hear all the shouting, they hurry outside to see four Tully canoes escorting the returning heroes to shore. The autumn sky is darkening to violet; a three-quarter moon the shape and color of milkweed is flowering near the horizon.

In the diluted softening light, Ellie and Vita stand with dozens of others watching and cheering as Vinsky struts ashore followed by a clutch of men and women in tattered clothes, and then others on stretchers or crutches or with bandaged heads, all acknowledging the crowd's greeting with lit faces.

Vita's eyes rivet on a tall man hunched over crutches, his left foot wrapped up in a ball. At first she's sure she only imagines it to be Alex. But, it is.

Through the brief welcoming ceremony, Vita trembles in the background. She doesn't want to imagine that he has come to her. But what's he doing here? She's furious, her hurt seethes. She imagines a dozen angry words of dismissal: "how dare you come here to torture me again," "take your so-called love back to your wife," "don't imagine you'll ever touch me again," "I'm going to tell everyone here how you treated me and you'll run away in shame." Even when she and Ellie bring their prepared dishes to share at the communal dinner, she sits as far away as she can, fuming, not able to eat, fixedly avoiding looking his way. But the guests are exhausted, so celebration is postponed for a few days. Even swaggering Vinsky looks haggard and cuts his speech short.

Vita watches Marcel greet Alex warmly, and the two men start towards Marcel's cottage. She turns and begins helping clear the tables, has her arms full of plates when she hears Alex's voice. He touches her shoulder.

"Here you are," he says.

He's darkly tanned, leathery lines frame his mouth, his hair and beard are chopped short. He curls over the crutches that are too short for him. Vita puts the dishes down carefully. She's suddenly very aware of her clothes, the soft blouse and airy skirt she'd donned for her sisterly celebration. She feels breathless and chilled. He says, "You look beautiful. As beautiful as ever, Vita."

"What are you doing here?"

"What do you think? I wanted to see you." He stops smiling watching her grim, anxious expression. "Vita, Gloria is dead. The flu."

"Meaning?"

His face falls and he bites his lips. "Oh, Vita, don't!"

She's full of barbed words, wants to wound. "You've made promises before, broke them all. Why should I ever trust you again?"

"I never lied to you. I loved you and I still do. Please."

"You killed me. You broke my heart."

"I'm sorry, I'm so sorry, Vita. I wish you could understand that I couldn't abandon Gloria. I had to take care of her."

"Then you should have stayed away from me! Why did you have to come into my life and tear me to pieces!"

Alex staggers on his crutches, drops one, leans on the table for support. Vita picks up the crutch. In handing it to him, she braces his shoulder, feels his muscle, remembers.

"You should sit down," she says. She brings a chair. "What happened to your foot?"

He maneuvers into the seat. She places the crutches against the table, pulls over a chair for herself. The light is dimming with sunset, a breeze sweeps up off the water. The tables have been cleared; the only remaining people around are out on the dock busy with boats.

"Lost a few toes," he replies. "Frostbite."

"Oh, Alex!"

"Not too serious. I'll be able to walk again pretty soon, just a little limp, that's all, so they tell me."

"It must've hurt like hell."

"After it stopped being numb, it sure did. But it was worth it. Mother Nature creamed the Zorians."

"So you were with the Credos in Keene?"

"Garth was there too...and I saw Lorna, Vita."

"I know what happened," she replies curtly, dismissing his apprehensive expression. "Ellie brought it here. The child."

"Yes, I heard that."

"How did she look?"

"She looked beautiful, Vita. She was in bed, resting, well, a little feverish, but that was three months ago. I'm sure she's fine now. I've been told they, she and Garth, went west to join the Credo cell near Albany."

He has her full attention now, her face glowing with love and fear for Lorna. As she leans forward he can catch the smell of her, roses and earth, ocean and spice, so intoxicating he sways in his chair. He keeps on talking about Lorna, just to maintain the moment, the illusion of her friendship and trust. He even gets a grateful smile.

"So her hair is growing long again," Vita says dreamily.

"Yes, and it's lovely as ever. Garth is watching over her, as captain I was able to give him extra time with her. The doctor said she was basically perfectly healthy. Just weak. I hope to keep getting reports of their whereabouts here."

"I hear from her sometimes."

"Don't worry."

Now her face darkens. "You're telling me not to worry? You left me in Boston just when we were planning to rescue her together." He opens his palms and takes a breath to apologize, but she goes on angrily. "And then you left me again at River Bend when you promised to help me look for her. So, when are you leaving here?"

"I'm not leaving, Vita."

"I've heard that before."

"How can I make you believe me?"

"You can't."

"Oh, Vita, no."

His hands ache with wanting to touch her. She looks so bitter and sad, her beautiful face crumpled in pain. He sees that her hands locked together are trembling. He feels a surge of hatred for himself, a corroding lava of guilt. How could he have so abused this beloved soul? He wishes she'd strike him, draw blood, inflict him with tortures. In the strained silence he chooses his next words carefully.

"Vita. Let me try to explain. Or at least get you to pity me instead of scorn me, Vita."

Remnants of sunset still glint the lake, but on the veranda of the old mansion the solar lamps stand out against darkness. Snippets of quiet conversation come from various directions out of the shadows. Music is playing somewhere, a subdued and mournful twilight tune.

Vita waits for him to go on, leaning back now with her arms folded, skeptical, wary, frightening.

"Here's what's been happening with me," he starts, but then bites back word after word. None of them suits what he needs to say. "I was lost," he tries. Lowers his head, shakes it, looks up again straight into her eyes. "I thought you'd never take me back."

How can he convey to her the suffering of his heart? He'd actually welcomed the physical agony radiating from his foot. With Gloria gone, his personal duty erased, he saw that because of his mother, he'd grown up defining his manhood as caretaker of a helpless woman. He longs to explain, Vita, you terrified me, you made my life a lie.

"I never loved Gloria," he hears himself state. The truth of it releases, soars. He finds no guilt in it. "Not as a woman, my woman. That's you."

Too blunt. In the silence while he waits for her retort, she instead reaches out to touch his hand.

"It's ok."

He rushes on. "I thought I loved my wife. But I never really had a wife. My passion for you knocked down the whole house of cards."

"I do forgive you, Alex."

But her words come out with chilling finality, a closing door.

"I'm so sorry, Vita."

"I'm sorry for both of us."

The pain he's caused her is melting away, but there's nothing in its stead. Only a great lassitude, drained of all emotion. The wounds are closing, but so is her heart.

"We've all been through so much," she intones, "so much suffering."

She can tell from his expression, his softening eyes, that she has given him hope. She hadn't meant to, this glow in his face jolts her. She envies him.

"There's Tully," he says. The perfect answer.

326

"Yes, here we are."

She looks away, to the necklace of lamps edging the old house, up at the black sky wild with stars.

Alex leans closer. "We'll raise Lorna's child together."

His strong, quiet voice, the love shining in his eyes, his breath, the feel of him even though they're not touching. The shards of gray in his hair, the sad new lines at his mouth, the slump of his shoulders, the pleading in his open palms. She puts her hands in his.

Acknowledgments

I especially want to thank Anthony Arkin, Amelia Arkin, James Battat, Duncan Campbell, Helen Snively and Alison Woodman for their invaluable and enthusiastic help and support. Heartfelt thanks also to my wonderful writers group: I couldn't have done it without you.

An excerpt from *Human Scale* appeared in the April 2008 issue of Harvard's *HILR Review*.

About the Author

Kitty Beer's stories and articles have appeared in print and online in the U.S. and Canada, including her work as an environmental journalist. Her screenplay, *Home*, placed in the 2004 International Screenwriting Awards contest. She is a member of the National Writers Union, PEN New England, and the Society of Environmental Journalists.

Kitty Beer grew up in New England and raised her two children in Canada, Germany, and upstate New York. She holds her B.A. from Harvard University, and her M.A. from Cornell University. She now makes her home in Cambridge, Massachusetts, where she is active in political and environmental efforts.

Human Scale is her second novel, a sequel to *What Love Can't Do* (2006), which took place in the 2040s. The main characters are new, but some minor ones reappear, and what's left of Boston continues a major backdrop. She is currently at work on the third novel in the trilogy.

Please visit her website at http://www.kittybeer.net, and her blog, http://planetprospect.blogspot.com.

CPSIA information can be obtained
at www.ICGtesting.com
Printed in the USA
FFOW03n1804130814
6829FF